GOOD NEWS

GOOD NEWS

edward abbey

E. P. DUTTON   NEW YORK

Parts of this novel, in somewhat different form, have appeared in *New Times,* the *Tucson Weekly News,* and *Tri-Quarterly.*

For information contact:
Elsevier-Dutton Publishing Co., Inc., 2 Park Avenue, New York, N.Y. 10016

Library of Congress Cataloging in Publication Data
Abbey, Edward
Good news.
I. Title.
PZ4.A124Go 1980   [PS3551.B2]   813'.54   80–12815

ISBN: 0–525–11583–8 (cloth)
ISBN: 0-525-03467-6 (paper)

Published simultaneously in Canada by
Clarke, Irwin & Company Limited, Toronto and Vancouver

Designed by Barbara Cohen

10 9 8 7 6 5 4 3 2

for my daughter
Susannah

Politics is brotherhood.
—WILLIAM BLAKE

*This is the real world, muchachos, and
you are in it.*
—B. TRAVEN

GOOD NEWS

It may have been, as the man on the Tower would say, a failure of courage. Or to use his preferred cliché, a failure of nerve. It may never have happened at all. There was indeed, in those fading years of the doomed century, a sense of overwhelming illusion in the minds of men and women. The cities became unreal. Not so much unbearable as unreal. To the millions crowded within them—for it seemed they could not live elsewhere, in a landscape owned by corporations and dominated by gigantic machines—the ever-growing cities assumed the shape of nightmare. Not a nightmare of horror but a nightmare of dreariness, a routine and customary tedium. Reality became personal, individual, limited to the walls of a room in the center of an enormous hive. The blue eye that *glowed from the center of the wall opened only into deeper realms of loneliness. Friends clung together, then were torn apart. Men and women feared one another and searched for safety in isolation. Families withered, scattered across a continent, attached by the thinnest strands of brief, tenuous, one-dimensional, and unreliable communication. To leave the illusory safety of the room was only to find oneself in a corridor without windows leading out into the corridor of the streets, where the walls were of glass and steel, the floor of concrete and asphalt, and the ceiling a dense umber haze through which a pale sun, ever more feeble, shone rays without warmth and little light. At night the layer of smoke and fog and industrial gases cut off all view of the stars, reflecting the vast illuminations of the cities, which extended for hundreds of miles in all directions. The streets were jammed with clamorous machines, crowded with endless hordes of silent humans, most of them wearing air-filtering masks; one saw only the eyes of others, and all eyes were wary, alert with fear, or blank, withdrawn into the inner space of abstraction. A terrible restlessness infected every movement, every gesture.*

The disintegration was personal and, at the same time, international. The fear that paralyzed the emotions of men and women in their lonely rooms also poisoned the reaction of nations to one another. As each solitary human sought to preserve his own integrity, so each nation strove to ensure its survival at the expense of all others. The fragile webs of a planetary economy frayed apart in an ever-intensifying struggle for the resources to support a worldwide industrial system. One breakdown in a small Mideastern nation led to massive dislocations, anger, and panic in great nations thousands of miles away. War became continuous, limited in scale but never ceasing, breaking out in a new locality as it subsided into chaos and civil war in another. Nuclear weapons were used, as they had been used once before by the first nation to develop them, not on the grand and universal scale envisioned by the most fearful, but in local and regional strife, a practical application of means always available, for ends deemed reasonable by military and diplomatic minds. The unthinkable had always been thinkable. In the effort to compensate for losses abroad, each industrial nation attempted to supply its needs by exploiting to the limit—and then beyond—its own resources of land and forest, water and metals and minerals. The fuel needs of the machine were considered paramount, but the effort to keep the machine operating led to destruction of basic resources needed for the production of food. Agriculture itself had long before been mechanized, industrialized, assimilated into the corporate empire, the farmland submerged beneath the growing cities or mined and stripped to produce the power needed to keep the cities functioning, the machines in motion, agribusiness alive. The immediate result, as certain cities vanished, was the economic strangulation of others. Religious fanaticism joined with nationalism and secular ideologies to destroy and sometimes to self-destroy the sources of power on which the overindustrialized nations depended. Invisible poisons spread through the atmosphere, borne by the winds from the guilty to the innocent. But all were innocent, all were guilty.

The majority of nations had lost the ability to be self-sufficient, even to satisfy the elementary needs of their people for food. Now every nation was losing this ability. The cities could not feed themselves; they were largely abandoned as urban millions spread into the countryside in search of food. Those who suffered least were those accustomed to poverty and hunger; those who suffered most were the inhabitants of the rich nations. And in the richest nation of them all the harshest changes came to the few but precarious, monstrous cities that had once appeared, briefly, in that nation's arid West; in those desert lands where, as the cautious had foreseen, "cities were not meant to be." Most of the people had disappeared, fleeing to the greener regions from which, as everyone knew, their packaged food came. But even in the most desolate and devastated of the remote cities a few men

4 -

and women survived, clinging to the ruins, trying to rebuild the simple farming and pastoral economy that had been destroyed by the triumph of the city, trying to re-create a small society of friends in a community of mutual aid and shared ownership of land. For a few years they were left in peace, forgotten by a world that seemed, for all they could tell, to have forgotten itself—and then the gates of the citadel were opened and certain men came forth with aspirations far more grand than those of farmers and herdsmen and hunters. The oldest civil war of all, that between the city and the country, was resumed.

Two men sit on a rock halfway up the slope of a desert mountain. Sundown: The air is still, caught in the pause between the heat of day, the cool of evening. Doves call in twilight, testing the tentative peace. Downslope from the men a rattlesnake slides from its dark den, scales hissing over stone; the yellow eyes glow with hunger—death in its glance.

The men are roasting the remains of a small mammal—too small for goat, too large for rabbit—on a bed of mesquite coals. Their horses stumble nearby, hobbled, browsing on thorny acacia, prickly pear, bursage. The feed is scanty here and the horses look ganted and weary; like the men they have come a long way.

One man pokes at the fire with a stick and turns the meat over. "How do you want it, boss?"

The other man, staring at something far in the west, does not immediately reply. His gaze is fixed on the fires of a burning city, where towers of dark glass stand in smoke and dust against the yellow sky of sunset. "What's that?" he says. "What'd you say?"

Patiently the first man says, "Rare, medium, or well done?"

"What was it?"

"Part Airedale, maybe. Part coyote. Maybe a few other things."

"Oh God, Sam, I don't care. Any way you like it."

The one addressed as Sam shrugs his bare shoulders and draws a big knife from his belt. "I'll have mine rare, boss. This here warrior is hungry." He lifts the roast dog from the embers with the point of the knife, lays it on the rock, slices off a thin steak, puts the rest back on the fire. Lifting the meat to his jaws he looks again at his companion. "You got to eat, boss. Keep up your strength. You're going to need it."

From nearby comes the clash of steel on stone. The second man says, "Those horses need it. Look at them poor devils."

"I know, boss. We'll take them down in the canyon after dark. Safer then." Sam chews on his supper, grunting with pleasure. He is a short, heavy, shirtless fellow; his brown skin, smooth and nearly hairless, shines with an oily gleam; the hair on his head is blue-black, rich and coarse, bound in a club at the nape of the neck. Neither the body nor his face—a round, full, saddle-colored face, wily, wise, humorous—offers much clue to his age. He could be thirty, he could be fifty-five. He could be a shaman, a wizard, a witch doctor, altering his age from time to time to suit the circumstances.

The second man is hard to see, hard to make out. In the twilight of evening he might be a ghost. But he is clearly old, well advanced in his mortality—the sunburned beak of nose projects above a narrow, pointed, cadaverous jaw that bristles, like cactus, with stiff frosty stubble. Under the shadow of his broad-brimmed hat the eyes, set deep and wide in cavernous sockets, look out on the world with asymmetric intensity: one eye clear, bright, lifeless, the other old and dark and tired but alive, all the same, with a melancholy passion. The left eye is glass but the other—his shooting eye—is living plasm, wired to the circuits of the mind and soul.

"Eat, boss." Sam proffers at knifepoint a chunk of burned flesh. "This dog is good dog. This dog died for our sins. If we do not eat him his death becomes meaningless."

"Ain't really hungry, Sam."

"You think too much, boss. Thinking is good but you must not think too much. You are very thin—turn sideways I can hardly see you. Look at me."

"No." The old man stares at the sunset, the burning city, the phantoms of memory. "And you don't need to call me 'boss' anymore."

"What shall I call you?"

"You know my name. We're partners now. You come as far as you had to."

"Look at me."

"No."

"Look at me, Jack Burns. Look at my hands."

"Oh Christ . . ." Reluctantly the old man turns toward the Indian. "No more of your goddamn tricks, Sam. I ain't in the mood."

"Watch. See this knife?" Sam waves the greasy, glittering blade back and forth, slowly, with the weaving motion of a snake at bay. "Now watch closely, boss." The blade glitters, flashes; there is a hissing noise, a sudden rasping vibration, and where the knife had been, a rattlesnake appears, its body draped over Sam's shoulder, tail a whirring blur, the spade-shaped head gliding forward over Sam's half-open right hand, toward Burns.

The old man lurches to his feet. "Goddamnit Sam, don't *do* that. Jesus *Christ* . . ."

"Don't be afraid." Sam strokes the snake with his left hand, murmurs a few words in a Tewa dialect. The buzzing stops, the serpent peers at Burns with half-lidded eyes, black tongue out and sensing the air. "This is our friend, boss. Someday this snake will save our lives. Touch him."

"What?"

"Touch him. Stroke his head."

"Come on, Sam. I know a rattlesnake when I see one. I know I'm crazy but I ain't that crazy."

"Are you sure?" Smiling, Sam speaks in Tewa to the snake. Then to Burns: "Hold your hand toward him, flat up."

"He won't strike?"

"He will not strike."

Fascinated, Burns puts his left hand slowly forward. "You sure, Sam?" The good eye on the snake, the other eye on nothing. "You know what you're a-doin'?"

"Don't be afraid. This is our friend."

Smiling a little in spite of himself, mesmerized, the old man pushes his hand slowly, hesitantly forward, to within three inches, two inches, one inch of the dark and heavy head. The black tongue flicks across his open palm. He sees and feels the head come to rest there. Gently he closes his hand about it; he is holding the leatherbound haft of Sam's big knife, the blade still in Sam's fingers. "No. No. Damn it, Sam . . ."

The Indian smiles. "Take it, boss. Cut the meat."

Burns sighs, relaxing, and sits down once more, cautiously, on the rock beside his companion. "Sam, you got to stop doing this. You're gonna give me a heart attack yet." He stares at the knife in his hand. Firelight shines on the glossy steel.

"You have a strong heart, boss. No ordinary rattlesnake will ever stop your heart."

"That was no goddamn ordinary rattlesnake."

"What was it then?"

Burns stares at the solid and substantial weapon in his hand, seeing, feeling, knowing its dogmatic reality. "I don't know. Do you know?"

"I was born into the Sun clan." Sam watches the fire, holding out his strong, open hands, spreading the clever fingers. "I was initiated into the One Horn Society when I was twelve. I learned many secret things."

"Where was that?"

"Down in the kiva. Many secret things. For ten years, before I went away . . ." He pauses. "Before I went away I was leader of the flute ceremony. The shaman taught me himself. Before he died. And then . . ."

A coyote begins to bark, far off, out in the desert. Answered at once by a second, in a different quarter. And a third. The barking passes, by slow degrees of modulation, into a quavering howl. The horses stop and lift their heavy heads to stare, through the dark, at something men cannot see.

"Well," says the old man, still studying Sam's knife, "then what?"

"Eat your supper."

Burns leans forward with the knife, picks up the meat. "You can tell me, Sam. What the hell, we're partners." He carves a hunk off the blackened roast of dog. "How'd you do it?"

"Holy secret, boss. You tell me something."

"Call me 'Jack,' damnit."

"You tell me something, Jack."

"Yeah?"

The Indian points toward the smoldering city, the scatter of fires and lights spread across ten miles of the horizon. "How do you think we're going to find him? In that dying mess? All those frightened people? You don't even know what he looks like now."

"I know his name." Burns chews slowly and grudgingly, with little appetite, on the unsalted meat. "I'll know him when I see him."

"You think so? You last saw him twenty years ago. How old was he then?"

"Rrrmmm . . ." The lean jaws make a clicking sound as the old man eats; he readjusts his loose bridgework. "How old was he? Hah . . ." Staring at the embers of the fire, Burns smiles. He draws an ancient wallet from his hip pocket, opens to a picture under cracked celluloid. Smiling, he contemplates the faded image of a solemn, towheaded, handsome boy of ten or twelve. "Good-lookin' devil . . . just like his daddy. We'll know him when we see him, Sam. No doubt about that."

"How do you know he's even there? In the city?"

Smile fading, the old man puts away the picture. "You touch on a tender spot, partner. We don't know. All I know is he was there four years ago when I got that last letter. The last letter anybody got, I reckon. If he ain't there anymore then I don't know where to look. We'll ride on to California. I'll find the little bastard somewheres."

"How do you know California is still there? How do you know he'll know you? Or want to?"

"All right, Sam . . ." Burns frowns at his big, powerful, interlocked hands. "You sure know where the fear is, all right. Don't you, you son-of-a-bitch. I don't know."

"Who wrote that last letter?"

The old man does not answer.

"Did the boy ever write to you himself?"

Burns makes no answer. He drops the half-burned, half-raw slab of meat back on the coals. Places a wad of tobacco in his cheek. After further pause, he says, "We better find some feed for them horses."

Sam places a hand on the old man's forearm. Then on his shoulder. "Jack," he says, "I'm not trying to be cruel. Too much hope—false hope—is cruel. Hope is the cruelest thing that Greek lady let out of the box."

"Sam, I know that. But I don't like to think about it."

The twilight condenses around them, thickening to night. A few stars appear, forming incomplete constellations—Scorpio, Cassiopeia, the Bear. The new moon, a sickle of silver, hangs low in the west. The lights of the distant city seem as dim as the dying coals of their campfire. Small bats dart through the gloaming.

"And that city," the Indian says. "That city . . . some strange things going on there."

"Always was. We'll find the boy and get the hell out."

"No politics."

"Politics?" The old man rises, resets the heavy gunbelt on his hip, tugs down his hat brim. "What do we know about politics? We're tourists. We don't even talk the same language. What do we care about politics, us ignorant aborigines?" He spits on the fire. "You coming or you gonna sit here all night?"

Sam sheaths his knife, wraps the remainder of the roast dog in a greasy rag, and gets up. He stuffs the bundle into a saddlebag, hoists his saddle to his shoulder, and grins at Burns. "Grab your saddle."

"Who's the boss around here? Ain't we coming back?"

"Somebody might have seen the fire."

The old man grunts in assent. He kicks dirt over the hot ashes, covering them, and follows the Indian down through the brush to the horses, which make little effort to get away. Giant saguaro cactus stand from the rocky slope nearby, lifting thorny arms, like supplicant humans, toward the stars. Sam the shaman bridles a docile pinto; Jack Burns saddles his mare, a gray-skinned, rack-ribbed, broom-tailed, towering specter of a horse seventeen hands high. Despite hunger and fatigue and long association the mare tosses her head high when he slips the bridle on; her big feet clang like frying pans as she sashays aside. "Rosie," he growls, hanging on to her neck, "Rosie, Rosie, you brainless hammerhead, stand still or I'll chew your goddamn ear off. . . ."

They ride down through starlight toward the shadowy cleft of a canyon, down to where the sycamores grow, and the hackberry, and the elephantine cottonwood—in the desert, the tree of life. A sound of spring-green trembling leaves. The smell of still water. The horses snort with anxious anticipation.

"You're so smart, Sam, why don't you conjure up a bale of alfalfa and a bucket of grain for these poor beasts?"

"What do you think I am, a witch doctor? A wizard? A miracle worker? I'm a magician, boss, a professional; I don't deal in the supernatural. Horses are wiser than you humans—they believe in what they can smell. Nothing else."

"Yeah? Is that so?" Burns ponders on this for a while. "Well, let me tell you something, Sam. I know bullshit when I smell it."

"A man knows what he can know."

"Yeah? God, there's nothing worse than a smart Indian. And that reminds me of something else. If you're really a goddamn Indian why the hell don't you talk like a goddamn Indian?"

"You're a bigot, white man."

"I'm no bigot, I hate *everybody*. Talk like an Indian."

"How? I don't know how. I'm a spoiled Indian. Harvard ruined me."

Burns ruminates, chewing his cud. *"My* daddy always said the only good Indian is a dead Indian."

"Mine would've said the only good Indian is a bad Indian. But he was a troublemaker. He was shot dead at Pine Ridge, South Dakota. By good Indians. His last words were, and I quote, 'Let me go, my friends, you have hurt me enough.' "

"Sam, you don't play fair. I'll say no more."

They ride on in silence, down over the rocks and into the trees. At first they cannot find the water; they give rein to the horses; the horses find it immediately, upcanyon, among the boulders, where the musk of startled javelinas floats on the air. The men fill their canteens and let the horses drink.

"If we could get one of them wild pigs," the old man says, "we wouldn't have to eat your mongrel dog."

"Bigotry again. There's more and better meat on a dog. Next best thing to a horse."

Burns looks at the horses. "Sure ain't much meat on ours. We better let them feed for a while, if there's much more here than up on the hill. Did I see filaree under those sycamores?"

They lead the horses back to the grove of trees and turn them loose, hobbled again, with trailing reins. The men squat against the comfortable bole of the biggest sycamore, deep in darkness, and listen with pleasure to the shuffling feet, the work of powerful jaws ripping up the sweet dry grass. Neither man is sleepy; they had slept earlier, during the heat of the afternoon. They will ride still farther tonight.

"That ole charger of mine," says Burns, "she ain't doing too bad. She'll make it yet." He ejects a stream of tobacco juice through the gap in his front teeth and onto the ground between his boots. "Since that raid she's the only horse I got left with enough sense and enough strength for a long march. She ain't much but she'll do."

Sam lights his little clay pipe. "I've seen uglier horses. Not many."

"Now Sam . . ." Thinking, the old man says, "We'll liberate a few on the way home. Should be lots of strays around the city."

"Is your son a rider?"

"Last time I seen him he was on a goddamn bicycle. But he's my son." That should be sufficient; but the old man adds, "Any son of mine can't ride will be shot, personally." Smiling in the dark, Burns looks at his partner. "You think I'm getting old, Sam? Old and creaky and cranky? Maybe a little touched in the head?"

"Yes."

"You're right. That's why we need him."

"We'll find him, boss."

"Jack! The name is Jack, for Chrissake."

"We'll find him, Jack. For your sake."

The horses stop suddenly, lifting their heads, nostrils flexing. From miles away, upwind on the barely moving air, off in the mountains dark against the stars, comes the sound of a high, faint, inhuman wail. They listen. The sound is not repeated. The horses wait, then lower their heads.

Jack Burns spits on the ground. "I ever tell you about my honeymoon, Sam?"

"Which one?"

"The first. That first premature honeymoon. Took this here city girl out camping in the woods. When it got dark we bedded down under the pines and then I told her about some of the things that creep around out there in the night. Trying to make her hang on tight, you see." The old man stares at the horses, smiling at his thoughts.

"Well? What happened?"

Burns' face wrinkles with a leathery, deeper grin. "She fell asleep. I was awake all night; every time a pine cone dropped I damn near jumped out of my skin."

The Indian nods in agreement. "Yes. We create our own fears. And at four o'clock in the morning we create the worst fear of all. The fear of living."

The horses shuffle about in the starlight. The old man says, "I look at it this way, Sam. If the worst thing that can happen to a man is death—then there ain't nothing that's worth fearing."

"Yes again. If that is the worst."

Leaning against the tree and against each other, they doze off. From far away, dim and distant, the wail sounds again, borne on the gentle wind, a cry of anguish or of ecstasy deeper than despair, wilder than joy. The men stir at the sound but do not awaken. The horses, after another pause, continue feeding. Bright stars burn, clusters of blue, red, green fires in random constellation turning on the wheel of space. In silence.

Hours later, well past midnight, roused by an inner clock, Jack Burns opens his eyes. He nudges his companion. They rise and grope through the dark of the trees toward the noise of their horses, catch them, and mount. They follow a path through the rocks, downcanyon, and come to a clear and definite trail. They follow the trail for a mile, two miles, and reach an old road, stony, deeply gullied, overgrown with brush and cactus. They ride the road, single file through the obstructions, over a ridge and into the next valley and come to a fence with open gate.

"Smoke," mutters Sam; "I smell smoke."

They go through the gateway, ride on for another mile, passing two abandoned, weed-grown automobiles on the way. Ancient and gigantic cottonwood trees loom ahead, their leaves making a constant rustling noise as of running water. Beyond the trees they find the ruins of a burned-out ranchhouse, a leveled barn; fiery coals wink among the ashes; smoke twists up from the charred, fallen timbers. The men look at the ruins and then at one another, through the fading starlight, and say nothing.

A gust of predawn wind flows down from the mountains. The tail vane of an unlocked windmill turns with the wind; steel grates on rusted steel. The sound is like that of a human groan. The Indian and Burns look toward the corral a hundred yards away and the tall tower—a skeleton of metal—standing within it. There they see, dangling on a rope, black in silhouette against the eastern sky, the first of the hanged men.

A. C. Dekker and his son Arthur ride across the desert southwest of the mountains. The noon sun shines on their backs; on shirts dark with sweat. Very tired, they seldom speak. A.C., in the lead, peers forward and up the hillside on the right, where the fluted columns of the giant cactus stand. These saguaros, thirty to fifty feet tall, resemble effigies of human beings; their thick limbs, like truncated arms, lift in warning, or salutation, toward the sky. Dekker's horse, head down and weary, follows the dust of a cattle path in winding course through brush and around half-buried boulders of granite.

The boy, sixteen years old, trails a few lengths behind on another tired horse. Hat pulled low against the sun, he surveys the terrain ahead and to the left. Like his father, young Arthur wears a holstered revolver on his hip.

The trail crosses a dry creekbed. They pass under a syca-more tree; spangles of light and shade float across their shoulders. Iron shoes clash on stone. Withered leaves, bleached pale by the sun, lie scattered on the rocks. A cloud of gnats dances above a pool of dark, stagnant water. A.C. pauses to let the horses drink.

"They're not far ahead," the father says. "We'll catch them now."

"How many you figure?"

"Three or four on horseback. And then those motorcycles—but they'll be gone. We'll never see them."

"Why not, Paw? They're the ones that done it. Most of it. They'll be in the city somewheres. Why not?" The boy stares at his father with dark-lashed cold gray eyes; a handsome lad, high cheekbones, a trace of down on his upper lip, wide shoulders, and long loose limbs.

"We'll see." A.C. spurs his horse away from the water. Arthur follows, gains, rides alongside. Their legs touch, the lathered horses rub shoulders. The boy is about to speak again but is forced to drop back by the lash of thorny mesquite across the trail. There is no room for two abreast. They ride on and reach the summit of a small rise. The father stops his horse, dismounting. "There they are, Art."

Looking down into the broad draw beyond, the boy sees the hovering dust, the long file of plodding cattle, dark riders herding the cattle forward. The father lifts binoculars to his eyes, studies the scene. "Five of them," he says. "God help us, there's five. With rifles."

"The more the better," the boy mutters.

A.C. leads his horse ahead, downslope below the ridgeline. They stop again, hidden among the rocks, in the slight shade of the saguaros that stand, tall as monuments, at their side.

"What are we waiting for?"

A.C. turns a grim and weathered face to his son. "You want to get them? Or you just want to commit suicide?" Arthur makes no reply. "Okay. Now let me think for a minute." A.C. watches the slow procession of cattle and horsemen down the draw, moving toward the old highway—four miles off—that leads to the city. He makes the decision and speaks long and quietly to his son. The boy nods, and nods again, unbuckling his gun belt and concealing it, with holster and revolver, inside the rolled poncho tied behind the seat of his saddle. Ready, he leads his horse back over the ridge, and disappears. A.C. waits, listening. When he hears, a minute later, the faint sound of boy and horse riding away at a fast trot, bearing for the highway, he leads his own horse on down the slope, following the cattle and the enemy.

Hidden by the ridge, Arthur urges his sweating mount down the drainage that leads, as he knows, to a junction near the highway with the wide draw on the west. When he gets there he pulls up in the shade of a big ironwood tree. His horse trembles with fatigue, the contagion of fear. The boy speaks to it, softly, and strokes the sweat-dark hide. The horse quiets a little as he tethers it to the tree.

The asphalt highway lies within sight, a transparent scrim of heatwaves shimmering above it. There is no traffic on that road. Scrubby weeds grow from cracks in the pavement. An abandoned Greyhound bus, once blue and silver but faded now to a lusterless gray, sits on deflated tires half on and half off the roadway; a small drab bird flies in through a broken window and out through the open door. Beyond the highway and the waves of rising heat, the desert hills to the south appear like islands floating on a sea without color. The world looks, in that direction, marvelously still and empty.

The boy waits, squatting in the shade.

The first rider appears, a tall man in khaki uniform, a flat-brimmed hat on his head, shading his face. Arthur stands. The rider halts his horse and draws a rifle from the saddle scabbard. Arthur holds both hands aloft to show that he is unarmed. The rider approaches. He speaks a few words into a two-way radio. The string of cattle comes in sight, flanked by the other uniformed horsemen, dark figures in the dust. As the first rider comes near, the boy lowers his arms and leans back, casually, against the side of his horse, covering the brand on the horse's hip. The brand—a rocking K—is the same as the brand on the cattle. The Dekkers' brand. Dekkers' cattle.

The leading rider comes to within ten feet of Arthur Dekker and stops. He wears a lightning-bolt patch on his shoulder, the gold bars of a lieutenant on his collar, a heat-weary scowl on his sweat-streaked face. "Well," he says, "who are you?" He holds his carbine in the crook of his arm, the barrel pointing at Arthur.

"I'm not feelin' too good," Arthur says. "You have any water?"

The officer inspects the boy with moderate interest. "How old are you?"

Arthur hesitates, on the verge of insolence. He reconsiders. "I'm sixteen," he mumbles.

"Get on your horse. You're coming with us."

"I need some water."

"You'll get water. Mount up."

Slowly Arthur turns, placing his left foot in the stirrup, his right hand on the saddle. The cattle are almost upon them now, shuffling along at a reluctant pace through the heat and dust, under a swarm of flies. Two of the other four horsemen come close, two remain in the rear.

As Arthur is about to obey the lieutenant's order he hears a shout and the sound of a running horse. His father is coming down through the brush and cactus, on the flank of the column. The officer and the four men turn at once toward the new diversion. Arthur slips his big revolver out of the poncho, cocks it, aims point-blank at the officer's broad back. He fires, the officer falls, one spurred boot caught in a stirrup; the horse rears and screams, plunges away through a thicket of bristling acacia. Holding his revolver in both hands, Arthur aims and fires at the second nearest man. And hits him; the soldier slumps forward, falls, a bullet in his neck. His father is already shooting on the run, from less than fifty feet away, and a third uniformed horseman drops clear of the saddle, sprawling on the hot sand, carbine trapped beneath his chest. Three men down in the space of seconds. The remaining two, confused and panicked by this sudden enfilade of gunfire, race off in opposite directions through the swirling dust, the milling uproar of the cattle, and vanish into the scrub.

A.C. gallops up, saws his mount to a brutal stop above his son. "All right? You all right?"

Arthur gapes at his father, unable to speak, his eyes wide with horror, the gun clutched in his shaking hands. He seems about to collapse. He cannot speak.

The father slips to the ground, staring at Arthur, grabs him by the shoulders. "You're all right? Hey? You're all right?"

The boy sags against his father's chest, tears starting from his eyes; he gasps for breath. Then feels his father stiffen with the impact of a heavy blow and hears at the same moment the blast of the gunshot. A.C. sinks to his knees, eyes dull with shock. On the ground ten feet behind them the third soldier lies, training his carbine on Arthur. And shoots. And misses, misses, as his elbows give out beneath his weight, his eyes glaze over, the muzzle of the weapon sliding into the sand. Arthur stares, unable to raise his revolver. The dying soldier makes a final effort to find and see the boy, his eyes blinking under a film of sweat. He lifts the rifle, the barrel wobbles in an arc through the air, swinging toward Arthur. Finds the target, too, and steadies the sights, but nothing happens; the soldier is unable to concentrate the strength he needs to pull the trigger. Slowly the rifle slants to the ground; the man swoons, mind and body relaxing into darkness.

A. C. Dekker, half crumpled to the ground, propping himself on one arm, holds his other hand to his belly. Blood trickles between his fingers. "Art," he gasps; "Art . . . bring me that carbine."

His son stares at the dead soldier, then at his father. Arthur takes halting steps, like a sleepwalker, to the soldier, picks up the small rifle, carries it to his father. A.C. takes the weapon. "Now get out of here," he orders. Holding his stomach with one hand, he crawls on his knees into the shade of the ironwood tree, sheltering himself within the low-drooping tangle of branches.

"Bring me that fella's ammo pouch," he says, with effort. Sweat glistens on his whitened face. "Then get out of here. Hurry."
Arthur does as he is bid, forcing himself to roll the soldier on his back and unbuckle the belt. The man's shirtfront is greasy with warm blood. He takes the belt with its two leather-cased ammunition clips to his father. "I better stay with you," he says, squatting beside A.C.
"No," the father snarls. "Those other two'll be coming back. Maybe with the motorcycle squad. You get out of here. Get on that horse and ride, goddamnit."
The boy stares at his father. "Where? Where is there to go?"
His father glares back at him. "Where? Where? God, Art— go home." Delirium in his eyes, his voice. "There's nothing there. It's all gone. They're all dead."
A.C. glares ferociously at his son, silent. In silent rage he looks away, toward the two soldiers inert on the sand, under the sun, the haze of dust still floating on the air. Out of sight but not far they can hear—or at least the boy hears—the frightened horses, the terrified cattle, thrashing around in the brush.
"Look," the father says. "Listen. Go to the city. Find some friends."
"What friends?"
"Find somebody. Get some of those kids you went to school with. Bring them back to the place. Then all of you—there's everything there you need. Rebuild it."
"I'm not leaving."
The father groans in anger, in helpless despair, in outrage. "All right . . ." He struggles to his knees again, using the carbine for support. "All right . . . Help me up. Get me . . . onto your horse."
Arthur helps his father into the saddle, mounting him from the right, the near side. The animal trembles, tugging at the rope. A.C. grasps the saddle horn with both hands, dropping the carbine. Arthur lets it lay, unties the horse. From out on the highway, toward the city, he hears the remote but growing

mutter of engines. For a moment he is paralyzed by fear, listening, then compels his frozen limbs into movement. He leads the horse into the pygmy forest of mesquite and cactus and ironwood, away from the trail and the highway, into the desert toward the mountains. His father sways in his seat but hangs on. They vanish.

The sun beats down on the two dead men. Interested flies congregate about the wounds, the blackening dribbles of blood, the stains and smell of human excrement. A cactus wren chatters with harsh vigor from the limbs of a cholla. A thrasher with long curved bill, perched on top of a saguaro, whistles like a human, alarmed, startling. One vulture soars a thousand feet above, black as charcoal against the sun, arrogant with indolence, patient, unhurried.

The roar of motorcycles grows louder, coming near. The birds fall silent. The roar becomes violent, tyrannous; five men in black uniforms and helmets painted silver, adorned with painted flames, veer from the decaying pavement and drive into the trailhead. The motors rumble, gearing down, the drive wheels thrash and fishtail in the dry sand. The leader, a man with the chevrons of a master sergeant on each sleeve, raises his right arm. The riders stop, letting their engines slow to a grumbling idle. The sergeant contemplates, only for a moment, the prone bodies. Swearing, he races his motor, lunges forward and circles the scene of the battle, but can make no sense of the tangle of tracks radiating away in several directions. He rides to the summit of the nearest hillock, and halts, peering toward the mountains. He returns to the others, glances once more at the dead, then turns and points at two of his men. His eyes are hidden by opaque goggles; white teeth shine in his sunburned face, beneath a heavy mustache, as he speaks. The voice is barely audible through the noise of the engines but the two men read the words on his lips: Bury those lads. They nod.

The sergeant signals to his other men: Follow me. Engines roaring, they churn through the sand back to the asphalt and charge westward, toward the city. The noise of their passage fades rapidly to a distant vibration on the air, to a whisper, to nothing. Left behind in the silence and the sunlight the burial detail look at the dead, at one another, and shrug. Slowly, they peel off black shirts, hang their helmets on the handlebars of the motorcycles. One man pulls a folding shovel from his gear, begins to dig. The other, an automatic rifle in his arms, climbs the small hill to stand watch.

Taking turns, they dig one shallow grave for the two stiffened bodies and roll them in, cover them up, place a few flat stones on the mound. They drink lustily from their water flasks, get back in full uniform, kick their engines into life, mount, drive off with bellow of exhaust and a flurry of sand. The dust and the blue smoke float on the air long after the sound of their departure has died away.

Again the scene is silent. Again the vulture resumes its spiraling descent. The birds begin to call. The shadows edge forth onto the trampled sand of the wash. The vulture's black image sweeps across the grave, disappears, comes back for another and closer pass.

The vulture lands, gently, almost silently. Dark wings trailing, spread for flight, it creeps cautiously, one step, then another, toward the grave. It roosts for a while on the flat stones, the bald red fleshy head twitching this way, that way, watching all quarters for sign of danger.

The flies buzz in the heat, murmuring over the spoor of caked blood, the scraps of flesh, the scattered fragments of bone and viscera. The vulture dominates the grave, alert and watchful. Satisfied at last, it begins to scratch at the sand with quick, forceful movements. A man's hand is revealed, rigid fingers clenching the air.

A second vulture appears in the sky. A third. In the immensity of the desert, in the heat of the afternoon, there is no sound but the contented murmur of the flies, the scratching of the vulture, a few sweet and triumphant birdcries.

The old man and the Indian, Jack Burns and Sam Banyaca (Ph.D.), the searcher and the researcher, rise from their afternoon siesta under a spreading paloverde tree. They saddle their horses and ride on toward the yellow sky of sundown, the cool of evening.

On their right, to the north, stands a mountain shaped like a flatiron, or like a battleship, with near-vertical walls of volcanic rock, on its horizontal decks a crenellation of eroded towers, pinnacles, balanced rocks on pedestals—a voodoo landscape. Nothing seems to grow up there, in that waterless waste, but thorn and spine and claw and needle and spear. Under the evening light, streaming in amber columns through a mass of clouds, the ancient rock of the mountain takes on a sullen glow, a mass of mangled iron heated from within by deep, infernal, other-worldly fires. Old Burns, glancing at it from time to time, cannot repress his feelings of discomfort. "Good Christ," he mutters, "what a godawful place. Who could ever live up there?" The question is rhetorical, requiring no answer, but Sam responds anyway. "Nobody ever did. But men have died there. And women too. Hunting for gold, hunting one another. Hunting God, maybe."

Burns growls in disgust, squinting up at the burnt cliffs and jagged crags, the caves like eyeholes in a skull. "Ain't no gold in there. That's not gold country." He chews, ruminating, and spits a brown jet of tobacco juice over the pommel of his saddle. "Obsidian, maybe. Maybe turquoise. Pyrite, maybe. But you won't find no gold in that rock. Only fool's gold."

"All gold is fool's gold."

"Yeah? Is that so?" Old Jack turns his leathery face and one good eye to his mate, the hint of a smile on his lips. "Don't philosophize on me, medicine man." He pats the pouch inside his belt. "We can buy what we need with it. That's good enough for me."

"Only from fools."

"Bullshit, Sam. Don't you know nothing about economics? About medium of exchange? How long'd you go to that Harvard?"

"Two weeks. It was a long grind."

"Not long enough, seems like. What branch of higher learning did they teach you there anyhow?"

"They taught all the branches—but none of the roots."

"Sam, I ain't in no mood for philosophizing. What're you lookin' at?"

Sam has stopped his horse and is studying the ground. "Another wounded man," he says. "More blood on the trail. Fresh blood. Man on foot leading horse. Not far." He looks ahead, shading his eyes, into the thickets of brush and cactus beyond the next ravine. "Very close."

The old man pulls his revolver. "See anything?"

"Yes and no. I'm not sure."

The branches of the mesquite and catclaw undulate gently in the evening breeze. Vague shadows merge, separate, come and go, appear and disappear.

"Hello there," cries Burns. No answer. "Anybody in there? Speak up."

Silence.

"Whoever it is, we better back off and go around," says Sam.

"Yeah. But he might need help. Him, her, whatever." They hesitate, uncertain. "What the hell, Sam. Keep me covered. I'm going in there."

The old man nudges his mare. She steps forward. They proceed down over the rocks, between a pair of giant saguaros, across ten yards of open sand. Sam watches from the rear, "covering" Burns with his eyes; except for the knife, Sam carries no weapon. Burns rides farther, following the path through an opening in the mesquite jungle. "Hey," he says, the gun in his hand, "don't shoot. We're neutral here." He whistles a tune from the hymnbook of childhood: "Little Brown Church." "Anybody here?" He peers ahead through the dense brush. "Hey? Damnit, speak up. . . ."

He stops his horse. Another horse stands in an open area before him, a body draped across its back. A young man, hardly more than a boy, stands in the shadows waiting for Burns, revolver cocked and loaded. They stare at one another through the gathering twilight. "Well," begins the old man. He notices, as if surprised, the revolver in his own right hand. He lowers it. "You don't shoot, son, and I won't shoot."

The boy clears his throat. "I need your horse." He keeps his weapon trained on Burns. "Get down."

"Yes sir," the old man says. He holsters his revolver, shifts his chaw to the other cheek, spits, and eases himself, creaking a bit, out of the saddle and down to the ground.

At that moment the Indian appears, silently, on foot, and

steps forward beside Burns. The lad does not seem to see him. He keeps his eyes fixed on Burns. "Okay," the boy says, "now stand aside. Hand me those reins."

Sam Banyaca says, "Your gun is melting."

The boy stares in surprise at Sam, then at his revolver. To his eyes the barrel of it appears to be curving downward, drooping like taffy toward the ground. He tries to lift it; the thing dribbles out of his fingers like quicksilver and falls to the sand in a blob of gun-metal blue. The boy gapes at his useless firearm, then at Burns and the Indian. Mouth round with astonishment, the boy says, or attempts to say, "Who . . . what did you . . . ?"

"Don't worry about it." Sam steps forward again, picks up the revolver, hands it butt foremost to the boy. "Keep this thing in your holster until you really need it. We're friends." Turning his back, Sam goes close to the man doubled over the saddle of the boy's horse. He touches the body, only once.

"Yeah," the boy says. "He's dead. I know. I got to bury him. I was trying to get him to the city, find a doctor. But . . ." The boy begins to weep. "It was too far."

"We'll help you," Jack says. "You can come with us."

The ground is too rocky for digging; they lay the body of old Dekker on the ground in the shade of a mesquite tree and cover it with a mound of stones to keep off the coyotes and vultures. Jack binds two sticks together to make a cross and plants the cross in the top of the mound. They doff their hats as Sam burns incense on the topmost rock and recites a Hopi prayer, first in Tewa then in English.

Oh spirit of the desert
Of the mountains and the sky
We give our brother's body back to you
To feed this tree and the grass,
The deer and the lion,
And all other things, big and small,
That live in this land and need us,
As we need them.

Where this man's spirit has gone
We do not know
But we shall remember him
For as long as we can
And when we forget, as we must,
Everything that has happened,
We too will be part of the earth
And the worlds to come,
Until we arrive once more
At the beginning again.

Wiping the tears from his dusty face, young Arthur says, "I want a prayer for revenge."

"Tomorrow we'll talk about revenge," says the Indian. "Tonight we better ride on. The soldiers will be tracking us. They want revenge too."

"Everybody wants revenge," Jack Burns says. "That's natural."

Leading the fourth horse, they ride through the cactus forest toward the lights of the city. The boy tells his story. Hunting lost horses, he and his father had turned back at evening toward the ranch to see, from a distant hill, their home in flames, and a troop of motorcycle police in black uniforms roaring off into the dusk. When they got to the ruins they found the boy's mother gone, consumed in the fire, their one hired hand hanging dead from the windmill, and their cattle driven off, as the signs revealed, by a band of horsemen—the soldiers. Arthur and his father set out at once in pursuit of the soldiers, catching up to them the next day. Their plan had been simple: Kill the horsemen first, then hunt for the motorcyclists.

"And then what?" asks Sam.

"And then?" says the boy. "Well, then the Chief. The one they call the Chief. That's all."

"How?"

"I don't know yet. But I got the rest of my life to figure it out."

"Who's the Chief?" says Burns.

"Where you from?"

"New Mexico."

The boy tells what he knows of the Chief, not much. Sam adds the few details that he has heard, giving Burns the picture of a man once an Air Force general, then some kind of professor at the state university, who has made himself the master of the dying city before them. Ruler of the condemned. Boss of the survivors. Commander, with imperial ambitions, of a mercenary army.

"Nothing new in any of that," Burns says. "We been dealing with folks like him all my life. We can handle that type all right, no trouble atall."

"But we're staying out of politics," the Indian reminds him.

"Why sure, sure. We find my boy and clear out. I know that, Sam, don't get your bowels in an uproar."

Their slow progress through the desert brings them to the side of the former highway, now silent, untraveled. Under the cool stars, through the warm evening, Sam and Jack ride side by side, followed by Arthur Dekker and the extra horse. A chorus of coyotes breaks out suddenly in the middle distance, a frenzy of yapping and squawling, which stops as quickly as it began. A routine noise, requiring no comment from the riders.

Nor do any of the three say a word about the abandoned trucks along the highway, the derelict automobiles at rest on flattened tires, doors sagging open, mice, moles, birds nesting in the ruin of their interiors. Vines and weeds grow from the rotted upholstery of dead Fords, defunct Chevrolets, moribund Power-wagons, decayed Cadillacs, and wasted Winnebagos. Quiet bats flicker in, flicker out through the broken windows of tractor-trailer rigs, four-wheel-drive pickups, Blazers, Broncos, Scouts, Jeeps. One thing—besides futility—these machines have in common: All are facing east, away from the city.

Again no one of the three horsemen makes mention of the singularly unanimous orientation of the motor traffic. As if one-way traffic, in all four lanes, in flight from the city, were no more than a normal pattern out of nature, as in an expanding world each particle of energy flees every other. But now, at last, all flight has stopped.

A fat and poisonous lizard, thick as a man's forearm, scuttles across the broken pavement before them. The old man reaches for his revolver; Sam lays a restraining hand on his wrist. "A friend," he says.

"Friend?" says Jack Burns. "That thing? That's a goddam Gila monster if I ever seen one."

"Only the white man calls it a monster."

"Well I'm a white man."

"Try to grow out of it. The real monster is up ahead in those glass towers. Look at this junk along the road: these steel toys, these pet baby dinosaurs. Even they tried to get away from him."

Burns considers for only a moment. "Sam," he says, "don't kid me. If there's one thing I can't stand it's an ecological Indian. Why, back in the old days the worst overgrazed range you could find anywhere was on the reservations. The worst strip mines, too."

"Worse than Appalachia?"

"I ain't been there."

"I've been there."

"Well, anything the white folks did bad you Indians could do worse."

"We learned from you. Before you came we were doing all right."

"Yeah, I've heard about that. Fighting and stealing, torturing everybody you could catch. Maybe three million of you in a land that we showed could support three hundred million."

"But our way supported us for twenty thousand years. And then you came, your ancestors, that swarm of greedy peasants from the slums of Europe, and you made a commercial-industrial slum out of our America."

"Now Sam, I wouldn't call it a slum. Not all of it. And like I said, we fed a lot of people."

"And how long did it last?"

"Well . . ." The old man hesitates. "What of it? What does that prove? Which is better: a hundred and fifty years of fun, excitement, lots of money—or twenty thousand years of flies, filth, poverty, and stagnation with a mob of ignorant heathen savages? Hey? How about that, you red-skinned devil? At least we never ate dog."

"You ate one another."

"The times were hard, pardner. Times *are* hard. Look at that boy."

Young Arthur is slumping in the saddle, exhausted, half asleep. They turn away from the highway and make camp for the night near the ruins of a transformer station; slack powerlines, long dead, trail for miles across the desert sands. The boy goes to sleep on his saddle blanket, head pillowed on his forearm. Sam Banyaca and Jack Burns, still arguing to pass the time, squat by a tiny fire of mesquite twigs. The old man nods off. Sam opens his saddlebag, takes out a beaded medicine pouch, and packs his little clay pipe with the crushed leaves of wild marijuana. He smokes, keeping watch, as his friends sleep. The horses, tethered close by in case of need, browse wearily on jojoba, bursage, ricegrass, acacia. Not enough. But they are all hungry, men as well as animals.

Sam keeps watch, listening to the sounds of the desert night:·an elf owl in a saguaro; a horned owl hooting from its perch on a leaning power pole; javelinas scuffling through a thicket of prickly pear; a pack of coyotes miles away, snarling over the dismembered remains of a man in the rags of a uniform. . . . Peace, peace, peace and order everywhere that he can hear. They are surrounded by friends. Their enemies are silent.

Early in the morning, before sunrise, the Indian rouses the other two. They saddle up and ride on through the fading starlight. They pass more burned-out ruins, abandoned homes, empty trailerhouses in the suburbs of a suburb. They file beneath a pair of human bodies, of indeterminate age and sex, blackened in decay, dangling by neck from the crossarms of a rusted steel pylon. Neither the boy, nor the old man, nor the Indian find these presentiments of urbanized society worthy of comment.

Long before the rising sun begins to shine on their backs they see its light reflected, in fierce red glare, from the walls of glass and aluminum that form the aspiring cathedrals of the city.

"Open the drapes."

"Yes sir."

"But slowly." The Chief snaps his fingers; Corporal Buckley steps forward, opening the leather-covered case as he snaps to attention beside the desk. He watches with sympathy as the Chief selects a pair of sunglasses. The Chief's eyes are a pale recessive blue, large, sensitive, slightly protruding, the eyelids pink and delicate. A permanent frown creases the skin between his blond eyebrows. "Thank you, Buckley."

The corporal closes the case with a smart click and steps back three paces. The Chief sets the glasses on his nose, gently, and lowers the earpieces, with care, into place. His eyes disappear behind the opaque blackness of the curved and oversize lenses. Protected now, he turns for a moment toward the great single sheet of tinted Thermopane that forms the entire east wall of the office. Two soldiers, having drawn the heavy curtains, return to their places outside the entrance doors.

Hands clasped behind his back, the Chief gazes across the smoky city toward the vague efflorescence of rose and gold beyond the desert mountains. He wears a uniform of khaki, the shirt, open at the throat, devoid of any insignia or decoration other than the simple blue-and-white ribbon of the Medal of Honor. The Chief is a small man—slim, fit, beautiful, with a well-toned tension, under perfect control, in each movement, each gesture.

Two officers, standing at ease, wait in silence at the entrance, watching their Chief. Major Roland, Captain Barnes. Only the major, tapping a braided quirt against his knee, reveals any sign of impatience.

Ten stories below, a platoon of soldiers marches in open formation up a largely deserted street. Within the hollow square of armed men two prisoners stumble forward, half naked, their arms bound, hurried on by unsheathed bayonets. A few civilians, keeping silent, watch the procession from windows and doorways. A stray horse grazes on the weeds that grow among the sand dunes along the street, ignoring the familiar tramp of booted feet. The parade of soldiers and prisoners leads directly toward an open park at the intersection of two main avenues. This park, known as Unity Square, contains a few iron benches, the stumps of trees, some abandoned motor vehicles, and, as centerpiece, a gallows. Three bodies hang by rope from the main crossbeam. As the Chief watches, a soldier under supervision of a sergeant hustles up the thirteen steps to the deck, detaches two of the bodies, and closes the trapdoors. Some ravens, disturbed by this activity, rise flapping into the air.

Still watching the scene below, the Chief speaks softly: "Major Roland?"

The major springs to full attention, steps forward three paces, salutes. "Yes sir!"

His back to the major, the Chief says, "What's going on down there?"

The major takes an official glance through the tinted glass, returns to attention. "Execution, sir. Myers caught two more arsonists this morning."

"Incendiaries? You mean revolutionists?"

"No sir, I wouldn't call them that. They're only arsonists."

"Men or women?"

"Men, sir."

"How old?"

"One's about forty, the other in his fifties. Old-timers, sir. Real scum."

"Really?" The Chief snaps his fingers. "Buckley: binoculars." The Chief pushes the sunglasses up on his forehead and waits with one hand held out. The binoculars are brought at once. The Chief studies the marching men. "Husky fellows," he says quietly. "You talked with them?"

"What's that, sir?" The major strains to hear.

"You talked with them?"

"Yes sir. Your standing orders, sir."

"We need men, Major. All we can get. You know that."

"Yes sir, but these are real hardcases. Lunatics, sir. Anarchists."

"What were they doing?" Watching through the glasses, the Chief sees the formation approach the gallows, opening up and coming to a halt. The platoon commander, standing near the platform, shouts an order. The two prisoners are shoved toward the stairway. The older man stumbles, crawls forward on his knees until he is forced upright again. The other, proudly erect, waits for the steps to be cleared.

"Same old thing," the major is saying. "Trying to get into the courthouse, burn the archives. Lunatics, sir. They've been at it for two years."

"They?"

"That bunch, sir. You know. The squatters. They think if they burn the records—"

"I understand, Major." A thin smile on his lips, the Chief continues watching the prisoners. The first, supported by two soldiers, is led to his place, hooded, the noose draped around his neck, the heavy knot pulled snug beneath one ear. The younger prisoner shakes off a soldier's hand and strides beneath the second dangling noose. When the executioner's assistant attempts to place the black hood over his head the defiant prisoner twists away, cursing. The assistant looks to the master sergeant, who shrugs.

Down in the streets a few people watch. Others turn their backs and slink into doorways. The smoke from cooking fires drifts along the avenue, over the drifted sand and the wrecked automobiles. The lone horse wanders in the dunes, the stalk of a sunflower dangling from its soft muzzle.

"Major Roland . . ."

"Sir?"

The Chief pauses, binoculars held to his eyes, aimed downward. He watches as the assistant executioner lays the noose over the bare head of the younger prisoner and draws the knot firmly into position. The Chief, observing closely, can see but not hear the man's mouth opening and closing as he sings, or shouts, at the assembled soldiers and onlookers. The assistant steps off the trapdoor.

"Major Roland," the Chief says again.

"Yes sir!"

"Bring me that prisoner."

"Which prisoner, sir?"

"The younger one. The one without the hood. Hurry."

"Yes sir." Looking again through the glass, the major draws a portable radiotelephone from his belt, extends the telescoping antenna, and speaks into the mouthpiece.

Watching, the Chief sees far below the platoon commander, a young lieutenant, listening to another radiotelephone, sees him glance up once, briefly, toward the tower before shouting an

order at the hangman. The hangman speaks to his assistant.
Once again the assistant marches across the open stage of the
gallows.
Radio in hand, the major addresses the Chief. "Sir?"
"Yes?"
"Myers wants to know—Lieutenant Myers requests, sir,
what to do with the other prisoner."
"Hang him." The Chief turns away from the window, hands
behind his back. Softly, almost wearily, he mutters something to
Corporal Buckley. The corporal calls the two guards from the
doorway; the guards pull the massive drapes across the east
wall, darkening the office. Shaded lamps and a small window on
the north wall illuminate the room with a muted light. The Chief
removes the sunglasses, holds out the binoculars: Corporal
Buckley, alert as a pointer, takes both.
The Chief pauses, waiting for something. All the men in the
room wait intently, listening. A steel whistle sounds from the
square below, faint but clear through the distance and the heavy
walls. The Chief sighs; the officers allow themselves a measure
of relaxation.
"Orders carried out, sir," announces Major Roland.
The Chief retires to his chair behind a massive, nearly
empty desk, almost the only furniture in the room. He taps his
fingertips together, contemplating his clean, pale, shapely
hands, the long and slender fingers: the hands of an artist. Behind the desk is a bookcase of exotic authors: Froebius, Frois-
sart, Plotinus, Sri Aurobindo, Valentinus, Marcion, Mani, Simon
Magus, Saturnius, Cerdon, Aurelius, Epictetus, Ptolameus, Her-
acleon, de Chardin, Bergson, Boethius, Claudel, de Sade, de
Maistre . . . others. And esoteric titles: *The Immortalist; Seven
Chains to the Moon; The Analects; The Apocrypha; The Upani-
shads; The Philosophy of History; The Secret Sayings of Jesus;
The Bhagavad-Gita; Book of the Zodiac; Hermes Trismegiste;
The Thousand and Twelve Questions; Das Johannesbuch der
Mandaer; Philosophoumena; Koptische-gnostiche Schriften;
The Gospel* ["good news"] *of Truth; Mandaische Liturgien;*

The Coronation of the Great Sislam; Synergistics . . . and others, many others.

The bookcase is flanked by maps and mapstands: a large-scale map of the city, beautiful shaded topographic maps of the state, the region, the recent United States, the continent of North America. A globe of the earth, three feet in diameter, internally illuminated, finely detailed, rests on gimbals in a polished mahogany frame.

Mounted on the wall behind the Chief and his desk is the life-size figure of an eagle cast in bronze, seven-foot wings outspread, fierce eye and ravening beak *to the dexter*, the side of honor. Above the eagle, covering half the wall, is a flag. The flag, fringed in gold, depicts a copper sun rising (or sinking) above a field of blue; the six rays of the sun flare in gold across a crimson sky. The flag of the United States hangs furled on a staff set in a floorstand near the desk. There is a single unmarked door, without guard, in the blank west wall. Those who enter through the main entrance doors on the north find themselves facing at the far end of the great room a brilliant tableau of flags, eagle, books, maps, globe, and desk (and sometimes Corporal Buckley) centered precisely about the head and face of the Chief.

Exactly as he now confronts his aides Major Roland and Captain Barnes. "Gentlemen," he says, "excuse the interruption. Major, continue your report."

Fat, broad, formal Major Roland advances to the map of the city, and using his riding crop for a pointer, outlines the previous day's operations: a sweep of the University quarter again, where most of the arsonists and dissidents appear to be regrouping. No casualties; fifteen civilians conscripted for the field engineers; three deserters found and shot; two men enlisted for indoctrination and military training; five hundred gallons of diesel fuel and an arms cache discovered in Grid Block 17 . . .

"Arms cache, Major? What kind of arms?"

The major hesitates, coloring faintly. His bristling mustache droops a bit as he rechecks his notebook. "What kind, sir? Well—no firearms."

"No firearms? What then? Mortars? Rockets?"

"No sir. Hand weapons."

The Chief sighs, casting an ironic glance in the direction of Captain Barnes. "What kind of hand weapons? Broadswords? Rapiers? Fencing foils? Speak up, Major."

"No sir, I mean . . . clubs. Spears. Bows. Sickles and scythes. Pickaxes."

"Those are farming implements."

"I know, sir, but we also found some of these." The major digs in his tunic pocket, pulls out a spiked object the size of a golf ball, which he hands to the Chief. The Chief examines the thing, then tosses it across the floor toward Captain Barnes. It comes to a stop with one of its rigid spikes projecting upward. Captain Barnes picks it up and looks it over.

"What is it, Captain?"

"A medieval caltrop, sir. A museum piece."

"Right. And what is its purpose?"

"Injury. This thing could maim a horse or a man, if stepped on. Or puncture a truck tire." The captain rolls the caltrop again over the floor. Again it comes to a stop with a spike up. Corporal Buckley places the caltrop on the Chief's desk.

The major stares. "If I caught somebody dropping one of those things in front of *my* horse . . ." He gulps with horror.

"You'd what, Major?"

"What? Why—why, sir, I'd slash his head off."

"Healthy response, Major Roland. What else do you have to tell us?"

"That's all, sir. Then we caught those two this morning."

"Yes, the arsonists. Where is Myers and that prisoner, by the way?"

"They're on the way, sir."

"What's taking them so long?"

Major Roland clears his throat. "Sir, the service elevator— it's out of order."

"Again?"

"Yes sir."

The Chief is silent for a moment, his fingertips rapping on the desk. "Major Roland, I've told you before: I want everything in *this* building kept functioning. Our headquarters here is the one island of order and civilization we've got in this smoldering, decaying, rebellious city and I want it kept that way. Functioning."

"Yes sir."

"Get that elevator fixed."

"Yes sir."

"And one more thing, Major Roland."

"Yes sir?"

"That was good work yesterday. I commend you. Keep it up and we'll soon get this city in order and be ready to march. Carry on."

"Yes sir. Thank you, sir." His round, choleric face bright with a smile, the major stiffens his plump form to full attention, salutes, faces about, and marches from the room. As he reaches the open doors he pulls the visored cap from under his left arm and slaps it on his shaven head at a jaunty angle, just in time to return the rifle salute from the guards.

Lounging in his creaking swivel chair, the Chief smiles after the departing major. Then aware of Corporal Buckley hovering nearby, he dismisses him with the order to close the doors on the way out.

A moment of silence.

Captain Barnes, a tall, thin, young man with sun-bleached hair, sun-bronzed face and hands, waits at parade rest; he wears the uniform of a desert cavalryman: khakis, sidearm, boots and spurs, a broad-brimmed hat in one hand. His fine, green, intelligent eyes, grave and fearless, contemplate with equanimity the figure of the Chief behind the fortress of his desk.

"Captain Barnes!"

The captain comes to attention. "Yes sir."

"At ease, at ease." Smiling, the Chief rises from his chair, walks around to the front of his desk, and sits casually on the edge. "Come here. I want to talk with you. Seriously. No formal

"You're a general, sir."

"Oh Barnes, that was long ago." The Chief's pale face becomes radiant with his engaging smile. "And in the Air Force —of course. A lot of foolishness. Ever flown a B-52, Captain?"

"Sir, I never had a chance to fly anything but light planes."

"Yes, yes, how true. Ah, Captain . . ." The Chief's smile fades away, a cloud of longing and regret comes over his eyes. "What we have lost . . . can we ever regain it?" He falls into melancholy for a few seconds, recalling—not recapturing—the past. Then firms up. "But we must. We will." He places one strong hand on the captain's shoulder. "Now, for the other thing. You must not think of this as a personal vendetta, Captain, but there is one man in this . . . this city, one person, or even personage, we might say, a former colleague of mine at the university, whom I want to see before we depart. And when I say I want to see him"—the Chief points out and downward, toward the dark draperies of the east wall, toward Unity Square—"I mean I want to see him *down there*. On the platform. Center stage, where he always liked so much to be, preaching his rotten and corrupting doctrine!"

The Chief's voice has risen as he speaks, climaxing in an involuntary tone of exclamation. He stops suddenly, then continues in his customary well-modulated, somewhat high but pleasing voice. "Ideas, Captain, ideas. In the end, dear Captain Barnes, we will give up anything, sacrifice anything, our friends, our loves, our own lives, rather than surrender—our ideas. And the more absurd the idea, the more urgently we defend it. Right, Captain? And so it must be, or we forsake the glory of intellect and the essence of humanity."

The Chief allows himself and the captain a moment of silence to reflect upon this obvious truth. Barnes says, "Who's the man, sir, and what's the charge against him?"

"The name is treason!"

"Treason?"

The Chief smiles. "The charge is treason. Treason against the State. And against much more, I might say. Against Man and against the future of Man." A pause. "You think I exaggerate but you'll understand. As for the fellow's name, it's only Rodack. Noah Rodack, you never heard of him, he was only a professor. Another Jew professor. Don't be shocked, Captain, it's not a question of anti-Semitism; I tell you these things because there is no one else I can talk to. We are surrounded by innocents and thugs. We lead a regiment of innocent thugs—not an incompatible hybrid. Quite compatible. And indispensable. To us. Find that man. I want a talk with him before we leave. Before he makes his final ascent. Put Brock on it, he'll find him."

"Sergeant Brock?"

"Is there another?"

"Brock . . ." Barnes looks up at the eagle. "Brock, sir, he's a monster. A torturer."

"Indispensable. But not a torturer. I have forbidden torture. There is no torture in my . . . my authority."

"You are misinformed, sir."

"Interrogation is allowed. Scientific interrogation. But no torture."

"Sir—"

"Don't disappoint me, Captain Barnes. You have your orders."

"Yes sir."

"Good. Now go tell that idiot Buckley to stop tapping, gently rapping, on our chamber door. Have Myers bring the prisoner in."

"Yes sir." Captain Barnes takes his hat, draws himself to attention, steps back, salutes, wheels about.

"And Captain—"

Barnes halts. "Yes sir?"

The Chief comes close, puts a hand on shoulder again. "Captain Barnes . . . I understand your loathing for Brock. I share it. We're leaving him behind, too, Brock and his filthy little squad of motorcycle police."

"Thank God."

"But for these last two days—we need him."

"Need him?"

"We'll use him. *Use* him, Captain Barnes."

"Yes sir."

"Then leave him to roast in this desert hell. Let the Devil and the sun take care of Sergeant Brock."

"Yes sir."

The captain marches out. The double doors, opening behind him, reveal a glimpse of saluting guards, struggling soldiers. The doors are closed, then opened again, and the prisoner, a dark shirtless man gleaming with sweat, is shoved into the room with such violence that he staggers to his knees. Arms bound he glares at the naked bayonets poised at his throat. A short, anxious, harried lieutenant advances toward the flags, the eagle, the desk, and halts. He salutes. "Sir, Lieutenant Myers reporting with prisoner as ordered."

The Chief, leaning against the edge of the desk, ignores the lieutenant. The Chief's pale eyes are fixed on the prisoner. After a moment of silent inspection, he pushes himself erect, walks past Myers and toward the prisoner. As he approaches, the soldiers back off a little, opening a space around the kneeling man. The prisoner and the Chief stare at one another in silence.

The Chief says, "Let him stand."

Two of the soldiers put hands on the prisoner to help him to his feet. The prisoner shakes them off, struggles upright without aid. He is a stocky fellow, brown-skinned, hair black as coal; on his chest and back are streaks of dried blood from bayonet cuts. He sways in weariness but his eyes, as he glares at the Chief, are bright with hatred. He licks his lips, trying to speak.

"What's your name, man?" says the Chief softly.

The prisoner swallows. "I got no name," he mutters. He bares his teeth in what is meant to be a grin. "My name is man. Hang me for it."

"What is your name?"

The grin becomes wider. "My name is *libertad. Viva libertad.* My name is *tierra o muerte.* Hang me."

"I'm not going to hang you. I'm going to make you a soldier."

"I'm already a soldier. Hang me for that."

"I don't hang soldiers. I honor them." The Chief keeps his steady gaze fixed on the prisoner's eyes. "And I lead them."

The grin becomes defiant. "I fight them."

The Chief smiles. He turns to the soldiers. "Untie this man. And give me two bayonets."

The soldiers move to obey. Lieutenant Myers steps in hastily. "Sir," he protests in a whisper, "this man is dangerous. He's a lunatic."

The Chief turns to confront Myers. "A lunatic? You say he's a lunatic?" He takes a pair of gleaming bayonets from one of the soldiers. "What of it?" He grins in the lieutenant's face. "We're all lunatics here. We're an army of lunatics. That's the secret of our power. Take your men out of here."

"Sir—!"

"Leave us."

The lieutenant stares in dismay, his lips quivering. "Sir, he's twenty years younger. I can't let you—"

"You can't *what?*" The Chief stares with cold anger into the officer's eyes. "You can't what, Lieutenant?" A pause. The lieutenant lowers his face. "Now get out," the Chief says quietly. "You and your men. Close the doors. Stay out till I call you. You understand?"

Meekly the lieutenant replies, "Yes sir." He orders the guard detail out of the room, looks back once more at the Chief —a beseeching look—then leaves.

The Chief locks the doors on the inside. The prisoner, his arms now free, stands watching. The mocking grin has become doubtful, a little fearful, no longer a grin at all. The Chief, a bayonet in each hand, faces the man, steps toward him. Instinctively the other retreats a step. The Chief stops. "Here's your weapon," he says, tossing one of the bayonets, hilt first, toward the prisoner, who tries to catch it in the air, fumbles, drops it. Blood wells from his palm before he even feels the pain. He glances at the new wound in surprise, then crouches to pick up

the bayonet. The Chief advances, his naked blade weaving
slowly back and forth.

The prisoner straightens, weapon in his bleeding hand, and
stares with a kind of wonder at the slim fair man in the immaculate uniform coming step by step toward him. The Chief's eyes,
fixed intently on the other, glow with penetrating intensity. His
voice, when he speaks, vibrates in tones of passionate, overwhelming conviction. "Prisoner," he says, "whatever your
name: You are a brave man. You are a soldier. I don't want to
kill you. I want you to fight—*for me.*"

The prisoner stares, not moving, the bayonet held before
him in a frozen, defensive posture.

"You have a family?" the Chief suggests. "They will be
cared for. You want land? You will be given land—your own, in
your own name, in deeds patent and inalienable. You want liberty? I will give you the liberty of the warrior, the conquering
warrior; there is no liberty sweeter than that. And I will give you
things even better than any of this. I will give you honor. And
glory. We are going to make a nation again. You shall be a part
of it. We need heroes, my friend; you can be a hero."

The Chief gazes into the prisoner's eyes, waiting, watching.
The other does not move. The Chief continues in his quiet but
mesmeric tones: "What is your name, my friend?"

The man's lips move numbly. "Garcia . . ."

"Garcia, my friend, let me tell you one more thing. What we
do is for causes even higher than honor, glory, heroism, patrio-
tism. Even higher than the nation. What we do . . . is for God.
There is a higher law than human law, Garcia. And there is a
higher world, friend Garcia, than this world. Far better than this
stinking earth where we sweat and grunt for food, fuck our
women, make children, fight one another, grow old and die and
rot in a cold, stinking grave. Is that what we are here for? No,
Garcia, it is not. To live without God is to die without hope. We
are creatures with souls. Immortal souls, Garcia, with a purpose
higher than any earthly fate. Our purpose is to follow—the light.
The light that leads us to God, my friend. And by that light, if
we do not rebel against it like fools, or betray it like cowards,

by that light, my friend Garcia, we will meet God. We will become one in union with God. Forever. Beyond time. Through all eternity."

The Chief pauses again, probing with his burning gaze deep into the other man's eyes, into his mind, into his spirit. "Do you understand, my friend Garcia?"

The man breathes out the word. "Yes . . ."

The Chief allows his concentrated gaze to soften into a smile, warm with love. "Yes, you do. Now, Garcia, you are my soldier. I am your commander. Take these bayonets"—he puts his own into Garcia's free hand—"and give them back to the guard when I open the doors. You understand?"

"Yes . . ."

"Yes *sir.*"

"Yes sir . . ."

Smiling, the Chief turns his back on Garcia, walks to the doors, opens them, and speaks to the waiting lieutenant. "Lieutenant Myers!" The lieutenant stiffens to attention. "Take this man"—he points to Garcia—"Private Garcia there, to the supply room. See that he is issued a uniform. I put him under your command."

Myers stares in wonder at the ex-prisoner, now approaching Myers' soldiers with the bayonets held out, butts foremost, toward them. "Yes sir," says Myers.

"And one more thing."

"Yes sir?"

The Chief puts a hand on the lieutenant's shoulder. "You did well in finding this man for us. He'll make a soldier. I commend you."

"Thank you, sir."

The Chief lowers his voice, speaks in a quiet hiss. "Now get the wretch out of my sight. I'm sick of the smell of him. And if he gives you one bit of trouble shoot him instantly. Instantly. I don't want to hear about it."

"Yes sir."

D̶ixie Dalton, wiping glasses behind the bar, hears the horses coming near at a slow walk, down the street. She glances at the musicians on the bandstand at the rear of the barroom. The aging man called Bob moves to the window, his head barely reaching above the half curtains. He does not seem to be alarmed. Dixie stays where she is and reaches for another dusty beer glass. She is a plump, handsome young woman with dimples in her rosy cheeks, freckles, green eyes, a tangled mass of crisp copper-tinted curls framing her head.

"Who is it, Bob?"

"Dunno. Just bums." He returns to his mate at the bandstand where the two are rehearsing for the evening's performance. Bob has the pallid flesh of a night person; his head is bald, his nose a limp beak, his ears project like jug handles, and his gray, wispy adolescent beard, attached in mangy patches to his narrow chin, seems to be full of fleas—he keeps scratching at it. Like any male primate, he finds himself curiously attractive; on his way back to the bandstand he pauses for a furtive look into a mirror on the wall and a quick finger-comb of the fringe of hair around his God-given tonsure. He strums the guitar hanging at groin level from his neck. "Okay, man," he says to his partner at the piano, "one more time." He scratches the beard.

"Not again."

"We got a gig tonight, Glenn. We gotta eat." Bob crouches over the guitar strings, right hand swinging across his knees. They begin to play. Bob rocks creakily back and forth in a kind of dancelike caper. His mouth sags open at one corner, he snarls, a lyric comes forth:

> *Hey mister cool ice cream man*
> *Find some cream for me*

The pianist winces, sinking his head between his shoulders, and thumps with big hands on the yellowish keys of an upright grand. A half-empty glass of whisky sits on the lid. Glenn has the bulging brow of a Beethoven and a huge white Brahmsian beard that spreads, like a fluffy bib, across his chest. He sits slumped on a rotating stool screwed down so low that his hands, as he plays, are on a level with his strawberry-colored, rhinophymic nose. In his bloodshot eyes shines the light—not particularly noticeable in the eyes of his friend—of genuine human intelligence. With glints of exasperation, frustration, smoldering rage.

A hand-painted placard rests against the bandstand, identifying this musical duo:

> *Dance to the Solid Sounds*
> *Of "The Trail Drifters"*
> *Singin' Bob & Swingin' Glenn*

The barmaid jiggles on the boards behind the bar, polishing the glasses, her shoulders and hips twitching with the beat. From outside comes the sound of men dismounting, the jingle of spurs, the clump and clomp of tired boots on the walk. She stops, listening with care. The swinging doors swing open, letting in a blast of sunshine. The black silhouette of a lanky, long-connected man appears, like a target, in the opening. The musicians fall silent.

An old man with whiskers steps inside, followed by a lad of sixteen or so. Both come to a halt, blinded by the sudden dark, as the doors swing shut behind them. The old man waits, then gropes his way to the bar, leans on it, and peers through the gloom. "Anybody here?"

Dixie Dalton looks them over with caution, puts down a glass, steps forward. "I'm here."

The old man studies her with a bright merry eye of glass, a dark and solemn eye of living tissue. The boy stands back, alert and watchful, aware of the musicians, of a half-open door beyond the bar. "You're the bartender?" asks the old man.

"Guess so. There's no others around."

"Damn if you ain't the prettiest sight I've seen since we left Magdalena, New Mexico. Damn near the only one. Draw us a pitcher of beer, miss, and set up three glasses." He looks around again, spots the two men on the bandstand. They stare back at him in silence. He returns to the barmaid. "What's wrong with them fellas?"

Dixie fills a pitcher at the tap and sets it before him. The foaming head spills down the sides. "They're musicians," she says.

"Folks sure are nervous around here. The ones that ain't dead, I mean. Step up here, Arthur, and have a beer." The boy comes closer.

"That'll be three dollars," Dixie says.

"Three dollars? For a pitcher of beer?"

"Yes sir. How old is your boy?"

Arthur flushes angrily. "I'm as old as you are, lady. I'll be nineteen in August."

"Yeah? August of what year?"

"What difference does that make?" the old man says. "We're all grown-ups these days." He pulls a green bill from his money belt. "Keep the change."

"That's the wrong color," Dixie says. "We don't take paper money anymore."

"*Chihuahua . . .*" The old man fumbles in the money belt again and comes up with a coin that flashes like a sunbeam when he slaps it on the bar. "How about that there, my lovely little lady?"

Dixie weighs the coin in her palm, bites the milled rim, drops it on the bar; it rings like gold. "This'll do." She gives him seven big silver dollars in change.

"What's your name, miss?"

"Dixie Dalton."

"Dixie Dalton!" The old man marvels over the name. "Why a name like that, those fellas back there"—pointing to the bandstand—"should set it to music."

"It's only a name." Nervously, half smiling, she runs a hand through her thick curls. "What's yours?"

"They tell me it's Jack Burns." The old man gulps down his glass of beer. "But that's only hearsay." He wipes the froth from his mustache. "Goddamn but that's good."

"Mine's Art Dekker," says Arthur Dekker.

"Now Miss Dixie, tell me this. We need grain for our horses. Where can we get some?"

She tells him. Burns relaxes a bit, looking pleased. He pours another glass of beer for himself and the boy. A streak of tobacco juice leaks from the edge of Burns' mouth; he wipes it on his greasy sleeve. Both he and the boy smell like saddle blankets. How about a room with bath? She tells him: There is none. The old man shrugs, not surprised by this information.

The musicians resume their rehearsal. The glass of whiskey on the lid of the piano, jarred by the pianist's heavy attack on the keyboard, moves with each vibration closer to the edge. Glenn stands for a moment, playing with one hand, rescues the imperiled glass, and empties it with a flourish into his throat. Sighing, he slumps back down on the stool.

The Indian comes in, leans on the bar beside Burns and the boy. He smiles at Dixie. Burns pours him a glass of beer from the pitcher. "Looks all right out there," Sam says to Burns; "no sign of the black riders. Or anybody else. The streets are deserted."

"Anybody following us?"

"No sign of it yet."

Dixie looks at the Indian. He lifts his glass of beer in salute, smiling. She smiles back. She likes his broad, brown, earthy face, the big shoulders, the comfortable roll of fat around his middle. The first man she's seen in a long time who's neither too young, too old, or in a uniform. God, she thinks, he looks . . . almost human. They'll kill him for sure.

The boy is restless. "Let's get out of here."

"What's the rush?" says Sam, winking at Dixie.

Arthur claps his glass down hard on the bar. "You two can stay. I'm leaving."

"Easy, easy," the old man says. "First we got to get that feed. And one other thing . . ." He pulls out the antique leather billfold, extracts the faded photograph. "Miss Dixie, ma'am, have a look at this."

She looks.

"You know anybody resembles that kid?"

She looks again at the picture, then at Burns. "Well," she says, "you do. In a way."

"Right." The old man swells with pride. "That's my son—twenty years ago. Course he must look a sight different now."

Dixie nods toward the boy at Burns' side. "I thought he was your son. You said—"

"My name is Art Dekker," the boy repeats, a bit flushed with beer.

The old man smiles, putting an arm on Art's shoulder, con-

sidering the young man with a new regard. "He could be, by
God. I wish he was. But he ain't. Least he ain't the one we're
lookin' for."

Dixie says, "You said your name is Barnes?"

"Burns. My son's name is Charlie. Last time I heard
any word of Charlie was four years ago. He was in the Army
then."

"Everybody was in the Army," Dixie says. "I was in the
Army. I was a biker—a motorcycle messenger. Courier, they
called it. Got out just in time," she adds in a lower tone, as if
divulging a secret. She glances toward the long window in front,
the hot sunlight beyond, a strip of blue. With half her attention
she listens for sounds from out there.

"Then you never heard of him?"

"No sir, I don't know anybody by that name. You want
another pitcher of beer?"

"No," says the boy, "we're leaving."

"Yes," says Sam, "I'll have another."

Burns draws back from the bar. "You wait here, Sam. Me
and Art'll get the feed. We're gonna need all we can pack along."

"Mention my name," Dixie says. "That'll help."

Burns and young Art Dekker go out; the swinging doors
extinguish them in a flash of sunlight. Singin' Bob, picking at his
guitar, steps close to the window to watch the departure, then
returns to the bandstand. "Let's go through it once more," he
says, scratching the beard.

"Not again," the pianist says.

"Just one more time, man."

"Don't call me that."

"Huh? I didn't call you anything. What's the matter with
you? I mean, you know, we gotta do it, man."

"I want to play music."

"So play."

"I said *music. Partitas.* Inventions. Variations."

"Forget it, man. You can't do that stuff any more and you
know it. Right? So come on. Once more."

The rehearsal goes on. Sam leans across the bar toward the bartender. "More discord than music back there."

"They always fight. I don't pay any attention." She fills his glass. "I'm Dixie. Who are you?"

"I don't know. Call me Sam. Why'd you tell Jack to mention your name?"

"So the guys'll know it's all right. Nobody trusts anybody around here. It's a scared town."

"You have to trust somebody. Sometime. Or you'll always be alone. Why do you stay here?"

"You mean a girl like me in a nice place like this? I don't know." She dabs at the bar with her rag. "You know any place that's any better?"

"Yes," Sam says. "If it's still there. My village. Our home." He stares for a while out the window, watching one white cloud afloat on the desert sky.

"You're an Indian?"

"I was. Now I'm just another Native American."

"You're lucky. God, I never had a home at all. Never will, I guess. Maybe I don't really want one."

"I know what you mean. I haven't seen my home for twenty years." Sam smiles into his glass of beer. "My people don't write letters. And neither did I. But I might go back there. After we find the old man's son." He places his brown hand on her white hand. "You could go with me, maybe."

She laughs nervously. "You're kidding. My boyfriend would kill me."

Sam withdraws his hand. "That's some boyfriend."

She laughs again, not looking at Sam. "Well, he's not really a boy. And not really a friend." She pauses to listen, not to Bob and Glenn, but for sounds from outside. "But he's all right, in his way. He's big, he protects me. A woman needs that around here."

"I believe you."

"You wouldn't like him. He's in the Army too. Like everybody else under sixty. Rides a big motorcycle." She runs a hand through her hair, then goes back to playing with the bar rag. "He don't come by very often but when he does—you know it. You wouldn't like him at all." She hesitates, twisting the rag, looking at her hands. "But if it weren't for him . . . I'd be in there." She points to the west, beyond the wall, toward the heart of the city. "With the others."

Singin' Bob, quiet for a time, claws at his guitar. Swingin' Glenn, morose, unmollified, rumbles up and down the keyboard with a cascade of polychromatic arpeggios. Bob stops.

Sam leans farther across the bar, closer to Dixie. "Hey," he says, "hoka hey. Cheer up. You want to see a trick?" He reaches for the silver dollars old Burns has left on the bar.

Dixie looks up at him, brightening. The dimples come back. "Oh yes," she says.

Sam spins a big coin in the air—it glitters in the gloom— catches it, slaps it down on the back of his left hand, keeping it covered with his right. "Heads or tails?"

"Oh . . . tails."

He lifts his right hand, holding it up and open, fingers outspread. The coin is gone.

"Well . . ." Dixie smiles. "Not bad. What else do you do?"

"Call me Sam."

"Okay, Sam. So what else? Where's the silver dollar?"

He reaches across the bar and behind her ear. "Here it is." The coin shines in his hand. "And here"—he reaches out again, plucks another from her hair—"here's another."

She laughs with delight. "Keep it up, we'll get rich."

"Whatever you say." Sam leans toward her, smiling into her eyes. Fascinated, she stares back at him, waiting. He reaches down inside her loose blouse and draws a third silver dollar from the warm cleft between her breasts.

"Oh," she says, "oh my, my . . ." A quick glance toward the window. The blue sky is still out there. The blazing light. The empty street. She looks back at Sam, smiling. "How'd you *do* that?"

"You want me to show you?"

"Show me."
The piano player pounds on his yellow keyboard, his eyes on the ceiling, and moans in polyphonic concord with the thunder from his fingers. Singin' Bob, overrun and discarded by the piano, lifts both hands in a gesture of dismay, scratches his beard, and sweetly smiles, across one narrow shoulder, at the two heads touching over the bar.

Onward then, thinks the old man. With or without our shaman, onward. After a long siesta in the shade of a looted shopping center, their horses rested, grained, watered, he and the boy proceed westward, into the shadows, into the endless ruins, toward the smoking city and the dark towers. They pull their hat brims low against the evening sun, against the red glow and the brazen glitter of twenty miles of broken glass.

"He ain't coming?"

"Said he'd find us later." Burns smiles on his thoughts. "Sam's in love."

"Love," the boy says scornfully. "That woman's a whore. I seen her kind before."

"She's no whore, not that Dixie. And even if she was, what's wrong with that? There's plenty things worse, and not many better. At least if she's honest."

"It's a sin. A sin against God."

Burns considers. "That might be so. But it's not a sin against us human-type folks. Such as we are."

"Well . . ." says young Art. He scowls into the evening glare. "Don't know about that," he mutters.

They ride on. Burns restrains his impulse to needle the boy. The kid is green—green with jealousy. Instead he checks their armaments. "That gun of yours loaded, Art?"

The boy touches his revolver, slides it in and out of the holster. "Sure is. You can bet your bottom dollar on that. What good's a gun that ain't loaded?"

The old man makes no answer. I'm riding with a lad who killed two soldiers yesterday, he reflects. Better treat him with respect. Even if he is in love. God, I'm in love too. When's the last time I saw a woman like that Dixie? Not for years. Not for many years.

They ride at a brisk walking pace, due west, up the broad avenue littered with fragments of paper and glass, flanked now with dehydrated palm trees, abandoned automobiles, decaying office buildings with sagging walls of lathing, chicken wire, stucco, crumbling bastions of cinderblock. Old voices speak from dangling signs, dead for a decade: *Lou Grubb Chevrolet: "the Friendly Folks"; Church of Jesus Christ of Latter-Day Saints; Ace Liquors; Goldwater's; Ramada Inn East; Fannin Makes It Move!; Big Surf; Food Giant; Yellow Front; Checker Auto Parts; McDonalds: "Over Two Hundred Billion Served"; Denny's; Valley National Bank; No-Tel Motel: "Adult Movies in Every Room"; Holiday Inn: "Welcome, Tulsa Jaycees"; Kon-Tiki Motor Hotel: "Free Beds for Hula Dancers"; Kum 'n' Go Inn; Apache Hideaway—"Cool Pool, Courtesy Coffee, Beautyrest Beds"; Friendship Motel: "No Vacancy"; Hospitality Haven: "Closed for Season"; and Welcome Inn: "Sorry."*

They pass more stores, looted, burned, ravaged: *Circle K;*

Seven/Eleven; U-Tote-Em; Go-Fer; and *B. Dalton, Bookseller.* They notice, without comment, a Lear jet with nose and forward cabin buried in the rubble of *Diamond's Department Store.* They ride past *Disco A' Go-Go: "Wet T-Shirt Contest Every Wednesday"; Pink Pussycat Massage Parlor: "Discount to Truckers"; Cat House: "Nude Girls—Live!—Onstage"; Honey Tree: "E otic* [sic] *Dancers";* and *Plaza International West: "Tonight! Singin' Bob & The Trail Drifters."*

Ruins. Ruins. All in ruins. Coyotes slink among the blackened walls, hunting rats. Anthills rise, Soleri-like, from the arid fountains of the covered mall. Young paloverde trees, acid green, and globemallow, and sunflowers, and tumbleweed, and the bright fuzzy cactus known as teddy bear cholla (cuddly and deadly) grow from cracks in the asphalt of the endless parking lots.

Stray horses browse among the sand dunes that are drifting fifty feet a year out of the southwest toward the mountains. Philosophical vultures on indolent wings soar above the deserted mansions of the rich, above the golf courses where cattle graze, above the zoological gardens, the sewage lagoons, the weed-grown runways of the international airport: Sky Harbor.

Occasional gunfire rattles down the stillness of the central canyons of glass and aluminum; the gallows creak and groan with their heavy load; bugles sound out, clear and shrill, from the barracks of the central Tower; and from beyond, from far beyond, surrounding the city's disintegration, comes the murmuring stillness of the desert, the eternal dialogue of the wind and the sands.

A great billboard looms on their right, speaking thus:

TIRED OF ARSON? MURDER? WAR?
READY FOR ORDER? LAW? PROGRESS?
SUPPORT OUR CHIEF!

The face of the Chief himself, blue eyes peering into the visionary future, a compassionate and hopeful smile on his lips, chin firm and nostrils proudly dilated, looms like a giant above the looming sign. A homemade arrow is lodged in his ear; bulletholes speckle his cheeks.

"Look busy," says Burns. "The boss is a-watchin'." Spitting his contempt, the boy draws his revolver. "No, save your ammo. You might need it on something real."

Speak of the devil. No sooner said than they hear, from a big shopping center on their left—*El Con*—the roar of motorcycles, the snap, pop, and crackle of small-arms fire. They stop, reining in sharply.

"It's them," says Art, "it's them. Them black-suited devils." He spurs his mount toward the noise of battle; waving his revolver in the air he canters wrong way down a one-way alley into a maze of walls, vanishing around a corner.

"Art," cries the old man, "Art—wait a minute. Not like that." He prods his mare into action; she gallops heavily after the kid, shoes thudding on the warm asphalt, farting from the sudden effort. Dodging around the first corner, Burns' leg brushes a cholla cactus; one jointed branch comes away, clings with its barbed spines to his shank. He ignores the stinging pain, searching ahead for the boy. Sees him loping around an abstract sculpture of welded auto bumpers and down a dark arcade into gloomy roofed-over depths beyond. The barking of guns, the yells of frightened men echo through the corridors of this commercial labyrinth. Burns saws his horse to a stop.

"Art!" he bellows. "Art!" A pair of nude mannequins with extravagant busts, cocked heads, rigid smirks, leer at him through the cracked plate glass of the shop at his side. *Frederick's of Hollywood;* nearby is *Farrell's Ice Cream Parlor; H. Cook's Sporting Goods:* rows of empty rifle racks, empty handgun cases; *Doubleday Books: Waldenbooks;* windowsful of bad news; Swiss Fair Deli; El Ciné Central: "*Star Wars Part Six,*" says the marquee; *Odyssey Records & Tapes: "All Prices Slashed."* Slashed, slashed, slashed. And slashed.

"Art Dekker!" howls old Jack Burns. "You get back out of there. Right—now!"

The guns reply. The falling crash of glass. The grumble of toppling masonry. A scream of pain soars through the twilight. Moments of startled silence, another scream—the smell of trauma. Burns hears footsteps running toward him, out of the unlit malls ahead. He hears a voice, hoarse but powerful, shout a command. The motorcycle engines, which had been quiet for a few minutes, roar again into violent life. Coming this way.

Burns pulls his horse aside, through the glass, over the low wall between the mannequins, into the dark at the rear of the store. He dismounts, draws his revolver, waits.

The running footsteps, faltering, come near. A young man lurches into the doorway, black silhouette against the light. No hat on his head, no gun in his hand. He reels through the doorway and into Frederick's, stumbles, falls, lies still on the floor amid the broken glass, shattered cabinets, fallen plaster, the headless, legless, pink torsos of plastic females.

"Art? Is that you, Art?"

The young man on the floor groans some kind of answer, tries to rise, then lies still again as the motorcycles come bellowing down the broad hallway. Burns watches them rumble by, not fast, the riders glancing left and right as they advance. Three machines, three men in uniforms of black, wearing silver helmets, bearing carbines slung across their backs. The leading rider wears, on his sleeve, the chevrons of a master sergeant. They go past, diminish in sound beyond the next turning, as other motorcycles, at the scene of the battle, continue to roar. Lions of steel thundering up and down the courses of a maze. But no more gunshots are heard, no more shouting or crying.

Burns waits a few moments. The bike squad, divided, seems to be going away. Tying his horse to a cash register, the old man fumbles toward the slim figure on the floor, kneels, touches the warm body. "Art?"

The body groans again, rolls over. Large gray eyes stare up at Burns. It is not the boy but a young woman, wearing a man's loose shirt, a man's overalls. "Who are you?" she says. And "It hurts."

"A friend. Where's it hurt?" She shows him, he feels the welling blood as he gently pulls down the oversize overalls. He sees the gash of a bullet through one buttock. He tears a strip from her shirttail, makes a compress, stanches the bleeding, binds the compress to her hip with another long swatch from the shirt.

"Shot in the ass," she mumbles, grinning over his shoulder. "Ridiculous. Right in the ass. How goddamn ridiculous."

"No, that's about as good a place to get shot as a body could ask for. Missed your tailbone by six inches. No permanent damage. You're lucky." He draws up the overalls, buckles the shoulder straps to the bib. Loaded ammo clips in the pocket. "We'll find you a doctor."

The girl laughs. "Doctor. That's good. We're all doctors. I'm a doctor of philosophy."

"That's better than none," Burns says. "That'll have to do. Until Sam shows up."

"What's your name, Daddy? You look like my granddad."

"Quiet now, quiet. . . ."

The motorcycles are returning. The rumbling of doom, approaching. Again the black riders file by, one two three, the sergeant and his silent men. Scarlet flames on silver helmets: holstered automatic on each hip, a carbine across each back: black-gloved hands on throttle grips: somber faces. The big motors grumble, through cannon-shell tailpipes, like Minotaurs with hungry bellies. No lights.

"The boys from downtown . . ."

"Quiet, quiet. . . ."

The riders pass by, and on, and away, searching. The engines fade gradually in the distance.

"They hunting for you, miss?"

"They're hunting for everybody, Grandfather. You better get out of here. Where's my Mauser? God, I'm thirsty, Grandfather, thirsty, thirsty." She attempts to rise.

"Lie still for a minute. I'll fetch some water." Burns gets up, shakily, and returns with his antique canteen. Cradling her head on his arm, he helps her drink. He takes a deep drink himself. "Let's go."

"I don't think I can walk."

"Find you a doctor." Again the girl laughs. He helps her up, supports her to the horse, loads her stomach-down across the saddle. "Hang onto the stirrup. No, don't try to sit, stay that way."

Burns leads his horse toward the doorway. Steel-shod hooves crunch on the limbs and trunks of scattered humanoids. He waits for a while, listening, staring, then guides the horse down the broad corridor. A few fresh stars glimmer above the skylight. Which way? he asks himself.

"To the university," the girl says, reading his mind. "North and west. Under the library. Return this book."

"But Art," the old man says, "what happened to Art?"

"Art is long. So long, Art." She giggles in delirium. "They killed him. They killed all my guys. Or worse."

"Don't talk." Burns decides to follow the route taken by the boy when he last saw him. This way leads down another gloomy concourse and out of the complex to one more immense parking lot, littered with immobile automobiles, grown up in desert flora. His first few steps remind him of the cholla joint fastened to his calf. He disengages it with difficulty, using two sticks; there is no way to handle the thing with bare hands.

He finds no clue to Art's disappearance—no riderless horse, no uninhabited body. The boy is gone: captured, shot, lost. He debates with himself the wisdom of trying to return to the saloon where Dixie Dalton presides at the bar, Sam Banyaca leaning ever closer toward her. Too far, too far, he must find help sooner than that.

The girl on his horse solves the question. Struggling, gasping from the pain, she has worked herself into a seated position in the saddle. "Not dead yet," she moans. "Take us home, Granddad, take us home. Got friends there, they'll help you."

"You're the one needs help, lady. Which way?"

"Lady? Lady? Nobody's called me that. Years. Go up that

next street, under the palms. Stay away from the stadium—
that's where they hold their pep rallies."

Burns strides forward as directed; the pain in his calf burns
like the sting of a dozen hornets. He sets the pain aside, forgets
it, marches on. The horse follows at his heels, the girl babbles
away, the stars wink and shimmer through the smoky haze.
Burns stops and silences her for a moment with another drink
from his canteen. Her hand, placed on his shoulder for support,
glows with a feverish warmth. The sensation of her warmth, like
the odor of her skin and hair, illuminates a constellation of
memories.

They stop once, and hide again, as the sound of the motorcycle patrol is heard on a nearby street. And the sound of marching
men, the groan of—a wounded prisoner? The sounds diminish
into the twilight, moving west toward the glass towers. Burns
and his horse and the girl continue north and west, through the
burned-out student ghettos, past block after block of black foun-
dations, dead trees, derelict motor vehicles, cleaned-out stores,
shops, gasoline stations.

He smells fresh horse dung and realizes that Rosie is defe-
cating on the move, marking their trail. He takes time out to boot
the stuff into the weeds, then goes on.

A shadowy hulk of a building, occupying an entire block,
appears ahead. "That way," she says. Burns obeys—and is not
too surprised, as they come closer, when a pair of young men,
masked like bandits, emerge from the ruins with shotguns leveled at his belly. "Halt," says one, quietly but firmly. Burns
halts; the second man steps forward, jerks the revolver from
Burns' holster, steps back again. "Okay, buddy: Who are you?"

Before Burns can answer, the girl in the saddle begins to
giggle. "You blind idiots," she says, "it's me. Me. Barbara. Help
me down."

They stare at her through the darkness; one moves quickly
to her side while the other watches Burns. Aided by the young
man, Barbara dismounts, stiffly, moaning a little. The two men
apologize to the girl but not to Burns. After a brief discussion

the men agree, reluctantly, to allow Burns into the library. The underground library. One leads his horse off to be hidden away from the building; the other, assisting the girl, nods to him to follow.

They move through shadows, among piles of rubble, toward the gaping walls of the building, down a passageway beneath the wreckage, crouching under low beams, and into deeper darkness, feeling their way. A steel door bars their path. The young man raps on the steel, in code; after a pause the door is opened from within. A large room is revealed, dimly lit by candles, a couple of oil lamps. What seems to Burns like a crowd of very young men and women stare at him. The boys are bearded, ragged, unwashed, apprehensive. Weapons are everywhere— shotguns, rifles, even lances and crossbows and sabers that must have been taken from a museum. Two of the women, after a moment of surprise, rush forward to take care of their wounded comrade, bearing her off, through canvas drapes, into some farther chamber beyond.

The door is closed behind Burns, closed with a firm meshing of heavy bolts, locked, barred. No one speaks, all are watching him. He stares back, not alarmed, feeling that he is among friends, but unwilling to speak first. They make a rough-looking crew, both the men and the women. Beards and headbands, bare chests, earrings and feathers, each with a knife or pistol stuck in belt. One girl, long-haired and handsome, wearing a velveteen skirt like a Navajo squaw, carries a sword in scabbard girdled to her waist. They might be pirates, gypsies, incendiaries— anarchists. But too young, too young, resembling art students in masquerade. Amateur pirates, a little self-conscious in their adopted roles. The silence is prolonged; then one young fellow clears his throat, essays a smile, starts to take a step forward, tugging at his red beard.

The drapes open again and an older man, crouching, enters the big room. He straightens, pauses in silence, looking grave, and stares first at the young people, then at Burns. He is a heavy, stocky man with gray beard, a bald professorial dome. He offers a hand to Burns. "My name's Rodack," he says. "Thank you very much for bringing her back." He turns to the others. "Barb's all right," he says, "thanks to our friend here. She caught a bullet in the rump, through one cheek. Lost some blood but it didn't hit any bone. She'll be fine in a few days. But"— Rodack stops and lowers his gaze to the floor—"they got Will and Angelo. Both of them. She thinks they're probably dead. They ran into Brock's motorcycle squad."

The long-haired girl with the sword sinks to her knees, begins to wail. A contagion of sobbing spreads among the girls; the boys, those rosy-cheeked, bearded pirates, look bleakly at one another, muttering curses.

Rodack looks at Burns. "There was somebody else there, Barb said. A kid on a horse, some crazy kid who charged right into the middle of the fight, blazing away with a revolver. They got him. Captured him, I mean. Alive." Rodack faces his students. "You know what that means."

A silence comes over the little group; the sobbing dies away. Rodack turns again to Burns. "Do you know who she is talking about?"

"Yes sir, I do."

"Who is he?"

"A boy I met yesterday. His name is Arthur Dekker. Just a boy with a grudge, far as I know, out for revenge."

"Does he know about us?"

"No sir," says Burns.

"He knows nothing at all?"

"He never heard of you. Found him way out east in the desert. Them motorcycle soldiers had killed his paw and his whole family. That's what he says, anyhow, and I guess it's the truth."

Rodack pauses again, pulling at his beard, watching Burns. They all watch Burns. "And who," says Rodack, "are you, if I may ask?"

"The name is Jack Burns."

"Jack Burns . . ."

"Yes sir. And now if you folks'll excuse me . . . and give me back my old cannon, and that worthless horse, I think I'll be going on."

"Stay with us tonight."

"I better find my boys."

"Your boys?"

"Yeah—two of 'em now." Burns pulls out the old wallet, passes around the faded photo once again. Of course, no one knows anything about a man, as he now would be, named Charlie Burns.

"There's Captain Barnes," suggests the red beard. "One of the Chief's honchos. But no Burns."

Politely, Burns inquires about this Captain Barnes. He listens attentively to the little that is known, nodding with interest. Again he announces his intentions of departing, requesting again the return of his property.

"What do you think you're going to do?" asks Rodack. "You can't find them tonight."

"I'm gonna start looking."

Rodack informs the old man of the Chief's curfew: Anyone found on the streets after sundown, without authorization, will be arrested; will probably be conscripted into the military or labor forces; and very likely tortured—to extract information, if possible, and if not for information then on general principles: for the fun of it. Sergeant Brock is a devil; and his assistant, a half-breed Apache known as Mangus Colorado—Red Shirt—is a demon.

Burns is properly impressed but still anxious to leave. Rodack says, "Then we'll have to *insist* that you stay. Not for your sake but for ours. If you go wandering into the city on a horse you will certainly be seen and caught. You'll probably be tortured and if you're tortured you might give away our location. We can't take that chance."

Burns makes a move toward the door. Two of the boys intercept him. Burns smiles, shrugs, and eases himself down to the floor, hunkering on his heels. He pulls the plug of tobacco from his shirt pocket and bites off a chew. He notes a pistol nearby, stuck in a boy's sash; he thinks he'll leave when ready, with little difficulty.

Rodack smiles at him. "We appreciate your cooperation, Mr. Burns. Now"—he turns to the group of solemn young men, the huddled and weeping girls, all watching him—"now," he continues, "we shall make tribute to our murdered comrades. For Angelo and Will, who died fighting tyranny." He nods to the red-bearded fellow, who clamps a pair of cables to a wind-charged storage battery under a table, which stands, altarwise, against the center of the north wall.

Rodack removes the cloth that covers an object mounted on the center of the table, revealing an antique record-playing machine—a stereophonic phonograph, flanked by a pair of speakers. Red-beard and one of the girls set the speakers wide apart in corners of the room, trailing the thin cords that connect the speakers to the machine. Two other girls place lighted candles on the table, one on each side of the phonograph. The four young people join the circle on the floor.

Rodack—Professor Rodack (enemy of the State)—takes a record album from among the books on a shelf in the wall. "We were able to save," he says to Burns, "only this one recording." He holds it up so that the old man can see the defiant face, the heroic name, on the cover. "Only this one. It's therefore quite precious to us. Although—even before—this music was precious to millions. Was always precious. But you understand." He pauses, sighs. The young men and women sitting on the floor and leaning against the walls have again fallen silent. "And because this recording is so precious to us, and because it may be the last of its kind in this demented slaughterhouse of a city, because of that—we play it only on rare occasions. On very important occasions. To celebrate a marriage, a birth, a victory. Or a death. Or a defeat. We have so few victories"—he smiles wryly at Burns, at his students—"that we must be willing to celebrate our defeats as well."

Standing before the phonograph on its candlelit altar, facing the flickering shadows on the wall, Professor Rodack removes the record, delicately, from the album and from the inner sleeve, taking care not to touch the microgrooves. The black polished vinyl disc gleams in the amber light. Holding it by the edges he lifts it above his head, in both hands, like a chalice, toward the ceiling. The students gaze at it with reverence, hushed and solemn as a congregation of worshipers. Old Burns notes the tears staining the cheeks of the girls, the frowning concentration—and tears—of the young men.

"Tonight," says Rodack, holding the record high, "we dedicate this performance to our guest and new friend, Jack Burns, who brought Barbara back to us alive. And also, with all of our hearts and minds, we dedicate this performance to our brothers Angelo Diaz and William Slade, who died fighting the new tyranny that has risen up in our midst like a shadow from that past which we thought, for a while, we would never have to see again."

"Yes," murmur several of the boys in unison. "Yes," murmur the girls.

The professor sighs again, and concludes his invocation. "For Will and Angelo, who fought for liberty, for decency and justice, for the right of every man, every woman, every living creature to live life in freedom from the madness of nationalism, the brutality of militarism, the greed of industrialism . . ."

"Yes, yes—"

". . . Who fought against the domination of the State . . ."

"Yes!"

". . . Who fought for a world where no man can be another's master; who fought and died—for anarchy!"

"For anarchy!"

Rodack places the record on the turntable, turns a switch. He picks up the tone arm, takes a deep breath, and sets the needle down precisely, softly, in the preliminary groove. The students stop their breathing, waiting in absolute attention.

Scratch scratch click . . . scratch scratch click . . . scratch scratch click. . . .

Rodack bends forward and with a forefinger gives the tone arm the slightest touch, the most exquisite and gentle of nudges. The needle escapes the obstructed microgroove and slides over to the next.

A moment of hesitation.

Now: Quite suddenly, out of the past, with harsh vigor, a four-pronged bolt of intellectual lightning crashes through the mist of two centuries, explodes like a revelation in this underground room of stubborn hope, opening a wide doorway to the sun and the light. The clenched fist that hammers on the prison door, announcing the supreme music of human liberation. (Somewhere. Somehow.)

Burns thought he had forgotten so much. He had thought he wanted to forget even more. But now, as the students, smiling grimly through their tears, breathe out in unison a single word—"*Yes!*"—old Jack Burns feels the world of his youth come flooding back upon him, and with it the lost youth of a legend he once loved, the broken resolves and lost promises of the revolution that—did not fail, but—never was completed. Was not completed!

Triumphant music breaks like a wave upon his head. "Oh yes," the old man mutters, shocked, touching the dampness trickling into the stubble of his beard. Astonished, he finds himself weeping with the rest of them.

The motorcycles shine in the firelight, engines mute but potent even in their silence. Two machines, parked beneath a giant catalpa tree. Abandoned buildings stand close by, black against the stars. An owl calls softly from a citrus grove. The dark city, surrounding them, seems peaceful—for the moment—as a cemetery.

Sergeant Brock leans against the trunk of the catalpa, one booted foot on a log. His face is in shadow; he holds his silver helmet, like a football, in the crook of one arm. Another man crouches near his feet, a small fellow also in uniform, gnawing on a roasted sparerib. Corporal Mangus Colorado, Jr.—Red Shirt.

On the other side of the fire, bound and trussed, lie the two young prisoners. The first moans fitfully, semidelirious, moving feebly in his bonds. Blood trickles from his lips, from his ear; his ragged clothes are soaked with sweat and blood. Like Corporal Mangus, he has the dark smooth skin of an Indian; but whereas Mangus is Apache, the prisoner is Mexican. Cousins. Blood cousins.

The other prisoner is a boy, downy-faced, clear-eyed, unharmed. He wears the long-waisted shirt, close-fitting jeans, scuffed boots of a cowboy. But no hat, and his belted holster is empty. His face, despite windburn and suntan, is pale; he chews nervously on dry, trembling lips; he is tense with fear.

"Finish your supper?" says Brock kindly.

The Apache grunts, wiping his mouth on the back of a hand so dark it appears nearly black. Silver rings, set with turquoise, flash on his slender fingers.

"No? Well hurry up. Can't fool around here all evening."

The Apache mumbles, and with bright teeth skins the last sliver of burned fat from the bone. He tosses the bone away, over his shoulder (for the dogs: an instinctive Neolithic gesture), licks the grease from his fingers, wipes his palms on his thighs, and belches with satisfaction. Gracefully, he rises and steps across the fire. "Which one first, Sarge?"

"The spic. He won't live long."

Mangus nods, stoops, grabs the Mexican by one foot, and jerks him closer to the small fire, so close that one shoulder lies in the hot coals. The Mexican gasps, attempts with convulsive effort to roll away from the pain. The Apache keeps him in place by planting a foot on his chest. The prisoner writhes with agony; the smell of scorching cloth and flesh floats up with the smoke.

"Talk to him," Brock orders.

The Apache bends down toward the Mexican. "Where are they?" he asks. "Where's Rodack? Where're your buddies?"

"*No se,*" the Mexican groans, "*no se. Madre de Dios, no se.*" The sweat streams across his face, his eyes bulge as he strains away from the fire.

"*¿Dondes los banditos? ¿Dondes sus amigos?*" The Apache, with childlike impetuosity, accompanies his inquiries with a kick.

"Easy now, easy now," says Sergeant Brock. "Don't hurt him too much, for chrissake. We want him to talk. Bring him here. Out of the fire."

Mangus shrugs, drags the prisoner to the log. Brock sits down, close beside the prisoner's face. He waits for a while. He puts down his helmet and unscrews the cap from a canteen, lifts the Mexican's head—gently—with one hand and offers him water. The Mexican drinks, swallowing in desperate gulps. Water, blood, sweat pour down his chin. He stares up into Brock's face, his eyes dazed but grateful, lips attempting a smile. Mangus Colorado adds a few more sticks of mesquite to the dying fire. The boy named Art Dekker stares at the passionate flames.

"Now," says Brock, softly, sweetly, to the dying prisoner, "how are you, Angelo? ¿Como está, compadre? Eh?"

Angelo manages a feeble smile; his sick eyes search the eyes of Brock, hunting for—succor? identity? an end?

"I want to take you home, Angelo. Home. ¿Comprende, cuate? Su casa, sus hermanos, su padre—¿comprende? Eh?" Dígame, Angelo—el professore . . . ¿ Rodack? ¿Rodack?"

The smile fades, returns. "¿Mi casa? Ah, si, si . . . Nogales."

"No, no, Angelo," says Brock patiently. "Not Nogales. Where you live now. Ahora. Aqui, en la ciudad. La casa de sus compañeros. ¿La casa del professore Rodack? ¿Rodack, Angelo? ¿Comprende? Dígame, por favor: ¿Dónde esta el professore Rodack? Por favor, Angelo. Estoy su amigo. . . ."

Angelo stares into the face of Sergeant Brock, concentrating through his pain on the effort to understand, to recognize. All at once his smile broadens, becomes radiant with pleasure. Brock smiles in return, awaiting the young man's next words. Angelo says, "Fuck you, Señor Brock. Aye—chinga tu madre." His eyes roll up, showing the white. He stiffens a bit, passing out, and then relaxes.

Sergeant Brock, no longer smiling, lets the head drop. He

draws his automatic, hesitates, puts it back. "All right," he says to the Apache, "we've wasted enough time on this little shit. Finish him off."

The Apache draws *his* automatic.

"No, no, not right here, you stupid nigger. Not with a gun. Take him out there"—Brock jerks a thumb toward the darkness of the citrus grove—"and use your knife. Don't play around. Just get rid of him."

Obediently, Mangus grasps the Mexican by one ankle and lugs him away. Brock sits on the log, waiting, gazing at the flames, the glowing coals. Art Dekker watches the sergeant. After a moment they hear a series of grunts from the darkness, a stifled scream. Then silence. The Apache comes back into the firelight, wiping knife blade on his sleeve. He comes close to the fire, halts, puts the knife away, waits for orders.

Sergeant Brock, sighing, raises his heavy head and gazes across the fire at the boy. Brock has a weary, lined, middle-aged, fatherly face, the square, handsome features of an actor, an ample brown mustache with drooping handlebars, rather like the mustache of an old-time, near-forgotten, much-loved Russian dictator. Or like Guru Mehar Baba.

"Well, young man," he says to Art, "it's your turn. Anything you'd like to say before we begin?"

Art fights down a fit of trembling. Tightening his jaw, he whispers, "Yes sir."

"Don't 'sir' me, son, I'm only a sergeant. You 'sir' officers (those scum). No, listen, before you get any brave ideas, let me tell you what my little buddy Mangus here likes to do to boys."

The Apache grins shyly at Art when he hears his name mentioned. Except for a couple of missing front teeth and a corrugated scar across his nose and one cheek, Mangus is a presentable enough fellow. He adds more fuel to the fire as the sergeant explains the procedure.

"What old Red Shirt here likes to do," he says, "is hang people up by the heels above a nice bed of mesquite coals, like he's building up now. Mangus is a Chiricahua Apache and this kind of slow brain roast is an old Chiricahua specialty. It takes a long time, this way, many hours, but then that's the custom. The Chiricahuas are an easygoing people; you can't rush them with anything. That's enough fire, Mangus, what the hell you doing? Now as I was saying—what's your name, anyway?"

Art mumbles his name.

"As I was saying, Art, or was about to say, we can skip this whole business as far as I'm concerned if you'll just answer a few questions."

"Yes sir. . . ."

"Don't 'sir' me!" For a moment a bizarre rage overwhelms Brock. Face red, he bellows, "I'm a sergeant, can't you see?" Tapping the golden stripes on his sleeve. "A fucking goddamn master sergeant. Do I look like a goddamn fucking officer? Do I?" He pauses, rhetorically, for an answer.

"No sir," Art whispers.

"Forget it!" Brock pulls a bandanna from his hip pocket and wipes his brow. Exasperation makes him sweat. "Where was I?" Relaxing, he looks gently at Art, smiles, says, "Ever ride a motorcycle, Art?"

"Yes sir, Sergeant."

"My friends call me Sergeant. Recruits call me Sergeant *Brock*. Get the rope, Mangus." The Apache rises and goes to the motorcycles, opens a saddlebag. Brock stares glumly at Art. Mangus comes back with a coiled rope, lashes one end about Art's ankles and tosses the coil over a branch of the catalpa, draws the line taut, and looks to Brock, awaiting orders. Brock holds up one hand, signaling delay. He speaks to the boy who lies, stiff with terror, in the dust and ashes near the fire. "Would you like to, Art?"

The boy says nothing, eyes fixed on the fire.

"Would you like to ride a police motorcycle, Art?"

No answer. "I'm talking to you, Art."

Hoarsely, Art says, "Yes."

"Yes, Sergeant Brock!"

"Yes, Sergeant Brock. . . ."

"That's better." Brock glances at Mangus. "Let off a bit."

The Apache slackens the rope. "It's easy, Art. All you have to do is answer a few questions. One question, really. Where do we find Rodack and his gang?"

"I don't know, Sergeant Brock. I never heard of them."

"Never heard of them? You were in there shooting with three of them this evening. You were shooting at us. At me and old Mangus, Jr., here. Your friends."

"I thought you . . . were somebody else."

Brock laughs quietly. "That's pretty good. But you were shooting at us. Who'd you think we were?"

Art hesitates, then tells the truth. He thought the motorcycle troopers were the men who had attacked the Rocking K, burned down the house and barn, murdered his mother, hanged Eloy Peralta to the windmill, and stole their cattle.

Brock grins. "So you were out for revenge? You've got some guts, Art. That's good. But you don't know for sure that I was there, do you? Or Mangus here? You didn't actually see us personally, did you?"

Art admits that he did not.

"That's called leaping to conclusions, Art. A bad habit. And how did you meet Rodack's gang?"

He didn't; he'd never seen them before, didn't know who they were, didn't care.

"You wouldn't lie to me, would you, Art?"

"I'm telling the truth."

"You're lying." Brock jerks a thumb upward. "Hoist him." The Apache pulls on the rope, elevating the boy's feet, legs, entire body off the ground. Art swings above the coals of the fire. Gritting his teeth, winding all of his strength and courage and hatred into one compact ball of resistance, he determines that he will not cry out, will not whimper, will not yield.

"Last chance, son. Where's Rodack?" No reply. "Okay, Mangus, you can rake more of those coals under his head." The Apache ties the free end of the rope to the trunk of the tree and looks about for a stick. "Where's Rodack, Art? In about five seconds your hair's gonna be on fire."

Art says nothing. The Apache bends to the fire with a stick, pushing a mound of embers toward a spot beneath Art's head. The glow illuminates Art's contorted face, his closed eyes, his dark hair. Waves of heat rise around his suspended body.

"Where's Rodack, Art?"

The boy does not speak. Sergeant Brock gets up, comes close, kicks away the fire. "Let him down," he says to Mangus. The Apache shrugs, disappointed but basically indifferent. Art is lowered to the ground, the rope removed from his ankles.

"I think you're telling the truth, boy. And I like your guts. We're taking you to the Tower. I'm going to join you to the Army. When you finish basic we'll give you a chance at the motorcycle squad. How's that sound to you?"

Art lies back on the ground, sweating, face red, gasping for air, unable to speak. But he succeeds, after a moment, in making a slight nod of assent. And has difficulty, after another moment, in suppressing a grin of triumph.

Brock rambles on. "About that ranch-burning and all, I wasn't there. It must've been some other bike squad. My boys wouldn't do that kind of work. What do you think we are, a bunch of hoodlums? We're soldiers, and you're going to be one too. Turn him loose, Mangus."

Mangus obeys. Arts sits up and rubs his chafed wrists, his numbed, bruised ankles. "Thanks," he mumbles, "thanks an awful lot."

Brock smiles benignly and rolls a cigarette. "That's all right. We treat our friends good. Now listen, I want you to report to the Security Forces building tomorrow morning at oh-eight-hundred hours sharp. Got that? Ask for me. I'll get you inducted personally. Tonight you're free to go home, get cleaned up, get some rest. See you in the morning."

"Where's my horse? And—" he adds, "—my gun?"

"Your horse? That old antique of a six-shooter? Well, you'll get your property back when you report tomorrow, don't worry about that."

Art stands up shakily, flexing his limbs, and looks around, out of habit, for his hat. Gone. Still uncertain, he looks once more at Brock. "I can go?"

"Go on. Get the hell out of here." Brock grins, offering a big hand to the boy, who hesitates, then takes it. "No hard feelings, eh Art? We're going to be buddies. You're going to be a motorcycle trooper. We need men with guts." He slaps the boy between the shoulder blades, "Now take off!"

Art totters off in his high-heeled boots, walking northward up the street, fading into the darkness. Brock and the Apache watch him go. Brock says quietly, "Follow that punk. Don't let up till you find out where they are."

The Apache nods, takes a canteen of water, and glides off into the night.

Brock waits for a few moments, puffing on his cigarette, watching the embers of the fire, listening. Then he kick-starts his motorcycle into action. The engine roars, transmission in neutral, as Brock toys with the throttle, accelerating then slowing the engine as if he were shifting gears and driving away. Letting the engine idle, he starts up the second motorcycle, his corporal's, and does the same. He shuts off the second, bestrides the saddle of his own machine, and pauses in thought.

The new moon is down, the stars shine beyond the branches of the catalpa tree. Dim fires smolder in the west where one great tower of glass and metal, alone among its dark companions, glows with electricity, tapering upward from broad illuminated base to a bright beacon at the apex. Headquarters: the pyramid of power.

Sergeant Brock contemplates those lights with a vague, abstracted, half-cynical smile. His thoughts are elsewhere, his plans, at least for the night, centered on a different object. He buckles on his helmet, flips the cigarette away. Without turning on the headlight he directs his machine, in low gear and at half throttle, down another street that leads past the dying citrus grove into the eastern suburbs of the city.

His arm around her shoulders, her arm around his waist, they descend the rickety wooden stairs, feeling their way through the dark. A rectangle of lamplight outlines the door that leads to the barroom. They pause, facing each other in the gloom, embrace and kiss. A melancholy languor fills her senses, weighs on her mind and heart.

"I wish you wouldn't go."

"I'll be back," says Sam Banyaca. "If you want me back. Soon as I find that old man—and his kid."

"I want you back."

"And you'll go with me? Home to my village?"

"Oh God, Sam"—Dixie sighs and leans her face against the Indian's chest—"I don't know. Maybe. I'll have to think about that. I don't know."

"You'll be welcome there. My people will be good to you. The women will be kind, I promise. They'll make you a member of the sunflower society. You'll learn the songs, the dances, all the secret ceremonies. Even the language. And if you're not happy—"

"Yes?" She looks up at him again through the dim light. The round, solemn face of Sam, his dark eyes looking down at her. She strokes his bare arms, the broad solidity of his waist and hips. "Yes? . . ."

"We could always leave. Go somewhere else." But at that thought she detects the doubt in his voice.

"Where?"

Sam is silent for a moment. "Yes. Good question. I don't know, Dixie. Come back here, I suppose. Things are bound to get better someday."

"Are they?" She turns toward the outlined door, the murmur of voices beyond, the whine of Singin' Bob and his guitar. "Who knows? They could get even worse."

Sam lifts one hand in the dark, a gesture of impatience. "Then we won't come back here."

Both are silent. Dixie says, "I can't make any promises. Not right now. But—I do want to see you again. I do, Sam."

He hugs her tighter, kisses her again, gently, on the brow, on the eyes, on the lips. "That's good enough. I'll be back. In a day or two. Very soon." He releases her, steps back, lifts something from around his neck and holds it toward her. "Wear this while I'm gone. It's good medicine."

She takes the necklace, trying to see the heavy medallion suspended from it. "What is it?"

"An amulet. Turquoise and silver. It'll protect you from the dark spirits while I'm gone." His white teeth shine in the gloom. "The dark spirits with the pale faces."

Dixie smiles in return. "You think I'm superstitious?"

"Maybe. Why take chances?"

"Well you're right, I am." She starts to drape the thing around her neck; he does it for her, kissing her on the tender juncture of neck and shoulder. "Oh God, Sam, don't do that again. You know what that does to me. Not if you're really leaving."

"I'm really leaving."

A pause. She fingers the cool stone and metal resting on her bosom. "Maybe you should keep it. You're going to need this more than I will."

"I've got other magic. Powerful medicine. You know that." Smiling, he runs his hand through her thick curls, caresses her bare shoulder.

Dixie sighs again, mixing pleasure with her anxiety. "Oh Sam . . . nobody's been so kind to me . . . so good . . . for such a long, long, long time."

"It's easy." He whispers in her delicate ear: "This here Indian's in love."

"Is that so?" Teasing, she says, "Who with?"

"You'll think I'm a liar. But it's a girl I only met about six hours ago."

"You work fast. A woman can't trust a man like that."

"That's right, she can't. But"—he stops for a moment, listening, then lowers his head—"but wait and see. You'll see. Will you be here when I get back?"

"Of course I'll be here. Where else? Where could I go?"

Sam hesitates. "You've told me where. I don't want that to happen to you."

"I'm tough. I can take care of myself—in any situation."

Caressing her hair and shoulders, he says, "I believe that. But that can get you into trouble too."

"Then hurry back."

"Right. I will." Again, reluctantly, he lets go of her, steps back. "All right, my sweetheart—"

"Follow this hallway to the rear," she says, turning him gently away from her. "Don't go through the bar. There's another door back there."

"What are you afraid of in the bar?"

"You can't trust anybody. Go on. That way." She clutches him once more around the neck, draws his head down for a final kiss, then pushes him away. "Go. Go. If you're going, go." He slips suddenly away, noiseless as a shadow. She listens for the sound of the back door opening and closing. Can barely hear it. But when she does, she opens the other door, into the bar, and enters. Swingin' Glenn stands behind the bar, pouring himself and two customers another round. Singin' Bob, alone on the bandstand, sees her come in; a little languid smirk appears on his narrow face. Aware of his eyes on her, Dixie pulls up the puffed sleeves of her blouse, covering her bare shoulders. Nervously she touches the necklace and goes behind the bar. Glenn salutes her with uplifted glass, bows and kisses her hand, and sidles past. "Back to my cross," he murmurs.

Dixie serves the two men leaning on the bar, wary-eyed old-timers. One is dressed in a pin-striped business suit; his companion, a plump, red-cheeked, white-haired old gent, wears a suit of tropical linen, striped shirt, broad floral necktie, and snap-brim Panama with matching hatband. The first man, lean, tall, gaunt as a cadaver, listens with grim humor to the leading questions of the one-time dandy.

"So you think we'd be better off without our Chief?"

"Not so loud. Yeah, I do. Don't you?"

"As a matter of fact, yes. How do your friends feel about it?"

"About the same. How about yours?"

Dixie overhears but ignores this dangerous conversation. Instead she watches, without seeing, the two old women dancing together on the open floor, the only other clients in the bar. Swaying together cheek to cheek, eyes closed in dreamy reminiscence, they move in half time to the rhythm of Singin' Bob's guitar, the heavy beat of Swingin' Glenn's piano.

It's okay, Paw,
I'm only prayin'. . . .

"I'd like to meet your friends." The white-haired man's blue eyes are alight now, bright with eagerness; his red-veined nose and fat, rosy cheeks radiate enthusiasm. "We have a lot to talk about."

"That we do," says the cadaver. "Bring your friends too."

The dandy lapses for a moment, with alcoholic self-pity, into candor. "I haven't got any," he admits. "They're all dead."

The cadaver grins. "Who turned them in?"

"What?" The dandy fumbles in his inside coat pocket. "My friend," he says, "I have something to show you." Fumbling about, he inadvertently reveals the fact that his handsome blue-striped shirt is, in fact, only a fake—a dickey. Pale and flabby flesh, hairless as a babe's, sags beyond. "It just so happens, my dear good fellow, that I. . . ."

Grinning, the gaunt man watches and waits.

A bellow of outrage from the bandstand. The crash of dissonant chords. "No!" shouts Swingin' Glenn. "No! I can't play this garbage anymore."

Sudden silence. The two ladies stare in surprise at the musicians.

Singin' Bob lets his slung guitar hang to his knees. "Can't?" he says. "The old joints too stiff, man?"

"Won't," says Glenn. "Won't play this garbage anymore." He spins on his stool and sits facing the wall, kneading his hands together.

"So what do you want to play, man?"

Glenn faces the wall, muttering furiously. "Man. Man. Man. What do I want to play? What do I want to play, *man*. Good Christ. Good Christ."

"Well, what do you?"

"Music," snarls Glenn in a furious undertone. "Music! *Music!* For the love of God, some real music!"

Bob laughs. "You can't play that stuff anymore, man. You're burned out. All burned out. Now come on. . . ." He nods toward the two elderly women. "These ladies want to dance. Come on, man. . . ."

"Boy! Boy!"

Bob shrugs; looking toward Dixie he makes a rotary motion with forefinger close to one ear.

"Music!" Swingin' Glenn swings around on his stool, facing the piano, his chin almost touching the keyboard; he lifts his hands, holding them poised above the keys. He glares ahead, at nothing, or at some internal vision. "Time," he mumbles. "Space. Yes, time is the mind of space. The mind of space." He turns his burning eyes on Singin' Bob. "Listen, boy. Listen to this."

Bob smiles wearily, waiting.

Glenn's large, pale hands descend. Softly. Like memory. They touch, depress the keys; the hammers strike the taut strings inside the frame. Gently, gently. A wordless song rises through the stagnant air of the barroom, a strange kind of music —precise, eternal, remote but intimate—never heard before in Dixie Dalton's Bar & Grill. The first voice completes its phrase and goes to the next as a second voice enters, imitating the first. The second is followed by a third and fourth, each voice singing, in counterpoint, the same clear melody. There are no vertical chords; the interweaving voices, flowing on, create a different kind of harmony, like that of braided waters pouring toward an ultimate, unimaginable sea.

Dixie hears, not watching, and thinks of Sam moving through the night, looking for one old man and two lost boys. The two women clasped together in the middle of the dance floor stare in wonder at Glenn, their dance forgotten. And even the dandy in the white suit, and the gaunt fellow in the dark suit, forget for the moment their mutual investigations.

Swingin' Glenn goes on, head back and eyes closed. Above the flying fingers and the music comes another sound—sound of a man moaning, groaning in ecstasy: Swingin' Glenn sings along, humming the theme. The music rises, winging higher and higher, and then—falters. Misses. Something is wrong.

Glenn's old hands grope like a blind man's, feeling in the dark, seeking the lost strands of the composition. Can't find them. He cannot find them. He can't remember, can't recompose the thing again. The groping hands come to a halt. The music is gone.

Silence.

"No!" howls Glenn. He slams his fists upon the keyboard. A couple of splintered keys fly up over his shoulder and clatter on the floor. "No!" he cries, letting his broad forehead crash down like a sledge, square on middle C and adjacent notes. This last chord of unCaged anguish, sustained by Glenn's foot on the pedal, floats for a time on the lamplit air of the barroom.

Singin' Bob waits, tapping irritably on the box of his guitar. "Okay," he says at last, with a glance at his partner's head sunken on the keyboard, "that was a nice try, man, nice try. Now you ready to finish the gig?"

Slowly, Glenn raises his head, reaching for his glass on the pianotop, empties it, nods to Bob. They continue with the interrupted ballad.

> *It's okay, Maw,*
> *I'm only dyin'. . . .*

"As I was saying, sir," continues the dandy, drawing a smart (if aged) cordovan passport case from inside his coat, "I have something here that should interest you." The cadaverous man waits, watching with grim amusement. The dandy flips the case open with a flourish, displaying on the inside a formal photograph, stamped and certified, of himself; the photograph—signed by bearer—is attached to an embossed red, white, and blue identification card, with serial number and golden eagle, signed by no less than Major Roland himself. The dandy smiles at the expression of horrified amazement on the bony face of the other man. "Yes," the dandy says suavely, "allow me to introduce myself: Inspector Wolfe, Internal Security. And you, sir, whatever your name, are under arrest."

The gaunt man seems stunned. "What's the—what's the charge?"

Inspector Wolfe beams with satisfaction. "Treason, sir. Remarks of a treasonous nature directed against our Chief of State."

The gaunt man relaxes. A grin, composed principally of

foul, yellow fangs, transforms his mask of a face from tragedy to comedy. He draws forth his own pocket case, opens it, and reveals a card identical, except for photograph, name, and number, to that of Inspector Wolfe's. "My name is Fox," he says, "and I'm an inspector too—you fruity little shithead. Now *you* buy *me* a drink."

The dandy gapes at the cadaver's ID. He stammers, stutters, gulps for air. Dixie waits at the corner of the bar, indifferent to all present.

Out of the night, out of the distance, comes the familiar roar of a motorcycle. Approaching fast—a single machine. Singin' Bob hears it first, and as he does, his close-set eyes turn, accusingly, toward Dixie. Feigning indifference, she dabs with a rag at the bar, where Inspector Wolfe has spilled part of his drink. The two old women scurry through the swinging doors in front; Glenn hastily gathers his music and shuffles into the dark hallway at the rear, blowing Dixie an apologetic kiss as he goes. The others remain, frozen in place.

The motorcycle thunders near. They hear it gearing down, hear it rumbling up the steps and over the boardwalk. The doors burst open and Sergeant Brock appears, mounted, engine bellowing between his legs. He skids the machine to a ninety-degree halt, knocking over a table and two chairs, races the motor in a final carburetor-flushing howl—a shower of sparks from the cannonshell exhaust—and cuts the ignition. He dismounts, giving the motorcycle a shove toward Singin' Bob, who springs forward to catch it.

Helmeted, goggled, Brock advances on the bar, white teeth flashing under his mustache. He puts down his helmet and slams one hard hand on the mahogany. "Bourbon!" he shouts—"and a kiss!" He grins like a tiger.

Smiling a little in spite of herself, Dixie comes near with a bottle, places it before him. Singin' Bob and the two security officers watch. Brock takes a gurgling swig from the bottle and bangs it down, exhaling a cloud of flammable gas. He looks at Dixie. "Now," he says, "my kiss."

She smiles but remains aloof, out of reach, looking down at the glass she is polishing.

"Now!" snarls Brock, lunging across the top of the bar. Cupping the back of her head with one paw, he yanks her close and plants a prolonged kiss on her mouth. Dixie tries to free herself but Brock pulls her tighter as she struggles. Releasing her, he discovers the new necklace, the silver and turquoise pendant. "What's this?" he growls, turning it over.

She plucks it from his fingers and staggers back, flushed and angry. "What do you care, you goddamn pig."

"Where'd you get it?"

"That's my business."

"No, it's my business." Brock appears, for a moment, to be on the verge of vaulting over the bar. But instead he laughs, takes another drink from the bottle. Setting it down, he becomes aware of the wet blue eyes of Inspector Wolfe watching him. Brock glares: "What're you doing here, babyface?"

Inspector Wolfe draws himself up and smiles. "On duty, Sergeant Brock. Nice to see you again."

"I hate spies. You make me sick." Brock turns his fierce eyes on the other, the lean man, who studiously avoids his look. "God—you too. Two of them. I hate you sneaks. If a man's going to be a son-of-a-bitch let him be an honest son-of-a-bitch. Like me." He turns his head to grin at Singin' Bob, watching furtively from the bandstand. "Ain't that right, pimp?"

Bob smiles nervously in return. "That's right, Sarge."

Brock's smile becomes a scowl. "Only my buddies call me 'Sarge.' " He waits, staring into Bob's eyes.

Bob lowers his gaze. "Sorry, Sergeant."

"Sergeant *Brock!*"

"Sorry, Sergeant Brock."

Brock waits, watching Singin' Bob cringe. Satisfied, he swings back to the bar and takes another drink. He looks toward Dixie. "I'm lonesome tonight."

"No wonder."

"Lonesome, baby."

"You're always lonesome. When you come here."

"That's why I come here, baby."

"Don't call me 'baby.' "

"No?" Brock studies her, her glossy curls, the rosy face averted from his eyes. "You're in a funny mood tonight." She makes no answer. "Come here, you little whore. I want another kiss."

"I'm not a whore."

"The hell you're not. You always were a whore. You always will be a whore. And right now you're my whore. Come here, goddamnit."

"Go to hell, you bastard."

The gaunt man, Inspector Fox, rising from his stool, takes a stealthy step toward the door. Brock reaches out and hauls him back, forcing him down on the barstool. "Stick around, Fox. I said I'm lonesome. We're having a party here and I want nothing but happy faces all around me."

Inspector Fox nods, permitting himself a timorous grin.

"You're forgetting your place, Sergeant Brock," says Inspector Wolfe. Astounded by his own audacity, Wolfe turns quickly back to his glass for another gulp of Scotch.

Brock regards him with scornful amusement. "Yeah. That's right. Forgetting my place. You sneaks are officers, aren't you? Fucking officers!" Brock turns toward Singin' Bob for sympathy and understanding. "And if there's anything I hate more than a spy it's a fucking officer. Ain't that right, Bob?" Bob nods sympathetically. "I can't think of anything I hate worse than an officer." Brock grins, staring Bob down again. "Except maybe a pimp. And guitar players." Singin' Bob smiles shyly, with lowered eyes.

Brock's smoldering eyes light upon the piano. "Where's Glenn?" he says. Nobody answers. "I want some piano music. I feel like piano music, goddamnit." He draws his forty-five—the heavy, blind, blunt Colt automatic—and points it toward the piano. Singin' Bob dives to the floor. Brock laughs and reholsters the weapon. "Jesus . . ." He turns back to the bar and his silent

audience of woman and spies. Takes another drink and stares at
Dixie. "Dixie, my darling . . ."

Refusing to look at him, she waits, saying nothing, hands
busy with the same glass she's been polishing for five minutes.

"Where'd you get that necklace?"

She returns his stare defiantly. "What's it to you?"

"Who gave it to you?"

"A friend gave it to me."

"You don't have any friends. Just customers."

"You're a filthy-mouthed bastard." She flings the glass at
him. It smashes against the bottle in front of Brock. The bottle
teeters; he steadies it and calmly, with his other hand, sweeps
the fragments of glass to the floor. He turns once more toward
Singin' Bob, beckoning the musician close with a forefinger.
"Come here, Bob."

Warily, the old musician sidles near, stopping just beyond
arm's reach.

"Closer, Bob."

Smiling, shrugging, Bob allows himself another step. Brock
snatches him by the shirtfront and jerks him close, face to face.
For a second Bob's toes are dancing clear of the floor. "Where'd
she get it?"

Bob hesitates, looking from the corners of his eyes toward
Dixie. "The Indian," he mumbles.

"What Indian?"

"The Indian gave it to her."

Brock shakes the little man, vigorously, with one hand.
"What Indian? The country's crawling with Indians. Which
one?"

"He was here all day; a guy named Sam."

"Sam who?"

"I don't know, Sarge. Honest, I don't know. If I knew I'd tell
you. A stranger. Never saw him here before." Singin' Bob is
sweating.

"Where is he now?"

"Don't know, Sarge. He must've left. They—they went upstairs a long time ago."

"Upstairs?" Brock glares from close range—six inches—into Singin' Bob's narrow face. He roars: *"Upstairs!"* He shoves the musician away, sends him reeling across the floor, and turns to Dixie, fury in his eyes. "So—you took him upstairs." Dixie stares back with level gaze. "You took him upstairs. You took some goddamn stinking greasy little goddamn—Indian—an *Indian!*—upstairs with you. And let him fuck you. Right? Let him fuck you?"

"That's my business," she replies.

Brock's lips twist in a sneering grin. "Yeah—that's your business all right. Whore!" He stands up, both hands on the bar. Dixie reaches for another bottle. The security inspectors start to sneak out; Brock checks them with a shout. "Hold it, you two. I got some business for you." Again to Dixie: "You want to be a whore, I'll put you where you can be a real *busy* whore."

Grasping a bottle, Dixie backs toward the rear door. Brock vaults over the bar and runs her down before she can reach it. She breaks the bottle over his head; unfazed, he grabs her arms. She slips free, runs to the middle of the dance floor, holding the broken bottle by the neck. Grinning, crouching, weaving like a wrestler, head dripping with blood and whiskey, Brock advances upon her. She looks at Bob, Wolfe, Fox. "Help me," she cries. They stare at her. She backs toward the piano, into the motorcycle; both go down. Brock pounces on her as she tries to scramble up; she slashes at him with the broken bottle, rips one sleeve below the yellow stripes, gashes his forearm. Not good enough; he is on her. Twice her weight, he twists her arms behind her back and propels her toward the security officers.

"Fox," Brock says, pulling a brace of handcuffs from his belt, "you take this whore to the Tower. You know where she belongs." The cadaver nods, a loose involuntary grin spreading across his face. Brock snaps on the cuffs. "Turn her over to Fannin, that'll take care of her." He turns to Wolfe and prods him in the belly. "You go along, make sure she gets there. Alive, you understand?" Wolfe's turn to nod an anxious assent. "Intact, you understand?" Wolfe nods. "Okay—now take this bitch out of my sight. She makes me sick." They start to lead her out the swinging doors.

"And one more thing—" The inspectors stop. Brock comes near and glares into their half-frightened, half-eager faces. "One more thing," he says with deadly emphasis, "this whore is still my whore, you understand. Until you get her there she's mine. And if either one of you scum so much as lays a finger on her—I'll break that finger. Understand? You put a hand on her and I'll break that hand. Understand?" Eagerly, they nod agreement.

"And as for you, you slut . . ." He grabs Dixie by the hair and forces her to look at him. "As for you . . ." He sees the necklace again; cursing, he yanks it over her head. "Get her out of here. Get her out of here."

They go.

Brock stands still, staring at the necklace. He hurls it at the piano and lurches toward the bar, wiping the blood and booze and sweat from his eyes. He sits on his stool and reaches for the half-full bottle of bourbon, clamping a powerful hand around it. Man's best friend. But instead of drinking he lowers his blood-smeared head onto his forearm and begins to cry.

Sound of an auto engine cranking up outside: the pathetic rattle, cheap and whining and un-American, of an ancient Volkswagen. The noise rises, sinks, and peters away, trundled off on four little asymmetric wheels.

Sergeant Brock weeps.

Singin' Bob creeps cautiously to his side. Extending a tentative and trembling hand, he dares to pat the sergeant's broad, bowed, heartbroken back. "It's all right, Sarge. It's all right. There's plenty more where she came from."

"No," Brock blubbers, head buried in his arms. "No there ain't. She was the last one. The very last one . . ."

On the roof of the Tower, on the terrace of his penthouse suite, the Chief stands alone, looking up at the stars. The great constellation Scorpio sprawls across the southern sky; far in the north, over the mountains, a scribble of lightning races among banked clouds.

The Chief is dressed in his slate-blue uniform, trim and immaculate; his black riding boots, adorned with the brass spurs, without rowels, of a cavalry soldier, shine like mirrors. As usual he wears no insignia of rank and no decorations but the simple ribbon of the Medal of Honor. Hands clasped behind his back, he gazes up at the crown of Heaven—Corona Borealis—directly overhead. Those inaccessible realms. Inaccessible? he thinks. We shall see.

He paces to the parapet and looks down into the dark streets, the whispering city, fifteen stories below. A few lights move about down there, not many—vehicular lights, electric torches, a few small campfires on the sidewalks. Three blocks south a building burns, unattended; the glow illuminates a vacant street, a glass wall opposite, the metal shells, like dead insects, of a mass of abandoned automobiles. One company of soldiers, commanded by an officer on horseback, approach the broad esplanade of the headquarters building, marching through the floodlit emptiness of Unity Square. Three dark bodies dangle on the gallows. From the bowels of the Tower, discernible from this height only as a steady, comforting, feline purr, rises the sound of the diesel generators.

The Chief returns to a small table on the terrace. He pours himself a dash of cognac (Three Stars), tastes it. Clasping his hands again behind his back, boots set well apart at parade rest, he opens his mouth and speaks, his firm, resonant tenor pitched toward the stars:

"Gentlemen: The Army is ready. Are you ready?" He pauses, hearing from the sky a chorus of manly cheers. "Good. Tomorrow we march. Motorized column in the lead, cavalry following, labor battalion marching in the rear—under escort. We shall keep parade formation until we reach the outskirts of the city, at which time motorized units will proceed at optimum speed to first designated base camp, there to await arrival of cavalry. Eventually, of course, we hope to find motor vehicles and fuel sufficient to motorize the entire Army. Until that time we shall advance in leapfrog fashion, with first the motorized column and then the cavalry taking the lead. Radio communication will be maintained at all times. The logistics of the entire operation, which as you know we have designated *Coronado*, will be under the immediate command of Colonel Barnes, until and unless we encounter organized opposition, at which time I will assume personal command of military and political operations. Are there any questions?"

The Chief pauses, tilting his head. "No, Captain Fannin, we

are not going to abandon this city. We are leaving it under the able command of my trusted friend, adviser, and aide, Major Roland, assisted by Captain Myers and his military police company, and by you, Captain Fannin, with your detachment of R&R specialists." Pause; the Chief smiles. "Don't laugh, gentlemen, don't laugh."

"No, no, no, that won't do," the Chief goes on, pacing forward and looking down. "Delete that passage." He looks up again at the stars, seeking nobler inspiration. *"Ad astra, ad astra*... Yes, indeed. Gentlemen, the first objective is a modest one: the city of Santa Fe. From there, augmenting our forces, we continue eastward to Amarillo, Oklahoma City, and St. Louis, overcoming whatever obstacles may appear. Since we have had no communications with any of those cities, we assume that conditions there are similar to conditions prevailing in this city —before I relinquished my studies, to establish order."

Pause. The Chief waits, smiling at the applause, then raises a hand. Instant silence. "At St. Louis we shall consolidate our position, multiply our forces many times over (I have no doubt), and prepare for the final push eastward. The goal, of course, is Washington, D.C., which we shall re-establish as the nation's capital. The overall plan, gentlemen, quite simply, is to rebuild America, to make her once again the world's foremost industrial, military, and—if I may say so—spiritual power, an example to mankind of what human beings, properly organized and disciplined, can accomplish."

Another pause, for applause. "As for New York City"—the Chief's thin lips form a condescending smile—"as for New York, if that wretched hive of moral degeneracy and ethnic pollution still exists, we shall erect around it a radioactive wall a mile high!"

Silent applause. "Thank you. Thank you, gentlemen. Now as to the grand design of our new American society, let me say this. This is not the time or place for a blueprint but let me say this: The new America will be organized along sound military lines. Not an oligarchy, as before, hiding behind a façade of democracy, but a hierarchy of power based on merit and ability. Meritocracy. Government of the people, yes. Government for the people, yes. But government *by* the people? Never again. We want a strong, centralized State, capable of dealing quickly and mercilessly with enemies, whether foreign or domestic. It will also be, out of necessity, a thoroughly technological State. The conquest of Nature, once far advanced, now temporarily interrupted, will be resumed and completed. Not a single square foot of soil, nor a single living creature, will ever again be allowed to escape the service of humankind, society, and the State."

The Chief clears his throat, pacing back and forth more rapidly as he becomes excited by his own oration. "A harsh doctrine, you say. Indeed, gentlemen, it is a harsh doctrine—but a necessary one. What is the function of Nature? The function of Nature is to serve the needs of humanity. And what is the purpose of humanity? The purpose of humanity is to serve the aims of society as a whole. As a whole, gentlemen, as a unified, living organism. You say that humanity as presently constituted is anything *but* a unified, organic whole. Quite so. It is our purpose, our duty, as leading and organizing element, to bestow that unity upon mankind. To impose it, if necessary."

The Chief strays near the table for another sip of cognac. He sighs thoughtfully, staring up at the stars. "The people, gentlemen, the people are like children. We must guide them. Lead them. Use them. Help them fulfill their inner purpose, whether or not they are aware of that purpose. It is not in fact necessary that they be aware of purpose. Even better if they are not—such awareness might stimulate the tiresome conflict of opinions familiar to us from our recent past. No, they—the people—must be instructed only in their duty, each individual assigned his proper place. Thus the need for hierarchy, central authority, unified command. Consider, gentlemen, the most enduring architectural structure that human ingenuity has so far devised. What is the oldest and best-preserved type of manmade building on earth, gentlemen?" Pause. "The pyramid. Yes, the power of the pyramid. Think about it, gentlemen. . . ."

They think about it. Allowing time for reflection, the Chief continues. "And what, you may ask, can be the purpose of this great social pyramid, this living, pulsating, integrated pyramid of human flesh, animal flesh, plant flesh? What is the point of a pyramid? The apex, the summit, of course. And to what does that great summit direct our attention? Think, gentlemen. Think carefully. . . ."

Again the Chief looks up at the sky, giving his invisible audience a broad hint. He waits for a few more seconds, accumulating intellectual suspense, then smiles richly—that fair, fine-featured face, those intense and interesting eyes transformed, transfigured by the radiance of his soul—and reveals the secret.

"To the stars, gentlemen. *Ad astra.* This earth, this gross material planet, this so-called Nature, this animal and human populace, these squirming masses of sweating, striving, copulating, ignorant, and self-obsessed bodies, all will be welded into one great pyramidal footstool—for our leap to the stars. The greatest adventure. The adventure for which all history to date has been merely a preamble, a groping, fumbling, confused, and semiconscious search. And when I say that our purpose is to sail among the stars I do not mean to limit our adventure at that point. No, gentlemen, not at all, not at all."

The Chief's voice rises to a new level of inspiration. "To the stars, gentlemen—and beyond. *Beyond!* For I speak no longer of the merely physical journey, the technological voyage—glorious as that will be—but of a spiritual voyage. I speak of transcendence. The transcendence of the physical. The transcendence of the flesh. I speak of the disembodied spirit of humankind, united in one indivisible and ultradimensional entity, rising like a wave to converge upon—the Absolute. Upon—Godhead Itself. That is what I am speaking of now, gentlemen: union with God. Think about it. Think about it. . . ."

The Chief smiles, pacing about, hands clasped behind his back. "Oh I've lost them now," he mutters, shaking his head with pity, "I've lost them now. Too far. No matter—they'll be-

lieve whether they understand or not. The less they understand
the more eagerly they will believe." He chuckles. "As always.
God, I love them." He returns to the table for one more sip of
cognac.

Young Corporal Buckley appears and raps gently, timidly,
on the penthouse door. The Chief ignores him. A pause. Corporal
Buckley raps again, more gently, more timidly. The Chief ignores him. Corporal Buckley waits for the prescribed thirty seconds and raps once more, even more timidly, even more gently.

"Buckley!" the Chief snaps.

"Yes sir!" Buckley snaps to attention.

"Come here, Buckley." Buckley advances toward the Chief
in a semi-goosestep. "Halt." Buckley halts. "Buckley, do you
consider yourself a loyal follower of your Chief?"

Buckley blinks. "Beg pardon, sir?"

The Chief repeats his question.

"Yes sir. Absolutely sir, begging the Chief's pardon."

"Will you obey any order I give you, Buckley?"

"Absolutely, sir."

"Good." The Chief swirls the cognac in his glass. He points
to the waist-high parapet along the edge of the roof. "Buckley
—I want you to go and stand on that wall."

Corporal Buckley turns pale. "Oh sir . . . sir, begging the
Chief's pardon, but I can't, sir, I can't."

The Chief looks stern. "That's an order, Corporal Buckley."

"But sir . . . I have this awful fear. I can't bear heights, sir."

The Chief looks very stern. "I know that, Corporal Buckley." He places a hand on the sheathed dagger at his waist. "But
I gave you an order."

"Yes sir." Buckley walks slowly to the parapet. He puts one
hand and one foot upon it, looking over and down into the
streets, the beguiling yawn of the awful fall. The parapet, built
of brick, is one foot wide on top. Buckley begins to tremble.

"Mount the parapet, Buckley."

"Sir, I can't."

"You're a soldier, Buckley. Mount the parapet."

Buckley whimpers, a doglike mewling of fear. He makes blind, pawing gestures at the wall, brings down the first foot and tries the other, then goes back to the first.

"Buckley!"

Buckley crouches, one foot on the wall. "Yes sir?"

"Come here, Buckley."

"Yes sir." Still shaking and pale, but immensely relieved, Corporal Buckley approaches his Chief.

"Do you love me, Corporal Buckley?"

"Oh yes sir. Very much sir."

"Come closer, Buckley."

"Yes sir."

"Kneel down, Buckley."

"Yes sir." The corporal kneels, his eyes on the Chief's boots. The Chief strokes the corporal's pale, thin hair. "Good boy." The Chief smiles sweetly, thoughtfully, at the corporal's lowered and waiting head. "Are you a homosexual, Corporal Buckley?"

"No sir."

"That's good. Homosexuals produce no soldiers. Are you a heterosexual, Corporal Buckley?"

"No sir."

"What is a heterosexual, Buckley?"

The young man hesitates. "I don't know, sir. Begging the Chief's pardon, sir."

"That's all right, Buckley. Innocence is a virtue. Chastity is an admirable virtue." The Chief pauses. "Kiss my boot."

"Sir?"

"Kiss my boot."

Again the corporal hesitates. "Which one, sir?"

The Chief considers. "You choose, Buckley."

The corporal bends low and, after a moment of indecision, kisses the Chief's right boot.

"Thank you, Corporal Buckley. I commend your sense of fitness. Your initiative. Someday you'll be a sergeant, Corporal Buckley."

"Thank you, sir."

The dull glaze of boredom appears on the Chief's eyes. "You may go now, Buckley." The corporal shuffles backward on his knees, rises, turns to leave. "By the way, Buckley—"

"Yes sir?"

"What did you have to tell me?"

The corporal has forgotten, but immediately remembers. "The woman is ready, sir."

"Which one?"

"Her name is Valerie, sir."

"Has she been up here before?"

"Ah—yes sir, I believe so."

"Haven't we got any new ones?"

"Not tonight, sir. Begging the Chief's pardon, sir."

"Very well. Now go, Buckley. Quickly."

"Yes sir." The corporal vanishes.

The Chief retires to his dressing room and removes his boots and uniform. Completely nude, he contemplates with justified pride the image of himself in the floor-length mirror on the wall. Though over fifty, the Chief has the figure of an athlete. His white body is shapely, well-muscled, sparsely haired, the shoulders wide, the hips narrow, the buttocks firm and small as a boy's; there is only the faintest classical roll of excess flesh around his waist. Although short, he looks (he thinks) like a god. (A short god.)

The Chief opens a wardrobe, puts on a blue woolen robe that sets off nicely the marble tone of his skin. He opens another door and enters the next room, the transcendence chapel.

The Muzak system, forever operational in the Tower, is playing, at the moment, a melody from an ancient musical—"Some Enchanted Evening." Dim rose-colored lights, recessed in the walls, cast an erotic ambience upon the furniture of the room: a straight-backed chair, a fireplace, the Chief-size bed draped in black velvet, and the woman.

She smiles but does not speak as the Chief enters and takes

his place on the chair, facing the bed. Letting his robe fall open, saying nothing, he looks at her.

She is young, beautiful, as required, fulfilling the simple needs of male fantasy: She looks like a virgin and moves like a dancer. Reclining on the bed, wearing a translucent gown that reveals the glow but not the details of her pink body, she smiles and makes a few subtle movements. The Chief watches and says nothing. She lifts one leg toward the ceiling, letting the gold-trimmed hem of her gown slip to the knee. The Chief watches but does not stir. The girl performs a simple dance, not rising from the bed.

When she stops for a moment the Chief says, "Come here, my child."

She slides from the bed and undulates toward him, sinking to her knees between his outspread legs. He lifts her lovely face in both hands.

"Your name is Valerie?"

"Yes sir."

"You are very beautiful."

"Thank you, sir."

"You were here before?"

"Once, sir. About a month ago."

"Are you afraid of me, Valerie?" He strokes her long hair.

"Yes sir. A little."

The Chief smiles. "Don't be afraid, Valerie. As you can see, I am quite harmless."

She glances down, murmuring, "I can change that, sir."

"Do your duty, my child."

The girl goes at once to her work, skillfully, eagerly, employing her lips and her fingertips, her mouth, her hands, her breasts, stopping now and then to whisper words of encouragement, of admiration, of provocative and extravagant invitation. But the Chief is not stirred. Is not moved.

Tiring of the game, he gently pushes her head back and turns up her face. "That's enough. You may go now."

"I'm very sorry, sir." She looks fearful. "I tried, sir."

The Chief smiles. "My dear, you are perfect. You are beautiful and sweet and perfect. My officers must love you. Don't be afraid, I won't harm you. But before you go I want to show you something." He turns the girl's face down toward his genitals again. "The secret of love, my dear Valerie, is not the flesh, but —the will. The *will*, my dear. Observe."

The Chief looks down at his penis. Limp, sluggard a moment before, it now begins to redden and stiffen and rise, as a cock should for a comely woman; the pale worm becomes the scimitar of manhood. Not a great cock, perhaps, a little less than average size, but clearly ready, hard, potent with power. Small, but— small is beautiful.

The girl moans with exaggerated admiration. She cups both hands around the Chief's tumescent organ, as if it were a delicate candle flame she would shield from the wind. Moistening her lips, she again leans forward.

"No." He pushes her back. "I don't need that. You can go now." Feigning reluctance, she murmurs a protest; he commands. "Go!" He points to the outer door. "Out!"

She rises and glides away, glancing back once with a coquettish pout on her lips. Useless: The Chief still sits on his chair, gazing with satisfaction at the rigid, supernumerary digit rising from his groin.

Mangus Colorado, Jr., follows the shadow far ahead. The boy blunders along in the middle of the street, carelessly, bearing toward the shopping-center mall where he had been captured. When the noise of the two motorcycles is heard the boy pauses for a second, then goes on. The Apache finds him easy to follow, undetected, even through the darkness, around and among the walls of ruined buildings. The boy makes no effort to conceal himself.

He enters the mall, the Apache close behind. Mangus sees him stop before a store called Porter's, go in, come out a few minutes later with a broad-brimmed cowboy hat on his head. The boy stops again before a broken bookstore window to peer at something in the darkness inside, then goes on. As he passes the bookstore the Apache also looks in, trying to see what the boy had seen. Nothing there but a lot of dust-covered books in disarray, scattered over the floors. Mangus is a reader of things more interesting than printed books. He reads the book of the world. The trail of a sidewinder on sand. The marks of an owl's wings in the dust, coinciding with the terminus of a wood rat's track. The freshness of a horse's droppings, the age of a campfire. The meaning of the smell of a man's sweat—whether fear, or stress, or pain, or merely physical exertion. The flight of doves toward water. The flash of field glasses on a distant ridge. The ripeness of acacia beans, the flavor of jojoba nuts, the location of wild garlic bulbs, the readiness, for roasting, of an agave's flower stalk. He reads the meaning of these drops of blood, not more than two hours old, weaving up the corridor of the mall, entering a smashed-up place called Frederick's. Entering but not leaving. The smell of a horse. The stain of tobacco juice on the floor. Interested, the Apache lingers here, but not long. He follows the boy, who is also following the spoor of the horse, which leads out of the mall and up a northbound street. Toward the old university.

The boy wanders on, stopping often to get his bearings, hesitating. For a while he changes direction, going east, as if thinking of returning to his origins. But stops again, resting and brooding, before resuming his generally northwestward progress.

The city is immense, stretching across the desert for thirty miles. Mile after mile of houses, shops, stores, bars, motels, car lots, boat lots, trailerhouse lots, vacant lots, parking lots, open fields, citrus groves, shopping centers, department stores, movie houses, office buildings, even an occasional (and very small) public park. In one of these the boy stops again, after taking a blanket from a store; passing over the blowsand and broken glass, he finds a patch of grass beneath an ancient mesquite tree, rolls up in the blanket, and goes to sleep.

The Apache squats nearby, watching and waiting, patient as a tethered horse. He takes a sip from his canteen, checks the squelch on his radio, chews on some jerky from his shirt pocket. The night is long, but not for Mangus Colorado, for whom time is meaningless. He wears no watch, he seldom looks up at the stars. He hears, however, the cry of birds, the stirring of the breeze among the tumbleweeds piled ten feet high along a wall, the approach and passage and disappearance, five blocks away, of a small sick car with one headlight, a clattering air-cooled engine, bound for the Tower ten miles to the west. And he hears, a couple of hours later, the mutter of a motorcycle, well tuned and powerful, following a single beam of light in the same direction. The Apache recognizes and identifies that sound, that particular engine, as belonging to Sergeant Brock. The Apache smiles, knowing where the sergeant has been. And keeps his watch on young Art Dekker.

The boy must be very tired. He sleeps for a long time after sunrise, and only the heat, building up in oppressive waves above the ground, finally forces him awake. Straightening his hat, leaving the blanket behind, he lurches to his feet and staggers off again through the suburbs, first north, then west away from the sun, then north again. The Apache stands and follows, silent as a ghost, keeping close to the shady side of the walls.

After an hour of erratic wandering, the boy stops, staring down a side street. The Apache stops and watches. He hears the sound of a horse at walking pace, shod feet clopping with hollow sound on hard pavement. The horse appears and its rider, a lean old man with a big revolver on his hip, a bulge of tobacco in his cheek, eyes shaded by his hatbrim.

He and the boy greet each other. The Apache cannot hear the words. The rider dismounts, leads his horse into shade; squatting on their heels, he and the boy consult with one another in quiet dialogue. The horse keeps looking toward Mangus Colorado, nostrils quivering, ears up. The Apache steals around a corner and approaches the man and boy from an oblique direction, downwind from the horse. The horse stands with lowered head now, munching at the weeds growing out of the asphalt. The Apache cannot get close enough to overhear the conversation so hunkers down again, deep in the black desert shade, and waits, observes. He sees the old man point once back the way he had come, toward the east. More inaudible talk. The old man draws a map in the sand of the street, which the boy studies. The talk continues.

After some time the old man stands up and scrapes away the drawing with his boot. The boy has a drink from the old man's canteen. They shake hands, the old man half embracing the other. The old man mounts his horse and turns to watch the boy marching off. A final wave—and they are gone.

The Apache looks after the man on horseback. No problem there: The rider is heading straight for the heart of the city. Straight for the slabs and monoliths, the upright packing cases, the vertical storage cells of what were, what once had been, the hives of law, authority, banking, information, medicine, finance, direct for the tallest of the glass cathedrals, the center of the power complex.

Let him go, thinks the Apache; suicide is no concern of Corporal Mangus Colorado. He doesn't even bother to lift the radio from his belt to inform the Tower guard that an armed man, unknown, is advancing toward them.

Instead, following orders, he follows the boy.

W̶hen Jack Burns awoke that morning he realized that he had been tricked. After the music of the phonograph he remembered a round of singing by the young people and personal testimonials to the memory of their two slain brothers. Engaged in sympathy, his emotions from a previous age—a previous life, it seemed!—surging through his mind and heart, he found he could not leave. And then exhaustion overcame him, he fell asleep on the floor of the underground hideout, dimly aware of others around him, some leaving through the steel door, bound into the night on foraging expeditions, raids, and revenge. Someone placed a blanket over him. The old man half slept, half dreamed through it all. He dreamed of a mountain valley bright with flowers, of a woman in a yellow dress walking up the trail toward him, smiling, singing. She's so far away, he thought in the dream; she looks so happy and so very far away. Yes, she replied, I am happy, and I am very far away. But I can hear you, she said in the dream, I can hear you. . . . He was overwhelmed by sensations of peace, happiness, beauty.

He awoke to the smell of food. A dozen of the girls and boys, armed and dressed like bandits, each with a spoon and a cup or bowl, sat cross-legged around a cast-iron Dutch oven full of hot stew. They were eating, talking somberly in low tones; when one of them noticed Burns opening his eyes, he was offered a share in the breakfast.

Afterward he again requested the return of his weapon and his horse. They tried to dissuade him from his plan but he was determined. Stubborn as stone. Red Beard, who seemed the most influential member of the gang—the professor was gone and apparently they had no leader; as one explained, "We are all leaders"—finally yielded and gave Burns his gun. Burns checked to make sure the cylinder was loaded; it was, except for the empty chamber under the hammer. Two others escorted him outside, into the dazzling sunlight, past their sentries to a fenced-in citrus grove where they had hidden his horse.

On the way they met Rodack and two of his bandits—one girl, one boy—returning from somewhere with heavy packs on their backs, mismatched rifles in their hands. They looked grim and pleased at the same time.

"No," Rodack said, "you're not leaving. Not already."

"Yes sir," said Burns, "I'm leaving. I thank you for the hospitality."

The professor smiled his wry smile. "Some hospitality—one night in a crowded basement. Sure you won't stay a little longer?"

"No sir, I can't. I'm on my way."

"In broad daylight," marveled the professor. "Like a free man. Like a citizen."

"That's my plan. I'm a-going right up main street straight toward them. Right into the devil's den."

"Maybe you're right. But they'll take your gun. And your horse. And draft you into a labor company. You'll be out digging irrigation ditches under the sun. For as long as you can stand up. Then they'll bury you, if they're not too busy."

"I reckon. I'm catching on to the system around here. But I guess I'll take my chances." It was the old man's turn to smile. "What else do I have to do? I sure ain't going home alone."

"Your home is with us—if you want it."

"Mighty kind of you, Professor. Maybe I'll be back."

"You'll have to hunt for us. We won't be here. Somewhere nearby, maybe. So if they torture you—when they torture you" —Rodack placed his free hand on Burns' arm—"tell them the truth. You'll do us no harm."

"I'm much obliged for that information."

"Good luck to you, Jack Burns." The professor embraced the old man; Burns could feel the hard stock of the professor's rifle against his back. The boy shook his hand. The girl shook his hand, as a man would, and then—her eyes starting to brim with tears—she hugged him around the neck and kissed his whiskery lean cheek, whispering in his ear: "Thank you so much for bringing Barbara home. Thank you, thank you, thank you." She let him go and passed out of his sight. The others were gone. The two boys escorting him pointed the way to his horse and left. He was alone, and found himself weeping. By God, he thought, I'm getting old, getting old, crying so easy again.

He found the horse; they were glad to see each other. He fed her grain from his saddlebags, spread on the blanket, cinched the saddle tight, mounted. This ceremony he was familiar with, he'd been doing it for about sixty years, and once again, as always, sitting in the saddle, he felt good, proud, as strong as ever he had been. That much, at least, had not changed. Would never change, he believed. How could that change? A man on horseback is different from a man on foot. Better? Maybe, maybe not; but different, that was for sure.

They stepped across a flowing ditch—Rosie disdained the water—and through the gate, which he left open; there was no other stock inside. He rode away from the wreckage of the library, past other bombed and shelled relics of what had been the university, and down a long avenue of dying royal palms. Dying from lack of water, lack of care, dying among the ruins.

He rode for an hour toward the center of the city, seeing no one but a few old folks and children lurking in doorways, staring at him in wonder. The sun blazed on his back, the heat waves shimmered before him in the streets, the harsh light, glancing from steel, concrete, shattered glass, hurt his eyes. He ignored these discomforts, riding straight for the distant towers.

He found the boy, wandering alone, dazed and lost. They talked for a while. Art tells Burns about the firefight. Two young men and a girl were trapped in a movie theater, besieged by a squad of motorcycle troopers. Art plunged into the battle, choosing the wrong side, the losing side. One of the boys was dead, the other mortally wounded. They were finished, almost out of ammunition. Desperate, he and the girl resolved to run. He covered her retreat, saw her get away. "To the university," she'd told him. He was reloading his revolver when two of the men in black, sweating, furious, eager to capture a live enemy, cornered him by a chained door. He told the rest of his story and revealed to Burns that his aim, now, was to tie in with the "Robin Hoods," as the girl had styled her group, to join them, fight for them, die with them.

Burns could think of saner, easier goals in life. Not many; some. But looking at the boy's passionate face, the urgency and love and hatred in his eyes, he did not even consider the notion of trying to suggest another way. What alternatives were there, in any case, here in this violent city, this oasis of passion?

He felt clearly his own growing love for young Art, this lonely and searching boy, who might have been, could have been, his son. Why not, he thought for one wild moment, why not give up the search for his own, take this lad instead, kidnap him if necessary, take him and the Indian and that girl—Dixie—take them back to his place, where they could hide and work and survive, together, until the madness of civil war passed by them?

Futile fantasy; it was already too late. He showed Art how to find the library and told him to hurry. They parted. When the boy was beyond recall, far down the littered street, Burns turned his horse and continued on his own way. . . .

Late morning now. The shadows contract toward the walls, toward the trunks of leafless trees; little living things—lizards, snakes, rodents, birds, feral cats, and wild dogs—creep into shelter, crawl under any shield available against the pitiless rays of the rising sun. Jack Burns rides slowly down a wide and lifeless street, through the wreckage and disorder, toward the Tower. Looking up, he sees the vultures circling against the blue —black-winged, fierce-eyed, melancholy birds, arrogant in their freedom, humble with hunger. He loosens the revolver in his holster, spits a jet of tobacco juice onto the pavement, and sings his little song,

The gloomy night
Before us flies,
The reign of terror
Now is o'er;
Its gags, inquisitors, and spies,
Its hags and harpies,
Are no more. . . .

His heart beats with fear. He wipes the sweat from his upper lip and listens to the echo from the hollow walls:

Are no more
no more
no more

Tunneling through the night, led by one yellow beam into the west, the cranky Beetle bumbles homeward. The cadaver drives, Wolfe sits jammed in the tiny rear seat; Dixie Dalton, hands chained behind her back, sits beside the driver.

Fox cannot keep his yellowish eyes on the road. His hands remain on the wheel but his eyes, loose and indulgent, keep straying to the woman at his side. His wide mouth twitches with nervous greed. Inspector Wolfe, anxious, alert, peers ahead, noting every obstacle on the way.

"Watch it, Fox, watch it. . . ."

Dixie ignores them both. What a pair of pigs, she thinks. Worse than pigs—reptiles. Gila monsters. Ugly, poisonous, creepy. But why compare them to an honest lizard? They're worse than anything unhuman. Ignore them. Think of—Brock. My lover. My *lover!* God, what a lover. I've had it now. They've got me now. I'm sunk. Dead. Buried.

She luxuriates for a time in self-pity. Then recovers. I can handle these cowards. Thank God there's two of them. Each afraid of the other. Both afraid of Brock. Afraid of me, too, I think. I can handle them. But where's Sam? Where's that Hopi when I need him? Floating off and leaving me. The magician. Some magician. His magic necklace. Big help that was. His crackpot friends—one crazy old man, one jealous kid. Where are they when you need them? I'll manage on my own. All by my lonesome, by God, if I never see them again. Who else do I have? Good question. Poor old Glenn? That little crawling Singin' Bob? Nobody, that's who. I'll make it on my own. If I have to. And if I have to I will.

She strains at the metal bonds, clamped painfully tight around her wrists. Impossible.

Inspector Fox, eyes rolling sideways, says, "Something bothering you, sweetheart?"

"You could open these cuffs a couple notches."

"That's not the only thing I'm going to open."

"Fox," says Wolfe, "watch the road. There's stray horses all over the place."

"Mind your own business. I'm driving."

"Then drive. Let the girl alone."

"Shut up." Fox drives on, grinning over the wheel. After a time he says, "You know, Wolfe . . ."

"Forget it."

"You know . . . we don't have to go back there."

"Are you kidding? Brock would hunt us down. Him and that Apache bloodhound. They'd kill us—if we were lucky."

"I'm not afraid of Brock." Left hand on the wheel, Fox's right hand is hidden near his waist.

"Yes you are. And so am I. Anyway, there's no place to go."

"Got a third of a tank. We can drive a hundred miles in this thing before it runs dry."

"Forget it."

Fox mumbles, licking his lips. Hunched over the wheel, he watches Dixie straining, twisting on her seat, close beside him. He lifts his right foot, letting the car slow down.

"Keep driving, Fox."

"Faggot," Fox replies; he grins at Dixie; she stares ahead, ignoring him, but planning, planning.

"I don't like that word, Fox."

"Queer."

"You bastard." Inspector Wolfe pulls a small pistol from his waistband and jams the muzzle of it into the back of Fox's neck. "Apologize, you bastard—and keep driving."

"Sorry," Fox mumbles, stepping hard on the gas pedal again.

"Apologize!"

"I apologize."

Wolfe sighs, relaxing a bit, and pulls his gun a few inches back. "That's better. Next time you call me that, you bastard, I'm going to kill you."

"Next time you won't have a chance."

"We'll see."

They drive on without further dialogue, no sound but the buzzing of the engine, the whine of the tires, the subdued mumbling of Inspector Fox.

The lights of the Tower appear. They drive through the floodlights of Unity Square, past the laden gallows, and into the gateway of the barbed-wire enclosure around the base of the headquarters building. Fox stops at the sandbagged sentry box, shows his face and pass. Wolfe does the same. The sentry, backed up by two other soldiers armed with carbines and fixed bayonets, looks inquiringly at Dixie Dalton.

"Prisoner," Fox explains, "for Captain Fannin."

The sentry nods, salutes, waves them on in, and picks up the telephone in his fortified box. Fox halts the car beside the main entrance; joined by Wolfe, he helps Dixie out of the car and hurries her up the steps, where they are stopped, before the great brass-framed revolving doors, by a sergeant and two guards.

"I'll take your prisoner," the sergeant says.

"No you won't," Wolfe says, "we're delivering her personally to Captain Fannin." The soldiers stare at Dixie.

A brief debate; the sergeant yields. Escorted by Wolfe, Fox, and the guards, Dixie is hustled through the turning door and across the tiled floor of an immense lobby. She is dazzled by glittering chandeliers hanging thirty feet overhead, by the amazing chill of the air conditioning, by the hard heels of officers and soldiers clashing on the tile. Before she can see very much, however, she is crowded into an elevator. Inspector Wolfe pushes a button: No. 12. The floor lifts suddenly, silently, beneath her feet; hands still bound, she sways, nearly losing her balance. One of the soldiers steadies her with a hand.

She looks him in the eyes. Young, sun tanned, freckled like a farm boy, he averts his face from her level gaze. "What's your name?" she asks.

The soldier does not answer.

"Get me out of here," Dixie says quietly. "Shoot these two clowns and get me out of here." Looking away from her, the soldier remains silent.

"You better shut up," Fox says, "or you'll be in more trouble than you are now."

"Shut up yourself," Dixie says. "Rapist," she adds in a low clear voice.

"Shut up," Fox snarls.

"Tell Brock," she says to the two soldiers.

Fox lifts clawed hands halfway toward her neck, his face twisted with fury. "You liar!"

The elevator stops, the doors glide apart. "Don't forget," she says to the soldiers, as Wolfe and Fox push her into a broad, carpeted corridor. There they pause, looking around. Dixie becomes aware, for the first time, of the *pleasant listening* issuing from the walls, the ceilings, from concealed speakers wired to a remote tape-playing machine hidden somewhere in the depths—or heights—of the Tower. "Some Enchanted Evening . . ." "Good Christ," she murmurs, "it's a dental office."

"You'll wish it was," Fox whispers, "you lying slut." He shoves her toward another pair of magnificent, sculptured, brass-bound doors, flanked by a brace of guards.

More delay, more protocol. Finally they are admitted to what looks, indeed, like a waiting room. But a large one, with broad chairs covered in leather, soft lights, a tasteful display of fine old books on shelves built deep into the wall. They sit and wait. Feeling vaguely comforted by these unfamiliar but luxurious surroundings, Dixie relaxes enough to let her eyes take in the titles of some of the books: *The Pickwick Papers; The Essays of Montaigne; The Divine Comedy; The Republic.* . . .

"Maybe we better take the handcuffs off her," Fox whispers nervously.

"Right, right," Wolfe agrees. He fumbles in his pockets, comes out not with a key but a picklock, little more than a refined sixpenny nail; this he inserts in the keyhole of each cuff and taps with a pocketknife, delicately, precisely. The cuffs spring open. Wolfe hides them in a pocket.

Dixie holds out her arms, looking at her chafed, reddened wrists. She massages them gently and stares, as she does so, at Inspector Fox. "You're in trouble, Fox."

He starts to rise, flushing with anger. "Goddamn you—"

The inner door opens. A woman appears, tall, blond, handsome, about forty years old, dressed in a brocaded robe, smoking a cigarette. The two men spring to their feet, facing her respectfully. "Well," she says, hoarsely, surveying Dixie Dalton up and down, "what have we here?"

Wolfe clears his throat. "Captain Fannin, ma'am, this girl is a prisoner. A conscript, I mean. Dixie Dalton. Sergeant Brock sent her."

Captain Fannin smiles at Dixie. "You're a darling. Good old Sergeant Brock. He's a darling too." She blows a cloud of smoke toward Wolfe. "Get out."

"Beg pardon, ma'am?"

"Get out. You and your slimy-looking servant. Take off."

Head slightly bowed, Fox mutters, "We want a receipt, Captain Fannin."

"A what?"

"A receipt."

"Oh for godsake." The captain opens a drawer in one of the end tables, scribbles a note on a pad, tears the sheet off, and holds it out at arm's length, her eyes elsewhere. As Fox reaches for it she lets it drop to the carpet. He picks it up, starts for the door, followed closely by Wolfe.

"He wanted to rape me," Dixie says.

"What?" The men stop, Fox's hand on the door handle. "Which one?" asks Captain Fannin.

Dixie points to Fox.

The captain stares reproachfully at Fox, then at Wolfe, then at Fox. "You?"

"It's a lie," Fox snarls.

The woman looks at Wolfe. "Well—did he?"

Wolfe clears his throat, hesitates, unable to control a sudden giggle; he glances once at Fox, then looks at the floor. Fox watches him, pale with hatred. "I—I'd rather not answer that question, ma'am. Begging the captain's pardon."

The captain stares. "You don't have to. Now clear out. Both of you. Jump!"

As the door closes behind them Dixie and the captain hear the hissing rage of Fox, a squeal of pain from Wolfe. The doors close solidly, with a click and mesh of bolts, and the sound, from outside, of a guard's key turning in the lock. Captain Fannin picks up a telephone, calls down to the lobby: "Captain Fannin here. Detain that man Fox. Sergeant Brock will want to speak with him. Yes, that's right." She hangs up, smiles brightly at Dixie. "Come, my dear. You're having a bath."

Dixie follows the captain, thinking that she might as well play along with this game until she finds a way out of it. On the way to the bath she is passed by two young women, wearing the thin gowns that seem to be a sort of uniform; lovely girls with huge painted eyes and flowing hair, they smile at Dixie and murmur greetings. She smiles back, awkwardly, feeling too big, awkward, out of place here.

The captain speaks to one of the girls. "Send word upstairs we've got a new one in tonight. They'll be interested."

The bathroom seems gigantic to Dixie, bigger than any room of the sort she had ever seen before. A deep tub, seven feet long, steaming with hot water, foaming with *gelée*, is waiting for her. The captain sits on a chair near the tub, smiling at Dixie.

Slowly, reluctantly, Dixie undresses, shy before the woman, embarrassed by her rough and dusty clothes—the old boots, the jeans, the torn blouse, her frayed underwear.

"You don't mind if I sit here and talk, do you, dearie?" The captain lights a fresh cigarette from the smoking butt of her old one. "I'm sure you must have questions."

"Well yes," Dixie says, with a nervous laugh: "How do we get out of here?"

The captain laughs too. "I know, my dear, we get that feeling now and then. Put your things in that little chute there. That's right, there in the wall."

Dixie starts to obey, hesitates. "What is this, for laundry?"

The captain smiles, waving her cigarette. "Just put them in, my girl, they'll be taken care of. Your boots too."

"My boots?"

"Your boots."

"But—I'll need them."

"You'll get everything you need here. Push them in, now, that's a good girl."

With sinking heart Dixie sends her boots down the dark hole after her clothes. Before she lets the sprung lid snap shut she feels a breath of hot air rising from the chute. Goddamn, she thinks, goddamn it to hell.

The captain tests the water in the tub with her elbow. "Now, Dixie my darling, step in and relax, the water's perfect." She watches with appraising eyes, squinted against the cigarette smoke, as Dixie slowly and tentatively lowers herself into the thick foam. "You are a beauty, my girl, a beauty. They'll love you here. You'll be well treated." The captain slides her chair closer to the side of the tub and picks up a loofah. "We'll all love you here. Let me get your back."

Obediently, Dixie leans forward; the captain scrubs her back, her armpits, becomes more intimate. Gently but firmly Dixie pushes the woman's hand away, takes the loofah from her. "I can—I'd rather do that myself."

"Of course, of course." The smiling captain leans back, holding the cigarette and blowing smoke rings at the ceiling. "Yes, Dixie girl, you'll like it here. Much better here than—out there, you know. Not only more comfortable but much, much safer."

"I suppose." Dixie lolls in the tub, keeping all but her head and shoulders under the suds. "But I would like to go out now and then. In the day, I mean."

The captain considers. "Later, perhaps. When we get to know you better. Meanwhile, you'll have everything you could possibly need right here on Floor 12. You'll have a room with one other girl. We've got a kitchen, a dining room, a nice little bar and library, a game room, a jacuzzi, a balcony when you want some sun—not that you'll want any of that for a while, with summer coming on. And if you're nice and good you'll be invited to parties up on the roof sometime. You will even"—the captain smiles sweetly at the ceiling—"be invited up there alone. At any time. For an hour with—him."

"Him?"

"The Chief, of course. You'll enjoy that. He's very kind. Very gentle. He'll like you, I'm sure."

"Will I like him?"

Captain Fannin laughs. "Darling, you say the strangest things."

The door opens, the girl named Valerie looks in. She smiles at the captain, at Dixie.

"How was it?" Captain Fannin asks.

The girl makes a face. "SOS," she says. "Same old shit. For a few seconds I thought he was gonna weaken. He threw me out."

The captain frowns. "Oh dear . . ."

"He scares me. You never know what he's going to do. I don't want to go up there anymore."

"I know, Valerie dear. You go now. I'll think about it." The girl withdraws. The captain flicks ashes on the floor. She looks at Dixie. "How old are you, darling?"

"Twenty-two."

"Twenty-two. Of course. Just a child." The woman sighs, rolling her eyes at the ceiling. "You've missed so much, so much. You and the others. You'll never know. . . ."

Dixie finds herself beginning to doze off in the warm and ample tub. Exhaustion, long denied in her nervous excitement and fear, begins to claim her limbs, her mind, her heavy heavy eyelids.

". . . It was a golden age," Captain Fannin is saying, lighting another in her chain of smokes. "It was *the* golden age, my dear. You can't imagine. Nothing like that"—she makes a gesture toward the wall, indicating the outside world—"like that horror you see out there now. Madmen and arsonists, hangmen and rapists everywhere, sand dunes in the streets, wild dogs in the alleys. No, my dear, what we had then—oh it's nearly indescribable. Before the collapse, I mean. When you were still a little, little child. The streets were lighted then with mercury lamps that turned night into day. And full of private cars, not wreckage. Every family had one, or two or three, motorcars with tastefully appointed interiors, foam rubber and plush upholstery, powerful motors under the hood, automatic transmissions, air conditioning, fingertip controls—flick of a switch and the windows went up, down, halfway, all the way. You can't imagine, dear, the delight of it. Padded dashboards. Reclining bucket seats. How pretty it was. Neon signs glowing everywhere in a hundred different shades of color, stores that never closed, traffic that never stopped. You should have seen the people then, darling. Everyone so smartly dressed. Men in tailored dress suits, not these awful uniforms you see nowadays. The women so chic—rich fabrics, gay patterns, an infinite diversity of cut and design. The nightlife, my dear! Disco, for example! But you've never even heard of it. And the bars, the nightclubs, the theaters, the restaurants."

Dixie listens, half asleep, to the captain's rhapsody. Sunk in the amniotic tub, soaking in comfort, she barely hears the captain go on. And on.

". . . Theater, opera, cinema, ballet, concerts, poetry readings, public lectures, a thousand different things going on every night. Vacations in Acapulco, Puerto Vallarta, San Francisco, New York, the Caribbean, North Africa, Spain, Greece, Anatolia, Paris, London—the whole world was ours with no more than a couple of good plastic credit cards. There was sport—oh *la sport!*—pageants of sport. Football, soccer, water skiing, downhill skiing, tennis matches, cabin cruisers swarming on every lake, houseboats floating up and down every river, sailboats, skateboards, roller skates, ice skates. Marvelous! The beaches so packed with lovely brown bodies you could scarcely walk on them. You could drive your car anywhere. Anywhere! We had drive-in movies, drive-in banks, drive-in liquor stores, drive-in eateries—yes, my dear, eateries, charming term, we had eateries galore, people were always eating, eating, eating, oh it was gorgeous—and drive-in churches even, drive-in homes. The quickie marriage and the quickie divorce, no hard feelings on either side, I went through several myself, there was always another partner waiting, by the pool, back at the condominium."

Captain Fannin taps a fresh cigarette from her little pearl-inlaid silver case, lights up, inhales, savors the dim rush through her lungs, exhales a languorous stream of blue smoke, watching with half-lidded eyes. Dixie finds her chin slipping under the foam; she sits up and yawns.

". . . The world was sick with envy. Our atom bombs. Our H-bombs. Our rockets to the moon. Our rockets to Jupiter, Saturn, and beyond, bearing messages for whoever—whatever—

waits . . . out there. (And may they come soon, soon come down, and makes us slaves once and for all or forever make us free!) No, my Dixie darling, you have no idea, no *idea*, how sweet life was in America then. Think of fifty thousand—no, a hundred thousand or even two-hundred thousand young people, my friends and I, jammed together in a park somewhere, an arena maybe, listening to four little guys on a stage half a mile away. For hours! All united, hearts and minds and bodies, screaming and yelling and shaking together. Happy, vibrating, multiplying bodies. Dear Dixie, it was wonderful, you'll never understand how good and sweet and beautiful our lives seemed then. How can I explain it? And the great cities over the land, growing greater all the time. Our Pentagon, inspiring fear and dread throughout the world. Our thriving industries: the steel mills! the copper smelters! the power plants belching their great plumes into the air! Everywhere! The big laboratories where every day somebody was discovering some wonderful new miracle cure for cancer, for the common cold, for lead poisoning, for emphysema, for heart disease."

Smiling at her vision, Captain Fannin shakes her large blond head slowly back and forth. Dixie turns a tap and adds more hot water to the tub; soap bubbles float on the air, iridescent globes of lavender and rose.

"... It was an age of riches, my dear. Two hundred and fifty million Americans rolling in the dough. A time of unlimited prosperity: our roads, rails, skies, and waterways roaring with traffic. Silver jets thundering every hour on the hour across the sky, no matter where you were. And even up there they were eating, up there in the sky, the people, I mean. Eating, eating. You can't imagine! The food we had, up in the sky, down on the ground, out on the water. Lobster from Australia! Crab from Alaska! Shrimp from the Sea of Cortez! Nuts and pineapples from Hawaii! Oysters and clams from—from, I forget. From somewhere. And the wines, my dear, the wines! From France, of course. From Spain and Portugal. From South Africa, Germany, Italy, Greece. Even from California—that poor doomed state.

And beef from corn-fed cattle raised in luxury and idleness in feedlots; steaks, roasts, prime ribs so marbled with fat you could cut them with your fork! Not like this dreadful range-grown meat they bring us nowadays. When we're not eating dogmeat, I mean. Which reminds me, Dixie dear . . ."

Dixie opens her heavy eyes. The captain is not looking at her but staring instead, wistfully, through weak and wobbly smoke rings, at the plastered bas-relief on the bathroom ceiling. The captain sighs again, continuing:

". . . What was I going to say? Oh dear. Oh yes. And of course we had all possible kinds of happy pills. Have a headache, pop some aspirin. Can't sleep at night, pop some Valium. Worries got you down, pop some Librium. Out for a good time, snort cocaine. Loafing away a lazy afternoon, smoke some dope. Trouble with your sex life, try Percodan. Bad pain in the kidneys, pop some Demerol. Seeking a higher spiritual status, drop some acid. Meeting friends, drown in alcohol. Dying, shoot up some morphine. Joining God, pop a holy wafer, and so on and so on. Where was I? The food? We discussed that? The bathrooms? Have I said anything about our bathrooms? You don't realize, Dixie my dear, how lucky you are to be here. For out there, out in that horrible burning city, there is no plumbing. No plumbing—are you aware of that? But when I was a girl, in those sweet and blessed times, there was a flush toilet—a *flush toilet,* mind you! —in every home. Two or three of them, actually. Flush toilets! —a simple twitch of the lever and all that nasty nasty icky-poo was carried away, out of sight out of mind, in one pretty swirl of blue-tinted water. Never to be seen again. And our beds: king-size, queen-size, princess-size, circular, pneumatic, electrified. (Those Magic Fingers!) And waterbeds! You'll never know what it was like to roll on a waterbed with your lovers— like oozing about in warm Jell-O—twice the fun with half the effort. . . ."

A pause. Smoke rings and bubbles. Baubles and gas. Baubles and bubbles and smoke rings and gas.

"Television! In color! Living flesh tones! Quadraphonic

speakers! Giant wall-size screens! Cable TV, free TV, public TV, porno TV. Portable TV—nobody ever went on a picnic in the hills without her porto TV, her blanket, her diaphragm, and her man of the hour. Or woman of the week. Gay times, my dear. High times. Hedonic wonderland. Of course, in some respects, we went too far. Our Chief, I'm glad to say, is restoring order and discipline. Still . . . all the same . . ."

She winks at Dixie, puts a finger over her lips. "The walls have ears. One must be discreet. But I'm barely getting started. So much you should know, so much we have lost. Power-driven lawn mowers with padded seats. Electric golf carts. Our private motor-cars. Our planes and buses and monorails and space shuttles—you could, if you wanted to, spend your entire life in a sitting position. When you weren't lying down."

Another sigh. "And the plans. Everything planned for, taken care of in advance. Social Security. Pension plans. Medical insurance, life insurance, burial insurance, paid vacations, maternity leave, child-care centers for working mothers, welfare subsistence for the poor—nobody was left out. Something for everyone. Even our Indians received free medical care, free education, free housing, free scholarships. (But look at them now; take away their pickup trucks and they revert to savagery.) And the personal services, available to everyone: psychiatry, sex therapy, assertiveness training, Esalen, Rolfing, est, Arica, Yoga, group encounter, body building, weight reducing, marriage counseling, child counseling, a whole supermarket of religious services: Buddhism, Jesus Loves You, Shiva, Sufi, Zen, Islam, Virgin Mary, Hare Krishna, A&P, Food Giant, Piggly Wiggly, Safeway! The wealth and abundance of it! You can't begin to comprehend. You'll never begin to imagine. Oh Dixie my dear, no one who was not alive in the America of those times can ever know the true sweetness of human life. . . ."

Again, the melancholy sigh. And then Captain Fannin speaks directly, positively, for the walls. "But our Chief, God bless him, is going to bring it all back again. The good parts of it, I mean. And more. And go beyond." She winks at Dixie.

Striving to stay awake, Dixie sits up straight in the tub. She looks about for a towel. The girl Valerie sticks her head in the doorway.

"Buckley is here, ma'am."

"Buckley?" The captain looks startled. "Again? What for now?"

Valerie points her rosy lips at Dixie Dalton, rising from the warm bath.

"Oh—I see. Goodness." At once the captain springs into action. "Out of the bath, my girl. Quickly now. Bring us towels, Valerie, and a brush."

Both women seem alert with anxiety. Dixie, center of sudden activity, is infected by their panic. "What's going on?"

"You're going upstairs, my dear. Up to the roof. Hurry now, hurry."

They rub her down with towels, then seat her—rosy and tingling—before a vanity table with illuminated mirror. On the table is an array of containers and instruments—puffs and powders, brushes, combs, tweezers, pencils, paints, creams, rouges, colognes, perfumes, hand mirrors—working tools of a courtesan. The two women beset Dixie, like trainers at a boxing match, combing and brushing her hair, painting her eyelids, penciling her eyebrows, rouging her cheeks with a blush of rose, tipping the nipples of her breasts with a touch of pink.

Jesus Christ, thinks Dixie, what the hell is going on here? But still waiting for the right moment, she offers no resistance.

"You've been honored, my dear," the captain says, spraying a mist of cologne into Dixie's armpits, groin, toes. "Your very first night here. Give her some of those mints, Valerie. Quickly. Quickly."

"What the hell am I supposed to do?" says Dixie.

"Whatever he says, my dear. But no more. Do be cautious. Don't look him directly in the eyes. Don't speak unless spoken to. Do your best to please him. But don't do too much."

"What does that mean?"

"It's hard to explain. It's kind of a test he sets himself every now and then. You must entice him, tease him a bit—but don't be vulgar. In no way. Oh God, Valerie, he must be in a mood tonight."

"Not too bad. He looked pleased with himself when I left him."

"Get Dixie a gown now, darling."

They slip it on her. "Is this all I wear, for godsake?"

"It's all you'll need, my dear. Now, out you go. This way."

They hustle her into the waiting room where Corporal Buckley, neat and pink and blond in his tan uniform, waits impatiently, looking anxious. He simpers at Dixie. A small man, only a little taller than Dixie, he wears no weapon, not even a pistol or knife.

"She's too fat," he says.

"She is not," says Captain Fannin. "She's a milk-fed country beauty. You be good to her or I'll cut your tongue out. Good luck, Dixie my sweetheart; we'll see you in an hour."

Not if I can help it, Dixie thinks. She follows the beckoning Buckley through the doors, into the corridor—where the guards, suddenly alert, give her full attention as she passes—and into a different, smaller, but richly paneled elevator. This one has a key in the switch on the control panel.

They rise three floors. The doors open automatically on an anteroom, sparsely furnished, ornately framed mirrors screwed to the walls. The bland music leaks from hidden speakers. She looks for a big book, a small chair, a heavy table lamp—anything handy. But sees nothing useful. The corporal opens a door, leading her into the bedroom. She notes a cold fireplace with three mesquite logs resting on a bed of unlit kindling. And two brass-headed andirons . . .

Corporal Buckley (always a bridesmaid) bends over the bed in the center of the room to straighten the black coverlet. A golden eagle, life-size, looks down from the ceiling with sheaf of arrows clutched in right talons, lightning bolt in the left: Nobility. Dominance. Penetration. Speed.

The andiron makes a soft but solid noise—*chunk!*—on the

side of the corporal's skull. He utters a little, quiet cry as he sprawls across the bed. Dixie reopens her eyes, drops the weapon, gets quickly to work. She pulls off the corporal's Wellington boots, unbuckles his belt, unzips and pulls off his trousers. The shirt takes more time but she gets it.

Listening carefully. No sounds from beyond either door. Dixie lifts the gown over her head and drapes it upon Corporal Buckley. She raises his feet onto the bed—compulsive gesture. Making him comfortable. The small man breathes heavily but steadily, as one in deep slumber. Sleeping in his underwear and socks, under a clinging negligee. Dixie yanks on the pants, the boots. Holding the shirt to her bosom, she draws a curtain one inch aside and glances through the French windows. A fair slim figure in a robe stands out there at the far end of the terrace, near the wall, staring up at the stars.

Dixie puts on the shirt, goes back to the anteroom, and steps into the elevator. The doors stand open, waiting for command. She looks at the array of buttons and pushes the one at the bottom, marked "B." She hears footsteps. The doors glide shut with a slick rustling noise and the floor sinks beneath her.

The Chief enters his bedroom without a glance at the recumbent form on the bed. He takes his place on the chair, letting his robe fall open, looking down at his pride. All is well. Passive, docile, and waiting. With a smile meant to be stern but not cruel, he lifts his gaze to the pale odalisque displayed on velvet.

"**Y**ou want to what?"

"I want to join."

Red Beard studies the boy. Two other young people stand near, holding weapons, staring at Art. "What's your name and where're you from?"

Art points to the east. "Arthur Dekker. I lived in Deer Valley. They killed my parents, burned our place, run off all the stock."

"Who did?"

"Them soldiers. Them motorcycle soldiers were in on it, too. I want to help, goddamnit. Why you giving me this hard time?"

"How'd you know we were here?"

"The old man told me."

"Ah-huh." Red Beard looks at the others, nodding. "I thought he'd be a loose lip," says Red Beard. "Better tell Rodack and the gang to get moving." One of the two, the young woman named Kathy, dashes off toward the ruins of the library, holding her ancient Mauser rifle at high port.

"He's no loose lip," Art says. "He knows me. He knows I'm all right."

"You don't have a gun."

"I'll get one. Give me a little time."

"You have to bring at least two firearms before you can join us, boy. That's the rule in our group."

"Don't call me boy." Art glares at Red Beard. "I'm as old as you, give or take a year."

Red Beard smiles. "Give or take about ten years. Now go on. Bring us some weapons and we'll consider you."

"How?"

"Well, the best way, if you're smart and careful, is to sign up with the Chief's Army. But you have to be careful. Give away your real feelings and they'll kill you. Or worse."

"All right," Art says, "I'll do it. And when I do I won't need you. I didn't figure you folks was much of an outfit anyhow." He turns away, out of the shade of the trees into the glare of the dusty street. Stops, ten feet away. "Tell that girl I was here. She's all right. She's a fighter." He turns away again, striding down the street.

"Hey," yells Red Beard, "wait a minute." The boy keeps going, resolute and fierce. "What girl?" shouts Red Beard. "Who do you mean?"

Art disregards him. Thirsty, hungry, but angry, he marches away. To hell with these dudes, he's thinking, I'll do it on my own.

A woman's voice pursues him. "Art! Art Dekker! Come back here!"

That stops him. He turns. The girl Barbara stands under the orange trees, waving. She leans on a pair of crutches but her smile is all for him.

Down in the cellar they feed him leftovers from the stewpot, fresh-made bread and prickly-pear jam. Real oranges, a ripe cantaloupe. But no coffee—no one here has tasted coffee for years. Instead they brew a kind of bittersweet tea made from the stems of green ephedra—Mormon tea. It seems good to Art. Barbara sits close to him as he tells, once again, his story. She slips an arm around his waist, hugs him, kisses his ear, his cheek, while the others watch, laughing. He feels like a hero. And it's a warm, lovely feeling.

Professor Rodack, holding the precious phonograph record, boxed, in one arm, the twin speakers under the other, stands there smiling and watching, but not relaxed. "Come on, people," he keeps saying, "we've got to get our baggage out of here. Time to move again."

There is progress. Several of the student guerrillas have already left with supplies. Rodack himself is heading for the door, arms loaded, when they hear rifle shots and a yell from outside. Red Beard comes tumbling in.

"They're here," he shouts, "they found us. Two armored cars, a truckload of soldiers. They've blocked the streets." Looking at his friends, his eyes come to rest on young Art sitting against a wall, fork to his mouth. Art stares back, uncomprehending.

"Okay," yells the professor above a sudden din, from outside, of heavy machine-gun fire, "everybody into the tunnel. Red, you lead the way. You know where to go."

Somebody pulls aside a carpet, another lifts a heavy steel manhole cover from the cement floor. A dark opening is revealed, large enough for a single human body. The smell of sewer gas rises into the room.

Red Beard stares at Art, about to speak again. Rodack breaks in, shoving the record and the speakers into Red Beard's arms, pushing him toward the tunnel entrance. "Take this. Hurry up now, hurry. Get them out of here."

Rifle slung across his back, holding the boxes, Red Beard climbs down a ladder into the tunnel. The others follow him, one by one. Barbara, leaning on her crutches, pushes a loaded clip into a rifle and shoves it into Art's arms, saying not a word, no longer smiling. Taking the rifle, Art notices for the first time the black band around her arm. She loads a second rifle and takes her stand facing the half-open door, where Rodack waits, peering outside, holding a shotgun at the ready. Through a cloud of masonry dust, running, comes another of their sentries, the girl Kathy, rifle in one hand, sword in the other. Standing beside Rodack, Art can hear the girl's desperate panting, can see the terror on her face.

She never makes it. A spray of bullets rips across her back, knocks her violently to the ground, twenty feet from the door. Art hears, for the second time in his life, the sound that bullets make plunging into living flesh. The girl lies still, too stunned to cry out, perhaps already dead. The bright blood pools beneath her.

Rodack stares, for a moment paralyzed. "Kathy," he says, and starts to go out. A burst of machine-gun fire explodes against the concrete walls above his head; the air fills with a haze of dust. Rodack reels back inside the door. "Who else is still out there?" he yells to the group bunched around the tunnel entrance. They stare back at him. "Kathy," says one. "And Paco," says another.

Art watches the outside, rifle aimed at the farthest corner of a wall. There is no human target. Yet. And then the snout of an armored car appears, olive green and rusty brown, with dark eyeslits in the steel for driver and gunner. A .50-caliber machine gun, radiating heat, dips toward him. Art aims and fires, unhesitating; sparks fly as his bullets glance off armor. At the same instant he sees the flash of light from the muzzle of the machine gun and ducks his head. Tumbling slugs of metal scream through the room, ricocheting from wall to wall.

Rodack slams the door, drops the heavy bar across it. The room becomes very dark, the only light coming from a pair of narrow windows high on the east wall. Art can make out three people still waiting at the tunnel entrance, one of them on his knees, while a fourth is disappearing down into it. Through the dust and gloom he stares at Barbara leaning in a near corner, holding her rifle. Art points to the square hole in the floor; she shakes her head. He hears a moaning, bubbling sound from the boy kneeling at the tunnel entrance; this lad—the one called Johnny—holds both hands to his face; blood streams out between his fingers.

Rodack opens the kit on his belt and goes to him, gently pulling down the hands. The eyes are gone, the nose is gone, the boy's whole face is a mass of blood. The others gape. "Into the tunnel," Rodack commands, "into the tunnel!" He holds a compress against the boy's ruined face and draws the head against his chest. Rodack's face shines with tears, sweat, the gleam of horror in his eyes.

A grenade crashes through the glass of the little window under the ceiling, bounces to the floor and rolls smoking and fizzing like a firecracker toward Art. Not a fragmentation grenade but a smooth-shelled canister of plastic, not much bigger than a beer can. Art grabs at the thing, misses, grabs again, flings it back toward the window. It bursts in midair, blinding his eyes with a phosphorescent blaze of white. The room is filled in a moment with the suffocating stench of nausea gas, vapor heavier than air that settles slowly toward the floor. A second gas grenade comes in the window, bouncing among the crates, boxes, and pots that litter the room.

All have fled into the tunnel entrance but Rodack, the mutilated boy, Barbara, Art. The air is opaque and thick with yellow gas. Rodack drops the wounded boy to the floor and drags the manhole cover to the opening; it clangs in place. The second grenade explodes. Blinking through the miasma and his involuntary tears, Art can see Barbara—without her rifle—crawling toward the door, reaching for the bar. He abandons his weapon and gropes after her, followed by Rodack dragging the boy Johnny. The gas is intolerable, unbearable, overwhelming.

Barbara gets the door open. The air outside is obscured by

dust; a voice bellows from an electric bullhorn: "I want prisoners. I want prisoners."

Anything seems better than the gas. Art crawls after the girl, his stomach beginning to turn in convulsions of disgust. He can't breathe—but he has to breathe. He can't see—but he has to find a way out.

They scramble up the steps outside on hands and knees, vomiting. They crawl over the rubble, past the inert body of Kathy, toward the boots and legs of men with guns, men wearing gas masks, steel helmets, green combat uniforms.

In the background, clear of the gas, a tall thin young captain stands in the open hatch of an armored car, watching the scene, holding the bullhorn. He has sun-bleached hair, thoughtful eyes, the alert stance of a commander.

The prisoners are so sick they cannot stand, even when kicked vigorously. "That's enough of that," the captain orders. He signals to a vehicle waiting down the street. "Throw them in the troop carrier. And search that basement room. Search every bit of it. Look for papers, books, weapons, food. Look for trapdoors, loose panels, a tunnel."

Slowly, cautiously, the masked soldiers enter the gas-filled room, introducing themselves with bursts of raking fire from automatic rifles.

The truck backs up to the prisoners twisting on the ground, writhing in their blood and vomit. Two big soldiers pick them up one at a time, by the arms and legs, and toss them into the bed of the truck. "This one's dead, sir," shouts a soldier, holding up the wrist of the bullet-mangled Kathy.

"Throw him in," replies the captain.

The Chief stands in the shade of an awning that covers part of the penthouse terrace; he looks down into the eastern streets, heavy black sunglasses with wrap-around lenses over his eyes. He holds a riding crop behind his back.

As always the streets are hazy with smoke and dust, but a brisk southwesterly wind has cleared the air above the rooftops. Raising his gaze he sees, beyond the city, the dun-colored slopes and porphyritic cliffs of the desert ranges that stretch away to the east; pinnacles of barren rock, forty miles away, stand hard-edged against the forenoon sky. Beyond the desert mountains are higher mountains, blue-green with forest, that rim the far-thest horizons a hundred miles away. Those distant scenes will soon be veiled by heatwaves but for the time being remain clear, intricate in detail, glowing with color, infinitely pleasing—because immeasurable—to the mind that can perceive nobility in the undisguised structures of the earth.

But the Chief finds only moderate pleasure in the tableau that forms the background of his triumphs. He taps the looped lash of the quirt against his knee, watching the eastern approaches to his palace of Thermopane and steel. He raises the sunglasses to his forehead, squinting in the harsh glare, and lifts binoculars to his eyes. He studies the broad avenue leading east but can see nothing, yet, of interest or importance. Except for a single shadowy figure slouching in the saddle of a gaunt horse, approaching slowly and from so far away that progress is imperceptible, illusory, the avenue is empty of life.

A gentle tapping sounds on the terrace door. The Chief disdains to register the petty interruption. After a decent interval the tapping is repeated. Again the Chief ignores the sound. A longer wait, a decenter interval, before the third rapping. When the Chief even then fails to respond, as against all custom, Corporal Buckley creeps out of the doorway and steps timidly, diffidently, toward his Chief. Buckley is in uniform again, with the addition this time of a mass of bandages, like a turban, taped around his small head.

He creeps toward his Chief and falls on his knees, humbly and silently. He reaches for the Chief's shining booted foot, lips puckered for a kiss. The Chief withdraws the boot, not looking down.

"Sir..." No answer. "I'm very sorry, sir." No reply. "Please forgive me, sir. . . ."

The Chief puts the field glasses on the table, beside what looks like a jewel box. He lowers the sunglasses over his eyes. "Buckley," he says.

"Yes sir."

"You are a fool, Buckley."

"Yes sir."

"An incredible, bungling, incompetent fool."

"Yes sir. Begging the Chief's pardon, sir, but he is absolutely right."

"Silence!" The Chief's voice is severe. "The sound of your voice makes me ill." A silent interval. "Have they found the girl?"

"Not yet, sir."

"Any word from Captain Barnes?"

"Not yet, sir."

The Chief looks stern. He deigns, at last, to glance down at the crouching corporal. His lips form an unspoken sentence: *I want to see you die.* "Buckley!"

"Yes sir."

"I want you to stand on the wall." The corporal, his face nearly touching the lacquered tile of the terrace, makes no reply, but his narrow shoulders begin to tremble. "Buckley!"

A whimper from the floor. "Please, sir . . ."

The Chief speaks firmly. "That's an order, Buckley."

"Please . . ."

"At once! Move!"

Moaning piteously, Corporal Buckley strives to rise. He looks with terror toward the waist-high parapet, twenty feet away, two hundred feet above the street. He crawls, on hands and knees, toward it. "Oh God, sir, oh God . . ."

"You cur," the Chief mutters. "No, you're worse than any dog." Abruptly losing patience, he lashes the corporal across the rump with the riding crop, then kicks him. "On your feet. Stand up like a man. Good Lord, Buckley, you sicken me." Stiff with revulsion, the Chief turns away from the creeping orderly, turns back to the sun and the east, gripping the short stock of the whip in both hands until he recovers self-control. He takes a drink of ice water from the pitcher on the table, picks up the blue case, snaps it open, contemplates with satisfaction the pair of silver eagles pinned to black plush, snaps it shut. He looks again down the avenue and this time sees a plume of dust in the distance, nearing fast. At the same time he hears the jingling of the telephone on the wall near the door. The Chief glances toward

Corporal Buckley, who is now endeavoring, feebly, clumsily, without success, but persistently, like a beetle, to climb onto the parapet.

"Get the phone, Buckley." The Chief picks up the binoculars.

The corporal scrambles to the telephone. The Chief watches through his field glasses the rapid advance up the avenue of an armored car, a truck, another armored car.

"It's Major Roland, sir," says Buckley. "He says Captain Barnes is on the way with four prisoners. One of them is a Professor Noah Rodack."

The Chief suppresses an impulse to break into a jig. Calmly but jubilantly he says, "Tell Major Roland to send Captain Barnes up here as soon as he arrives."

"Yes sir." Buckley relays the message, then stands at attention, waiting.

"And Buckley . . ."

"Yes sir."

"Get the *hell* out of here." Almost kindly the Chief adds, "Go have that headdress changed. You're bleeding again." Saluting, Buckley starts to go. "But first"—Buckley halts, looking frightened—"Bring a bottle of bourbon. Soda. Two glasses. Ice."

Happily, Buckley cries, "Yes sir!" faces about, and vanishes.

The Chief walks on springy steps to the wall and stands looking down through vaults of space; only a couple of ravens flapping past, below, on their way to early lunch at the gallows, mar the nihilism of the fall. He watches Captain Barnes' small caravan careering to a side entrance; the three vehicles disappear into the basement motor pool. Corporal Buckley comes and goes, performing his duties with humble but cheerful mien.

The Chief waits. Patiently.

Not for long. Captain Barnes appears, tall and brown in the open doorway, broad-brimmed trooper's hat in hand. Looking grim, weary, he raps on the doorframe with his fist. The Chief turns and comes toward him, smiling, right hand outstretched. Barnes salutes, the Chief returns the salute, shakes his hand, and half embraces him before stepping back.

"At ease, Captain, at ease." The Chief points to the chairs at the table. "Have a chair."

"Thank you, sir." Barnes sits down, pours himself a glass of ice water from the pitcher, and gulps it down; he pours a second as the Chief prepares highballs, doubles, in tall glasses sparkling with ice. Barnes drinks the second glassful of water, not stopping. Putting down the glass he breathes out heavily. "Thirsty . . . God, but it's getting hot down there."

"I know that, my boy. High time to leave this bloody desert. Forever." The Chief thrusts a tall cold glass into the captain's hand, sits down. "Cheers. Here's to our departure."

"Cheers, sir. Tomorrow." They touch glasses.

"Tomorrow, thank God."

They drink, pause, sit back. Barnes stares over the city. The Chief smiles at Barnes. "You look tired, Captain."

"Yes . . ." Barnes wipes sweat from his brow. "It was ugly. Ugly."

"Ugly? You mean your raid on the bandits' lair?"

The captain nods.

"That's war, Captain. Often ugly. But sometimes necessary."

"I can't call what we did war, sir. We were attacking children. Girls."

"That's not true. Those terrorists are college students. Or they were. They're at least as old as most of our men. Maybe older."

"Yes sir. But they're not soldiers."

"They're worse than any soldiers, Captain. Vicious, treacherous, fanatical. I know what students are like." The Chief drinks. "I had to deal with those scum many a time. Guatemala. Chile. Mexico. I know what they're like." Barnes remains glum and silent. "Cheer up, Captain. Drink up. We're celebrating."

"Yes sir."

"Any casualties?"

"We killed four of them, sir. Some others got away. Through a tunnel. Not a scratch on our side."

"Not a scratch?" The Chief smiles again and points to a tear in the captain's right sleeve. "That's a bullethole." Barnes glances at the hole, looks away, saying nothing. "How many prisoners, Captain?"

"We took four. One died on the way here. Bled to death—boy's whole face shot away."

"I see." The Chief nods sympathetically, restraining his eagerness to get on to the big question. "Yes, that sort of thing is unpleasant. I can understand." The Chief drinks again, waiting for Barnes to volunteer more information. But the captain says nothing. "I understand that one of your prisoners is my former colleague Professor Rodack."

Barnes nods. "I believe so, sir. He won't identify himself but I'm sure it's Rodack."

"They'll talk."

"Sir, I left orders that Sergeant Brock was not to touch those people. They are to be treated as prisoners of war."

"Why not, Captain? No irregular methods of questioning allowed here. Naturally. But"—the Chief smiles—"as you said, we are not at *war* with these ... people. They are revolutionaries and traitors, not soldiers. We'll hang them this afternoon and be done with them. Now let's talk of something interesting. Are all units ready for Operation Coronado?"

"Yes sir. All ready." The captain hesitates. "Sir, about these prisoners—"

The Chief points to the sun, overhead, and the new moon, a pale crescent of white, far in the east. "Good. The moon lags farther behind the sun each day, and waxes. Waxes fat, we might say. If we get started tomorrow afternoon we'll have a week of growing moonlight for the march east. We'll escape the heavy hand of summer here. The timing could not be better. Now that I've got Rodack as my guest there's no further reason for delay. And now, my dear Captain Barnes—" Smiling, the Chief places his white hand on the little blue jewel case. "A request, sir. Don't hang those prisoners."

The Chief, eyes hidden behind his dark glasses, looks solemn. "Traitors must die."

"Yes sir." The Captain nods. "Certainly. Hang Rodack. But spare the two young ones. They're only kids. Put them in a labor company. Give them a chance to think, learn, reform; they'll turn out good."

The Chief takes his turn to be silent. At last he says, "Captain Barnes, you're a generous man. I respect that. You have the virtues of a soldier: courage before the enemy, mercy for the defeated. I admire that. I will give your request serious consideration."

"Thank you sir. I appreciate your promise."

"Very well. Enough of this. I have something here for you, Captain, some news, which I think you will appreciate much more." The Chief picks up the case, releases the catch; the lid springs open. He holds the box toward Barnes. "Take these, Colonel Barnes. They are yours."

Barnes stares at the silver eagles, their wings outspread: the sign, the insignia, the dignity of full colonelcy. *Coronel—columna*—leader of a column—of a Roman legion. He cannot restrain a smile of pleasure. "Sir!" He turns the box in his hands. "But sir . . ."

"I know," the Chief laughs, "it's a bit of a jump. Not exactly proper procedure. Not S.O.P. But what the hell, this army of mine—this Army of ours, Colonel—it's the only one there is, so far as we know, in the whole West. Or anywhere. Why shouldn't we do what we like with it? I've been planning this little surprise for you for some time." The Chief smiles, pleased by the glow of delight on Barnes' face. "Damn it, my boy, we need a colonel in this outfit. You're the only man I've got worthy of the rank."

"Roland, sir . . ."

"Yes, yes, poor chubby tubby old Major Roland, he'll be annoyed by this. What of it? We're leaving him here in command"—the Chief sweeps one arm around the horizon, taking in the neighboring office buildings, the smoking ruins, the gallows below, the streets full of sand and dust and rusting wreckage. —"in command of our whole fair city!" The Chief laughs again. "And if he's still here and alive when we come back, or when you come back, Colonel, why we'll make him a bloody major general." The Chief lifts his glass, still half full of ice and the golden glow of whiskey. "Cheers again! To you, Colonel. My good Colonel Barnes."

Barnes lifts his glass. They touch. "Thank you, sir." Still marveling, he smiles at the silver emblems in his hand.

"Here," says the Chief, taking back the case, "let me put these little tin chickens on you, Colonel Barnes. Damn the ceremony, we'll do it here and now. Arise, Colonel Barnes."

Barnes pushes back his chair and stands up. The Chief, coming close, looking up, puts a hand on Barnes' shoulder, exerting a powerful pressure downward. For a moment Barnes entertains the silly illusion that the Chief expects him to kneel, like a warrior about to be knighted by his lord. Barnes remains erect, however, and after a moment of hesitation the Chief removes his hand from the young man's shoulder. He takes the eagles from the box and pins the first (removing the double bars) on the right side of Barnes' open shirt collar, opposite the crossed sabers of a cavalry officer. The second he pins—not regulation, but looking good—onto the front of Barnes' flat-brimmed campaign hat, which he takes up from the table. He embraces Barnes again, with both arms this time, like a European, shakes his hand, steps smartly back, and salutes.

Tears in his eyes, the new colonel returns the salute.

"To the East!" shouts the Chief, lifting his glass.

"To the East, sir."

"*Ad astra! Ad astra per aspera!* Through any difficulty, through all obstacles!"

"Through all obstacles."

They clash their glasses, drink again, empty the glasses, and toss them over the parapet of the roof. Mutually delighted, Barnes and the Chief grin at each other.

"And now, dear Colonel—"

"To work sir."

"Exactly. Back to work."

From far below comes a faint yell of anger. The Chief laughs, the Colonel smiles, takes his hat, salutes, performs a precise about-face, and strides off.

Alone and smiling, the Chief paces happily back and forth on his private terrace, out of the shade and into the sun, out of the sun and back in the shade. After a time he stops by the telephone.

"Get me Myers. . . . Myers? The Chief here. . . . Yes, yes . . . Now Lieutenant, I want that man sent up here. . . . Rodack, yes . . . No, not to the office, to the roof. . . . Can he talk? . . . Just barely. Can he hear? . . . You think so. Is he alive, Myers? Or can't you tell? . . . Well, send him up anyway. . . . No, not at once, later, in a couple of hours. . . . Yes . . . that's right, Lieutenant, Brock is not to touch him . . . not yet, anyway. . . . Yes, he may question the others. But nothing crude, you understand. No physical torture, is that understood, Lieutenant? . . . Quite . . . yes . . . Those three? The so-called Zapatistas? . . . Hang them, what else? Immediately after lunch. . . . The others? Later today, about sundown, as usual. . . . A trial, my dear Lieutenant? They've already been tried. Tried—and found wanting . . . Exactly . . . Yes . . . Very good, Myers. Carry on."

Pleased with the day so far, content and satisfied, the Chief prepares to descend to his office; all tasks delegated, he is free for an afternoon of study, planning, meditation. But first he pours himself one more glass of ice water and walks to the parapet for another look down into the city, far below him. His city—but only one, he knows, of the many to fall before him in the months to come.

Burns keeps to the center of the four-lane avenue, on the dirt median where the palm trees stand, casting a little shade. His big mare paces steadily ahead, not fast, not slow, but at a gait suitable to the distance remaining, the objective desired, the oppressive heat of the day, the nature of the time.

An hour after the parting with the boy he hears, miles behind, the bluster of gunfire. He halts, listening; it does not last long. The old man rides on. There is nothing else to do.

Shortly afterward he notes the sound of motors coming from behind, rapidly. Burns makes no attempt to hide but goes on as he is doing, down the median from palm to dying palm. An armored car rumbles past on his right, an officer standing in the front beside his driver. An open truck goes by, its bed half loaded with standing soldiers; one of them aims his rifle at Burns and laughs when the old man goes rigid for a moment. Then the second armored car—a blast of heat and iron and shouted conversation inside—and the quiet returns. The dust clouds sail across the pavement in spiraling whirlwinds, settle slowly, are gone.

Jack Burns rides on. Still far ahead the Tower that he is bound for rises from the square, the barren park that terminates the avenue. The convergent lines of street, buildings, ruins, wrecks, trees, meet at one nexus, and from there change course from the horizontal exactly to the vertical, following the slanted walls of the Tower, which point into the sky.

At night the Tower appears as a pillar of amber light, tapering to a spire capped by a flashing strobe more dazzling than any star. By day the building resembles a gigantic obelisk. The sloping walls present broad columns of burnished steel; recessed between the columns are walls of glass, a bronze-colored Thermopane that reflects the sunlight, concealing the interior. On the flat roof of this structure, where the pyramid would be on a true obelisk, is the penthouse. Rising from the penthouse roof another hundred feet is the spire of steel that supports the culminating beacon. Even by day the blinking strobe sends forth a sharp, bright, piercing signal—the pyramid's inescapable eye.

An irrigation canal, bearing a sluggish flow of brown water, parallels the avenue. Burns turns his horse aside for a drink, guiding her among abandoned autos to a mudbank at the side of the water. The horse drinks; Burns stares across the ditch at a man in a dirty business suit sprawled on the ground.

The man is long, lean, stinking. Flies whine about his swollen and yellow face. One hand clutches at the air, rigid, with fingers like claws; the other hand is on his neck, where a length of barbed wire has been tightened, with a stick, tourniquet-fashion, around the throat.

Burns rides on. A little red Volkswagen rattles by, one block on his right; vanishes.

He rides on, minding his own business. Two blocks up the

street he passes a second corpse, attended by flies. This is the body of a short, fat, silver-haired old gentleman in a white linen suit. The man lies on his face, two blackened bullet holes in his back. His straw Panama, fallen beyond reach of his outstretched arms—the man must have been running when he fell—begins to skate away on another slithering whirlwind as Burns rides by. The agitated flies regroup, return, resettle themselves with murmurous drone of contentment.

Hate them all, Burns thinks, I'm beginning to hate them all; all of them, all of us, the whole goddamned human race. But he rides on. There is little traffic on the avenue. In the heat of noon most humans have retired indoors, under shade or shelter. Even the starving dogs remain hidden during the midday hours, waiting for the relief of sundown.

He rides into Unity Square. Burns can see nothing animate but a couple of sentries lounging near the gateway in the barbed-wire compound before the Tower; and two men at work on the scaffold, releasing bodies from the taut ropes; and a few ravens circling above, clacking beaks, squawking in protest.

Burns stops his horse halfway across the immensity of Unity Square to stare at the Chief's capitol. Against his will, against his better judgment, he finds himself fascinated by the silent, brooding, magnetic aspiration of the great Tower. The bronze windows reflect the sky, the passing clouds. The tapered walls exaggerate the effect of foreshortening, so that to Burns, craning his neck and staring upward, the building seems even taller than it is, even more powerful than it should be. Like the face of a mountain wall, the Tower seems to lean back against the sky, to soar among the clouds, to rise—to be rising, with a grandeur both real and unreal—toward the noon sun.

And looking up, up, up, over the bronze planes of glass and the white columns of steel, he sees the tiny figure of a human at the convergent summit of the edifice, a man, black in silhouette against the sky, leaning over the topmost wall and looking back, down across the avenue of blazing quadrilaterals, at him. Two men staring at one another across the surface of a table two hundred feet long—a table that seems to be reeling into the sky.

Burns lowers his head, feeling dizzy. For a moment the world turns black before his eyes. He waits, gripping the saddlehorn until the spell passes. He lifts his hat to let a bit of air flow across the white mane of his head, cooling the outer surface of the brain and mind. He is sweating, the air feels good.

To his mission. He touches heels to the mare's flanks, rides toward the sentries. Talking, they disregard his approach until he comes to within ten feet of the open gate; one of them steps out of the shade, reluctantly, and bars the opening, leveling an automatic rifle toward Burns. "Halt where you are, old-timer. State your business."

Burns pushes his hat back with his right knuckle, leans forward on the pommel of the saddle. "I've come to see a young fella named Barnes," he says quietly. "Captain Barnes."

The guard stares. "Get down off that horse."

"Yes sir." The old man eases himself from the saddle; always edgy, and agitated by the manner of the guard, Rosie starts to shy away. Burns tugs at the bridle, strokes her sweating neck. "Easy, old girl, easy. . . ."

"Spooky horse you got there, Granddad."

"She's a good horse."

The guard grins. "Looks like bear bait to me." Burns says nothing. "Okay—what'd you say you want?"

"Want to see Captain Barnes."

"You do, do you?" The first sentry turns to the other, loafing in the shade of the guard station. "He wants to see Captain Barnes."

"Tell him we don't have any Captain Barnes here. Only Colonel Barneses."

"What's your business with him?" the first guard says to Burns.

Burns smiles. "Well—social. This is a social visit."

"That won't do it, Granddad."

Tired though he is, Burns feels the temper rising in his blood. For two cents, he thinks, I'd kick this young punk's ass right up between his shoulder blades. But he controls himself, with effort, and says quietly, "I'm his father." And as the guard continues to stare at him, he adds by way of explanation, "Captain—Colonel Barnes is my son."

This stirs some interest. The guard telephones a sergeant, who comes out to repeat the interview. "Colonel Barnes is your son?"

"Yes sir."

"And your name is Jack Barnes?"

"Well—that's what some say."

"Let's see some ID."

Burns pulls the old wallet from his hip pocket, opens it to the faded photograph under the cracked celluloid. The sergeant studies the picture. "Somebody's little boy. Very nice, mister, but this is not ID. I asked for ID." He looks through the wallet, empty save for the boy's photo, the photo of a young woman, and some faded, useless hundred-dollar bills. "There's no ID here, mister. Nothing at all. No driver's license, no draft card, no SS card, no credit card, no Internal Security card, nothing." The sergeant looks at Burns with challenging eyes. "And you're packing a gun. You got a permit for that antique?"

Old Jack Burns smiles patiently, groaning inside. Here we go again. After all these years. Controlling his ancient rage, he says, "You're right, Sergeant, and I sure am sorry. I guess I left all them cards at home."

"You're in trouble. We don't let anybody wander around in this city without identification."

"I don't live here, sir. I'm a tourist." Burns continues to stroke the trembling horse with his right hand, holding the bridle with his left, his body turned slightly aside from the sergeant and the watchful guards.

"Where're you from?"

"New Mexico."

"That's no excuse." The sergeant hesitates. "Let me give you some advice, mister. If I were you I'd get back on that horse. . . ." But something in the mismatched eyes, the sardonic smile on Jack Burns' face, makes him hesitate again. He nods to the guards. "Take him in."

Good thinking. But there's a hitch. During the fraction of a moment in which the sergeant glances at his soldiers the gun—the "antique"—somehow appears in Jack Burns' right hand. As if it had jumped, on its own, out of the holster and into the old man's grip. And the muzzle of the gun, thrust forward like a fencer's foil, makes little searching circles two feet short of the sergeant's belly. The mare rears back, trailing the untied reins, as Burns steps sideways, putting the sergeant between himself and the two guards. Burns pulls the sergeant's sidearm—a handsome automatic—from its holster. He cocks it. "Drop those rifles," Burns says to the guards.

"Shoot him," the sergeant says, his hands half raised, his eyes on Burns.

"Drop the rifles, boys."

Another moment of uncertainty. The guards unsling and lay down their weapons. "Now lie down. On your faces. That's right. Now you, young fella"—to the sergeant—"pick up that phone in there and call my boy. I want to see him. And I mean I mean to see him."

"Call him yourself."

"Pick up that phone or so help me I'll blast you right through the guts."

The sergeant studies his man for another moment. Convinced, he backs into the guard station, Burns right behind him, unhooks the phone, dials a number. The two guards lie prone in the sun, their rifles out of reach. Rosie the horse backs a few more steps from the gate, reins dragging, torn between her duty to stand and her impulse to run. High on the main entrance steps of the Tower, a few soldiers look on, amazed perhaps but making as yet no move to interfere. The sergeant speaks quiet words into the phone, hangs up. "The colonel's coming."

"Thank you sir." Burns takes a deep breath. "You just stand there, son, where everybody can see you. That's right. Put both hands behind your neck. Yeah, like that. Keep them there.

Face away from me. That's good. Just stand there." Burns sits down in the chair he feels behind him, keeping the pistol and the revolver aimed at the sergeant's back—two feet from the muzzles. He sighs heavily, feeling the sweat beginning to stream down his face. "Now we'll wait."

"They've got sharpshooters watching you right now," the sergeant says. "With telescopes. Put down those guns and you'll still get out of this alive."

Burns crouches down a little in his chair, so that only his hat remains showing above the level of the waist-high wooden walls. "We'll wait," he says.

They wait.

A man comes walking toward them from an unexpected direction, out of the shadows of the motor-pool entrance toward the guard station. A young man, tall, slender, bareheaded, unarmed, wearing the khaki uniform.

"Here he comes," the sergeant mutters.

Burns squints with his good eye past the sergeant's body. "I see him." He smiles with pride. "That's Charlie. Got to be."

The sergeant stiffens, about to move. Burns shoves the revolver hard into his spine. "Hold still now."

The sergeant shouts. "Stand back, sir."

The colonel, looking annoyed, keeps on coming. He steps around the prostrate soldiers on the pavement, giving them only a glance, and walks boldly to the open door of the guard station.

"Stay back, sir, this old fool—"

"That's all right, Sergeant, I'll handle it." He looks with cold green eyes at Burns. "Let him go."

"Go ahead," says Burns.

The sergeant slips out, whispering something in the colonel's ear as he sidles past him. "No," the colonel says sharply, "not yet." He stares hard at Burns, saying nothing. What he sees is a long, thin old man of about seventy, with snowy whiskers, a red, broken beak of a nose, one glass eye and one living eye, holding a pair of guns in large, bony, speckled brown hands.

Burns lowers the guns, staring back at the colonel; he notes the silvery twinkle of the eagle on the young man's shirt collar. "A colonel," he says, grinning, "a goddamned chickenshit silver bird. Charlie, you've disgraced us."

"That's Colonel Barnes to you, sir."

Burns cannot stop grinning. Delight and triumph surge upward from his heart. "Come on, Charlie. . . ." He starts to rise.

"I don't know you, old man."

Burns sits down again, the guns hanging loose in his hands. He shakes his head in dismay. "Doesn't know me. He doesn't know me. What do you know about that." He squints up at the young man. "Charlie, this is me. Jack. Your old man."

"My father died thirty years ago." The colonel's cold stare remains unmoved. "You'd better go."

"No he didn't," Burns says. "He's here. Me." He pounds his chest. "Me."

"My father was a lunatic. Deserted my mother. Killed himself trying to blow up a dam. Thirty years ago."

"No he didn't," Burns insists, getting excited again. "They thought he did but he didn't. He escaped. Look at me, Charlie. Goddamnit, boy, look at me, I'm your father. Can't you tell? Don't I look like your old man?"

The colonel considers. "How would I know? It was long ago."

Burns controls his sense of growing rage. With difficulty. "I'm your father! You're my son!"

"Prove it."

"I know it. I can *feel* it, just looking at you. Can't you feel it, Charlie?" The old man begins to get up from the chair.

The colonel motions him down. "My father's dead. And besides—his name was Barnes. Not Burns."

"That's a lie. Your mother changed the name."

"Show me proof."

Burns gestures outward, into the city. "There's papers here somewhere, pictures, records. . . ."

Colonel Barnes smiles thinly. "Your friends burned everything like that—years ago."

"My friends?" Burns is puzzled. Then remembers Professor
Rodack, the guerrilla students, the bandits. "Good Christ . . ."
For a moment he is troubled by doubt. Doubt of his feelings, his
intuition, his certainty. Doubt of himself. He looks with his dark,
troubled eye at the tall young man in uniform standing before
him. "Listen, Charlie. . . ." How to prove anything? How to
convince himself? "Charlie . . . I can tell you all about your
mother. Her name was Jill. Jill Maynard. She was born in Ore-
gon in, in—I forget the year. In the nineteen-fifties. Yeah, she
was twenty years younger than me. She was—small, kind of
frail, blondish, big eyes. Big brown eyes. She . . ."
     "My mother had blue eyes."
     "Blue? All right—yeah, that's right, blue eyes. Jesus
Christ!" In his exasperation the old man pounds his fists, still
holding the two guns, on the arm of the chair. "Yes, you're
right." Blindness. Misery. He stares at the floor, trying to remember. It *was* so long ago. "And she . . ."
     "You'd better go, old man. Before it's too late. I could have
you shot for what you've already done."
     "Shot?" Old Jack Burns glares up at the colonel. "Shot?
Why not hang me? That's your business, ain't it? Hanging folks?
Look at them over there!" He points to the gallows, where a
detail of soldiers are lowering two bodies through the trapdoor
of the scaffold floor. Under the floor, concealed by a skirting of
canvas and planks, a truck or wagon waits to haul away the
dead. An old red Volkswagen waits at the corner, two figures
seated within it.
     The colonel keeps his eyes on Burns. "Yes, I could have you
hanged. If you prefer."
     "Then hang me, goddamnit. Because I ain't leaving here till
you face the truth."
     The colonel gazes steadily at the old man. "I've faced
enough truth already, sir. My father left us when I was a baby.
My mother died when I was two years old. All the family I've
got and all the family I need are here—my men. And as for a
father"—he points upward—"he's there. Now get out."

"Charlie!" The old man stands, fury in his heart, hefting the guns up and down. "What do you mean? Who are you talking about? Don't tell me you're a Christer too. Bad enough being a colonel. Look at me! I'm your father!"

"I don't know you, sir."

"God, are you crazy? What did they do to you?"

"I don't know you."

Burns makes one last effort to regain control. Quietly he says, "Come with me, Charlie. Leave these murderers, that dictator Chief. Come with me. I got a little ranch back on the Rio Salado—old Salt Crick." The mocking grin appears on Burns' lips. "Stole it, of course. From the bank. It ain't much but a man can get by there. Two men—with families. Got some good horses, cattle, two good springs, a well. And lots of room. *Lots of room, Charlie!*"

The colonel smiles. "We've got the world, old man. Now for the last time: If you want to live—go. Get out of here."

For a moment Jack Burns feels an impulse to plead, beg, shake the boy by the shoulders, compel recognition. The impulse passes. Defeated, he reholsters his revolver, lays the sergeant's automatic on the desk. "All right. Here's your flunky's pistol. He'll need it. I'm going, Charlie. But I just want to tell you—I know who you really are. I can tell you all about your mother, everything about the first ten years of your life. But you don't want to hear it, do you?"

The colonel looks steadily into the old man's good eye. "No sir, I don't want to hear it. I'd rather forget." He adds: "And my father is dead. Let's keep him dead."

"Your father is alive." Burns steps toward the door; the colonel backs out of the way and stands aside. "And by God he's gonna stay alive, Charlie. For a long time to come."

The colonel says nothing. The two guards and the sergeant stand nearby, watching. A squad of soldiers watch from the Tower steps. The sergeant looks to the colonel. Colonel Barnes holds up one hand, shakes his head.

Burns pulls down his hat, looks about for his horse, sees her outside the barbed-wire gate, a hundred paces away. Sunlight flashes in his eye from the banks of enormous windows overhead. He looks up one more—one last—time.

Up the sloping wall of steel and dark glass, up to the summit of the Tower. And there he sees, fifteen stories above, still looking down, hands on the parapet wall, the silhouetted figure of a man.

Upward. He's there.

"No!" cries Burns. "No! No!" The blood of rage—of outrage —floods his brain. *"No!"* The big revolver springs again into his right hand, cocked and aiming upward in one unhesitating movement. The colonel and the soldiers gape at the old man with the gun, not yet believing what they see. Burns steadies the revolver with his left hand, taking care with his aim, centering front sight in the notch of the rear, and squeezes off the first shot.

The cartridge explodes, the copper-jacketed bullet sings spiraling into the sky. The man looking down seems to shrug one shoulder, as if touched by a fly, but makes no other move.

Old Jack Burns recocks the revolver. The loaded chamber revolves, aligning the next round with hammer, firing pin, the rifled bore. He aims with care, hands steady, his dark eye intent and unflinching, fixed on the target, while from the surrounding walls of Unity Square the first discharge still reverberates.

Burns is about to squeeze the trigger again when Colonel Barnes, awakening from a nightmare of disbelief, takes two long strides forward, knocks the gun away with one hand, and with the hard edge of his other chops the old man across the neck, under the ear, close to the jaw, slashing him in one stroke dumb, blind, deaf, down to the pavement.

feel so clean, she thinks. I feel so good. But scared. My God but I'm scared.

Button B. Button B. Whatever that means. As the floor sinks beneath her, she tries to pin up her hair a bit, make it look more manly. Or at least, more—Buckley. Rearranging pins. There are three mirrors in this fancy, gold-trimmed, private elevator. The Chief's elevator, no doubt. The ubiquitous eagle motif is here again, on the cherrywood panels, on the ceiling. And there's that key in the switch.

I need a hat of some kind. Looking at herself in the mirrors. She tries to remove the makeup from her eyes, using a clean little handkerchief from Buckley's hip pocket, but without complete success. And her breasts swell out, unbound, against the trim-fitting shirt. Goddamned big tits, she thinks—nice some-times but not very practical. She attempts a slumping posture, making her sexual identity slightly less conspicuous. It doesn't help much. Well, she thinks, as the elevator slows to a soft, hydraulic halt at Floor B—the letter illuminated—here we go anyway. What I really need is a gun. A machine gun. Her heart beats madly as the door slides open. She removes the key from the control panel and steps briskly out, as if she belonged here, as if she knew where she were going.

Two armed guards stand nearby. They spring to attention when the elevator door opens, then relax as they see only the corporal's stripes of Corporal Buckley. They stare at him—at her!—and look at one another in surprise. Dixie hastens on, ready to run, and turns the first corner. Dim lights reveal a narrow corridor of bare concrete, a low ceiling bearing pipes and ducts; from somewhere ahead comes the heavy roar of diesel engines. She hears a man's voice from behind: "Hey there! Wait a minute!" The sound of booted feet, starting to run.

The dim corridor stretches far ahead, into an obscurity of lights and shadows, steel doors and ductwork and ranks of mas-sive storage tanks. Refusing to panic, Dixie squeezes into the darkness behind the nearest tank, squats against the wall and waits.

The guard trots past, peering down the corridor, aiming his short M-16 ahead. Dixie slips out and back the other way, behind the tanks and past the elevator entrance, brightly lit but immo-bile. The second guard waits there, speaking into a phone. She gets by without being seen, hurries down the gray, overheated corridor toward closed doors.

She reaches a massive steel door. Locked. Through a small square window—double-paned, reinforced with wire mesh—she looks into another hall, glaringly illuminated, which is lined with rows of windowless, numbered doors—like cell doors. Each door has a slitlike opening at the bottom and a spyhole, covered with a movable, hinged lid, at eyelevel. As Dixie watches, two guards enter, armed with clubs; they unlock a cell and drag out a limp, half-naked man, hauling him between them to a door at the far end of the corridor. The guards and their prisoner disappear into a bright room with sterile white walls, suggesting a kind of operating chamber or laboratory. That door is closed. Dixie stares into the empty hall and hears, or thinks she hears—this underground world so dominated by the vibrations of the generators—a rhythmic chanting, human voices singing in unison, a drumming of hands on steel bulkheads.

Am I trapped? I'm trapped. Maybe. Maybe not. She will not panic. She turns again, back the way she has come, steals once more around the guard at the Chief's elevator, and this time finds another door not far beyond. This door opens to a cement stairway leading up. One flight of steps brings her to another steel door embedded in masonry: locked. She scurries up the next flight to the next landing. Another locked door. The stairway goes on, leading up and up—to what? To the roof again? To the Chief and his penthouse suite?

Dixie sags against the rigid door, feeling the first stirring of an uncontrollable terror. She thinks she's going to faint, or scream, or suffocate. She suppresses the urge to beat on the door with both fists. Voices approach.

The door is shoved violently open from the other side, pushing Dixie against the wall. Two soldiers storm by without seeing her, rushing down the stairs. She manages to catch the door before it swings shut and locked again, and looks through an inch-wide opening into the brightly lit vastness of the lobby on the main floor. A squad of soldiers tramps by not twenty feet away, eyes front, with a small sergeant barking orders at their side. Beyond, across the polished floor, officers stroll in consultation, weapons and visors and brass insignia glittering under the immense chandeliers of light blazing far overhead. A row of open elevators waits on one wall; halls and doorways lead to other offices, other wings of the building; and far away, on her left, she can see the huge bronze doors of the main entranceways, flanked by guards with automatic rifles.

Dixie slips through her door and walks swiftly, boldly, along the wall of the lobby, under maps of America and murals of industry forty feet high, toward the nearest of the side hallways. Soldiers, officers thronging everywhere. She lifts a visored cap from a table, where some officer had carelessly left it for a moment, and claps it on her head. Much too big; but her bunched, curly, springy hair keeps it in place. Face lowered, shoulders rounded, she hurries down the wide hallway, looking at nobody, seeing nothing but the green fatigues, the shining boots, the bayonets, daggers, rifles, pistols of soldiers and more soldiers. She passes the open doors of a dormitory: naked men, men in underwear are lounging there between rows of bunks, among lockers and weapons racks. Averting her eyes she hastens on and comes to the broad double doors of another exit from the Tower. Armed guards stand about smoking and talking; nobody interferes as she pushes through the doors and steps out into the floodlit glare of the compound and the sudden, startling heat of the desert night. Beyond a broad expanse of asphalt is the barricade, coils of concertina wire six feet high, and beyond that a steel-mesh Cyclone fence topped with four strands of barbed wire. No escape, no escape.

A column of tanks and open-bed military trucks is parked along one wall; but the trucks are guarded. Everything is guarded.

Dixie keeps striding along, following the base of the Tower, never hesitating. Buckley's boots are a size too big for her and she feels awkward, clumsy in them, but does not stop walking. Cannot stop moving; nor can she find a place to hide. No shadows, no darkness—nothing but bright lights everywhere. No wonder those diesel generators in the basement are working so hard.

Three quarters of the way around the building, three city blocks, she finds herself coming again toward the front entrance and the only opening in the barbed-wire enclosure: the gateway wide enough for trucks and tanks, barricaded for the time being with wooden trestles. Two men with rifles stand near the guard station, lighting cigarettes.

Unhesitating, Dixie walks straight toward them. They glance at her, continue their conversation. She walks directly past them, slipping between the trestles, and strides briskly on toward the edge of the floodlights and the nearest dark street beyond Unity Square.

"Hold it, soldier. . . ."

Without stopping Dixie looks over her shoulder at the sentries and signals for them to follow her.

They gape in surprise. One says, "We got to stay here, Corporal."

She hisses at them, gesturing vigorously, and keeps going as fast as she can without actually breaking into a run. One of the guards steps forward, as if thinking of following her, but the other detains him with a hand on the sleeve. She reaches the fading parameter of electric light, blending with the misty blue of the moon. The shadows of the streets are only fifty yards away. She glances back. The guards look after her but make no move to follow.

Dixie melts into the shadows. Frightened and at the same time enormously relieved, she runs down the dark street between unlit cliffs of glass and steel, through the sand and the weeds and among the hulks of useless Cadillacs, Peugeots, Daimlers, Jaguars, Mercedes-Benzes. Decomposing steel, glass turning blue as old bottles, fine-grained walnut and once-supple leather becoming dust. Becoming air. Becoming air and dust and history.

Six long blocks from the Tower, feeling safe at last, certain she's not being pursued, she collapses on a sand dune and pulls off the boots and rubs her aching feet, the hot spots at heel and ball that threaten to become blisters. Soaked with sweat, panting with fear and fatigue, she sprawls out on the sand, gazing up at the indifferent stars, and tries to relax, to regain breath and breathing, to recover a sense of sanity in a world that has seemed, for too many hours, to be a prisonhouse of nightmare.

She is exhausted, hungry, very thirsty. I must find water, she thinks, quickly. No easy thing to find in this maimed, murdered city. But first she must rest, and rejoice in her escape. She feels like weeping with joy, with relief, with pride in her audacity and luck, not surprised to find tears starting down her cheeks. She remembers lines from an ancient poem:

> *Stone walls do not a prison make*
> *Nor iron bars a cage. . . .*

What a lie, she thinks. What a barefaced, foolish, treacherous lie. She looks straight up, between dark canyon walls of steel, and thinks, on further reflection, But of course nobody ever did believe it. Half giggling, half crying, she thinks, And the guy who wrote it never expected anybody to believe it. Never believed it himself, for godsake. Unless he was crazy. A poet, or something . . .

Gonna pass out here if I'm not careful. Better get farther away from *that place.* That—Tower of Hate. She rolls on her side, props herself up. So tired, so terribly tired. She gets to her knees.

And hears the motorcycle. A motorcycle, one big motorcycle coming down the street, straight toward her. The Cyclops eye is aimed her way, bobbing now and then as the machine rides over a ripple of sand, a warp or pothole in the asphalt pavement. The machine idles along, wobbling a bit from side to side, as if its operator were drunk, or inexperienced, or playing a game.

Dixie stands, uncertain which way to run. She looks about for a hiding place. There are dark doorways and broken windows in the nearby buildings, a few abandoned cars along the street. She elects the nearest doorway, makes a dash for it. But as she runs the motorcycle's beam, swinging wildly, catches her in motion. She hears the motor roar as the rider turns up the throttle, hears the machine come bounding after her, a man's shout ringing out above the noise.

If only I had a gun, she moans, gasping for breath, if only I had something to fight with. Anything. She staggers toward the dark entrance, panting, ribs aching, overwhelmed by the nightmare sensation of trying to run through sand. The machine is close behind her as she reaches the portal of a wide doorway —and finds it boarded up. Crying with rage, energized by fear, she clutches at one end of a spiked-on two-by-four, wrenches it free, and turns swinging at the glaring eye. The dark figure in the saddle shouts her name again—"Dixie!"—as she smashes the light. The machine howls with racing engine as it falls, the rider slipping from the saddle and coming at her. The motor stalls, sputters out.

Dixie swings at the man but misses; he ducks beneath the blow. Half choking with laughter, speaking her name, the man comes in close and grapples with her, pries the board from her hands, and drags her to the ground. "Dixie," he says, laughing, "it's me, it's me. For godsake . . ." He straddles her, pinning her hands, holding her there until she stops struggling, until she finally recognizes, through the darkness and the floating dust, under the goggles and the silver helmet, the brown warm round smiling face of Sam the shaman.

They embrace. They laugh and weep together, while the old dying city coughs and groans around them, and meteors trace fiery signals across the velvet sky, and wild dogs and bold coyotes exchange challenges down the freeway, across the avenues, and over the cactus fairways of a dozen forgotten municipal golf courses.

Then they conspire. "Can you drive a Volkwagen?" says Sam. "I can drive anything," says Dixie.

The light blazes down, directly into his living eye, an inaccessible and hostile light, magnesium white, incandescent bright, burning into his soul, compelling full attention.

"You're all right, Mr. Burns," the voice says, from forty miles away, through clouds of confusion. His ears are full of echoes. His head seems like a cavern, haunted by ghosts, the wings of bats, echoes from forty years ago. Forty years, four hundred miles away, four thousand days of loneliness.

"Shade his eyes," says another.

A soft white hand rests on his brow. A girl's hand. No, not soft, not white—but a girl's hand. He can tell, he can remember that much, no matter how long ago it may have happened before.

"You're here with us, Mr. Burns," she says. "We're all in here together."

"Howdy, Jack," says a boy's voice.

He clears his mind of abstract hallucinations, the whirling galaxies of pain, and sees the girl's face, Barbara, beaming down at him. Behind her the face of young Art Dekker, fierce and unsmiling. The anxious face of Professor Rodack.

Burns tries to sit up and nearly passes out again. He lets his head come back to rest on the girl's lap. She strokes his hair, his sweating brow. The blazing light, far overhead, out of reach, glares into his eye. He tries to speak, the words are plain in his mind—*We got to find old Sam*—but only a groan issues from his throat.

"Take it easy, Mr. Burns. Don't try to talk yet."

He hears the clamor of steel doors sliding open, clanging shut. Heavy boots marching on concrete, the noise of a scuffle, the thump of club on flesh and bone, snarling voices. Burns rolls his head toward the sound and sees, through a grid of bars, men in uniform dragging a half-naked prisoner past a cell door. His cell door.

The prisoner is a Mexican, dark-skinned, with a mane of shaggy black hair. "Let me walk," he growls at the guards, "let me walk. I am a man, not a baby. Let me walk!" He struggles to free himself; the guards let him go for a moment. The prisoner straightens his pants, glares around, and sees Rodack, Barbara, Art, and Burns staring at him. His glare becomes a sudden smile as he lunges toward their cell, stretching forth his right hand. "*¡Compañeros!*" he shouts.

Rodack thrusts his hand through the bars. He and the prisoner outside grasp each other. "*Compadre,*" says Rodack. "*¡Viva la causa!*"

"*¡Viva la libertad!*" The guards fall on the condemned man, trying to drag him away. He and Rodack cling to each other.

"We'll be with you soon, *hermano,*" Rodack says. "Very soon. In a few hours. Wherever you are."

A club descends on their interlocked hands, breaking them apart. The Mexican is hustled away, out through a door that admits a bar of sunlight before it is slammed shut. Two more prisoners, a man and a woman, are marched past Rodack and his friends. Both have the stunned, unbelieving look of those about to be hanged. They are hurried out of the cellblock, given no chance to say good-by. The four friends stare after them, appalled into silence, as their minds edge toward a void beyond consolation.

"Are we next?" says young Dekker, unable to suppress a quaver in his voice.

Rodack puts an arm around the boy's shoulder. "They're saving us for sundown," he says. "We'll get out of here."

Jack Burns makes another effort to sit up and this time succeeds. His head rings with some ceaseless, internal vibration but at least he can see, can hear, can touch and feel. He finds himself in a narrow cell without window, sitting on a cement floor under that unshaded electric light far above. There are no bunks, no furnishings of any sort but a single battered bucket in one corner with a wad of ancient newspapers beside it.

He touches a hand to the side and back of his neck, finding the tender source of his pain, an inflamed and throbbing swelling. He blinks his good eye, feels for the other; it's still there. Which surprises him, given the force of the blow on his neck. He grins at the girl, Art, Rodack, the three concerned faces watching him. "Jesus H. Christ," he mumbles, "somebody really got me." He cannot yet remember what happened. He reaches out to grasp the steel bars of the door; the bars are cool, firm, solid —quite actual. A well-known sensation. "In jail again," he says calmly, without surprise.

"They said you tried to kill the Chief," Barbara says.

The old man pulls on the bars; there is no give. He looks blankly through the bars across the corridor at the barred door on the other side. The opposite cell is empty now. "Kill him? Kill that man?" He feels for his weapon. The revolver is gone, and with it his holster, gunbelt, the leather belt from his jeans. "Yes sir. Sure tried."

A sliding door bangs open at the end of the corridor. Four guards enter; one with bunch of keys unlocks the cell door. The other three stand nearby, armed with clubs, no guns. The cell door swings open. "Out," snaps the jailer, "everybody out."

Barbara starts to moan in sudden panic, then represses the moan, forces herself to be silent. She hobbles out of the cell on her crutches, followed by the others. Rodack and Art assist old Burns, who has trouble staying erect. He sways dizzily, the walls reeling around him. Then the walls come to a stop. He follows the girl on the crutches.

They are marched through the doorway at the end of the hall, into a storm of sunlight. A squad of soldiers armed with rifles and bayonets forms a hollow square around them. They are directed down an asphalt alleyway past a file of trucks, across the open court, through the gate in the barbed wire— Burns stares at the men in the guard station but sees no familiar faces—and into the great open space of Unity Square.

The stage and the gallows loom before them, dangling bodies twisting at the end of taut ropes. Three ropes, three bodies. The hangman, a master sergeant, and his buck-sergeant assistant release the dead, letting them drop out of sight through the trapdoors into the concealed area beneath the platform.

As the next three condemned persons are led up the thirteen steps, a canvas flap is pushed aside from beneath the platform and a team of mules appears, harnessed to a wagon. In the open bed of the wagon lies a heap of human bodies. The driver cracks his whip, the team and wagon move away across the square toward a southern street.

Rodack, Burns, Barbara, and Art are brought to a halt in front of and below the gallows. The soldiers stand behind them. All watch as the hangman's assistant busies himself about the three new victims on the stage. Their hands already bound, he binds their ankles, then drapes a black hood and a noose over the head of the first man, a pale numb lanky fellow with eyes kept firmly closed. The sergeant draws the heavy noose firm around the man's neck and goes on to the figure in the middle—the woman they had seen briefly down below, hurried past their cell. The woman has long black hair, braided like an Indian's, olive skin on a small-boned face, dark and frightened eyes. Neverthe-less when the buck sergeant comes near with the hood she spits at him; and when the sergeant tries to lower it over her head she shakes it off, throws back her head and screams, a piercing cry that carries above the rattling drums of the drum-and-bugle corps music broadcast from speakers mounted to walls around the square. The military Muzak.

The woman screams: "Burn all the records! Burn all the records!" The sergeant tries to muffle her with the black hood, pulling it down over her face. But she cries again: "Burn all the records! *¡Tierra o muerte! ¡Viva la libertad!*"

The sergeant forces the noose in place around the woman's head. He draws the massive knot close and tight under her ear, under her chin, cutting off her voice. He turns to the third of the condemned, the shaggy-maned Mexican staring out across the vast square. He seems to be searching for someone, a certain face, a friend, a wife, a child, a mistress—but before he finds that face the darkness is lowered over his eyes, the hard hemp drawn and tightened about his neck. The assistant steps aside. The three black-hooded ones stand motionless, waiting. The ra-vens circle overhead.

Lieutenant Myers, in charge of the execution detail, glances at his watch, nods to a sergeant at his side. The sergeant lifts a steel whistle to his lips, blows. The shrill, harsh, agonizing screech slashes through the air, the hangman pulls his lever, the trapdoors open.

The living bodies fall, two men, a woman, fall into and through the stage as if escaping, a triumph of magic over mili-tary law—but the escape is cut short by the unyielding ropes. The three jerk to a halt when only halfway down. The ropes grunt, the timbers creak from the abrupt strain, the system holds, the fugitives are stopped.

With broken necks and strangled windpipes their bodies struggle for survival, brains blacked out, minds extinguished, but muscle and nerve still clinging to life. No longer among the living, the three dead strive to return. Their bodies fight for one more minute of existence, spasms of dying energy rippling through the flesh as they seem to dance and leap at the end of the swaying ropes. But there is no return. No return is allowed. Bitterly, grudgingly, life retreats from cell to cell, the light fades from nerve to nerve. The darkness deepens. The darkness closes in, softly, finally, totally. The hooded bodies subside into fretful twitches, irregular and futile. They twist slowly first to one side, then to the other.

A moment of silence. Lieutenant Myers waves his saber in the air and shouts, "Thus die all enemies of the State! Thus die all traitors to our Chief!"

The soldiers cheer. Most of them. Far down the ranks is one on his knees, vomiting into the dust.

The hangman's assistant uncleats a rope; aided by block and tackle he hoists the executed high and into full view, where they can be appreciated. He hitches the free end of the rope to the cleat again and lets the dead folk hang there, closer to the sky. Closer to God. Closer to the ravens, settling on the crossbeams.

Rodack and Burns, the girl and the boy, huddle together, leaning on one another, holding one another up, until the sergeant barks an order and the soldiers herd them across the square again and into the compound and down the alleyway and into the basement prison where they belong. The guards and soldiers disperse, leaving the square to the dead, to the ravens, to the sullen blaze of the afternoon sun. The spectators disappear. There are none left to witness the three that hang, black against the vivid sky, none to hear the echo of a woman's voice vibrating through the empty canyons of the city, her words traced in fire across the golden air . . .

> *burn all the records*
> *tierra o muerte*

The hangman, taking a break, is detained on the corner by a drunken Indian; talking earnestly, they disappear into a doorway.

The glass walls tower above the square. Ten, fifteen, twenty stories high, they lean in convergent perspective toward the sun. They mirror one another, they mirror the sky: Images of hard-edged clouds slide over glassy, opaque façades, folding with surreal ease as in dreams around blunt corners framed in aluminum. The man who stands on the topmost floor of the greatest of the towers, staring into the East, cannot be seen from below, or from outside the glass wall, but he sees everything, he misses nothing, he knows all.

viva la libertad
viva la libertad
viva la libertad

"**M**angus!" he shouts into the wall telephone. "Get the hell out of the sack. Meet me down in the lab. We got work to do." Brock claps the phone back in its cradle, pulls on pants, shirt, boots. He starts to belt on his automatic pistol, then changes his mind. Not for the lab. He combs his dark hair, with care, admiring himself in the large mirror on top of the dresser. Afternoon sunlight streams in the window. He slicks down his hair with tap water, rubs his teeth with his forefinger, making a face at himself. If he, Brock, is not the best-looking son-of-a-bitch in this insane, decrepit, slaughterhouse of a city, then who is?

He leaves the silver helmet, his sunglasses and scarf, on the dresser. Won't be needing them either, not right now. Ready, he steps out of his room, locking the door. Soldiers in uniform trot down the hall. Every man in sight carries a weapon. "Tomorrow we march," he hears somebody say.

A dim depression, a cloud of nameless dread obscures the normally sunny surface of Sergeant Brock's soul. The depression is like a vague ache somewhere in general, nowhere in particular, floating through his nerves. A physical discomfort, as if mercury were bubbling in his blood. But the dread—the dread is in his stomach. But dread of what? He has no idea. Why the depression? He cannot remember. Then he does remember. His depression deepens.

Brock opens a fire door in the masonry wall and descends, by dim lights and concrete steps, into the basement of the Tower. A guard, half asleep in the heat below, jumps to his feet, presenting arms.

"Wake up, Willy," Brock says. "I want a look at these new prisoners Mangus caught this morning."

"Sure thing, Sarge." Slinging his automatic rifle, the guard gropes through a mass of keys hanging on his belt.

"Never mind," Brock says, pulling out his own. He lets himself into the prison office, where two guards lounge by a table, leafing through yellowed magazines and drinking lemonade from an iced pitcher. Soft bland music drips from the speaker on the wall: theme from an antique movie called *Love Story*. From beyond the walls, throbbing through the cinder blocks and plaster, comes the rumble, unceasing and semihysterical, of the diesel generators. The roar of power. Desks and file cabinets line the room, giving it the secure, homey look of any government office. A photograph of the Chief, blown up to life size, adorns the wall behind the jailer's desk. The Chief wears perfect white; his painfully sensitive, earnestly intelligent eyes gaze into an unlimited future.

Brock sits on a desk. The guards stand, waiting for orders. "How many prisoners left?" asks Brock.

"Only four," says the first guard, a paunchy fellow in soldier suit, corporal's chevrons on his sleeve. "The new bunch."

"Only four?" Brock looks surprised. "So Myers really cleaned the place out today. Hung them all?"

"Only the big ones. They shot the rest, I guess. Anyhow, they're gone."

Brock twists his great mustache, musing over the patterns of Fate. Alive only hours ago, now gone. Gone where the woodbine twineth, as we used to say. "And these four—that would be Rodack, right? And his young punks?"

"It's Rodack, and an old man with no ID, and two kids—a boy named Art Dekker and a girl named Barbara."

"Art, eh? Him again. Well, damn me. And what's the plan for them?"

"Rodack hangs at sundown. The others with him, I suppose, except for the girl." The corporal smirks. "They've got better use for her."

"Of course," says Brock, staring thoughtfully at the floor. "All right . . ." He stands, pulling a pair of leather gloves from his hip pocket and drawing them on. "I'll be in the lab with Mangus. Bring me the two young ones first."

The corporal hesitates. "The colonel said no interrogation."

"The colonel? The *colonel?*"

"Colonel Barnes. The Chief made him a colonel this morning."

Brock looks astounded. Then disgusted. Then resigned. "What the hell. Bring me the two young ones." He steps toward a door near the cellblock bulkhead.

"What about the order, Sarge?"

"Don't worry about it. Let me worry about it." He snaps his fingers. "Get them!"

The guards pick up their clubs. They carry no firearms. The corporal unlocks a compartment in the wall by the cellblock door, exposing a folded crank. He turns the crank, the door slides open with a clang. A corridor is revealed and a row of solid cell doors, each with its spyhole at eye level and the narrow grid at the bottom. The decor is elementary: green steel and gray cement, glaringly illuminated by naked light bulbs. The guards tramp down the hallway toward the barred cells in the middle. Sergeant Brock enters his laboratory, his intelligence research center.

This is a small room, compactly organized, windowless. Fluorescent tubes on the ceiling light up every corner making it a room without shadows. A padded operating table, bolted to the floor, equipped with straps, belts, and stirrups, occupies the center of the room. Two steel chairs are set nearby. Shelves mounted to the wall carry a limited assortment of interrogation aids: cast-iron brazier with charcoal briquettes, lighter fluid, branding irons, ammonia, K-Y jelly, clean rags, a large jar of aspirin tablets, a lady's hand mirror. There is a sturdy little leatherbound book, old, greasy, dogeared, bearing on its cover the official seal of the U. S. Central Intelligence Agency (classified document). There is also an array of brass, copper, black-plastic electrical equipment—electrodes, clamps, coils, a transformer, these linked by a tangle of heavy-duty insulated extension cord. From the speaker concealed among the lighting fixtures floats the music scientifically designed for pleasant listening; the selection, at the moment, is "Sentimental Journey."

Brock checks out the apparatus. He plugs the cord to a socket in the wall, flips a switch on the transformer, and pushes the voltage-control lever forward and back—ten clicks each way. The transformer makes a satisfying hum, the red needle on the meter flickers up, oscillates, comes down. Setting the control arm on the first click, at five volts, he touches an electrode to his arm and feels the thrilling pulse of electricity surge through his muscle. He shuts the machine off.

Mangus Colorado wanders in, shirt unbuttoned, sweat streaming down his chest. He nods to Brock. "Morning . . ."

"Morning? It's two in the afternoon. Button your shirt, asshole. You're on duty now. Christ, Mangus, you can't sleep all day. You dumb greasy aborigine."

The Apache mumbles an incoherent reply, buttoning his shirt and stuffing it into his trousers. He pours lighter fluid over the briquettes in the brazier, strikes a match, and ignites the charcoal. He places the business end of the two irons in the flames. He scratches an armpit and yawns. "Somebody stole my Harley," he grumbles.

"Nobody stole your Harley."

"It's gone, Sarge."

"Did you look where I left it?"

"Yeah, Sarge. It's gone. Somebody in moccasins took it."

"We'll find you another one."

"I liked that one."

"Don't worry about it, shithead. I'll get you another." Brock skims through the pages of his little book, finds the chapter he wants. Chapter 12: "How to Prevent Electrolytic Burns."

The Apache puts a cigarette in his mouth, pulls on leather gloves from the work bench, and lights the cigarette with the tip —already a glowing red—of one of his irons.

The endless tape glides on through the music system, playing "Holiday for Strings," followed by "Humoresque," followed by "Scarborough Fair," followed by "Edelweiss." . . .

The jail guards, grunting and sweating, drag the terrified girl, Barbara, into the lab. They force her onto the table and strap her down on her back, facing the old buzzing fluorescent lights in the ceiling. Bound to the table, she looks with wide eyes at the smiling Brock, at the shy leer on the Apache's scarred features, both of the men leaning over her. Her face is white with fear.

The Apache tugs at the girl's jeans, trying to pull them down. Sergeant Brock cuffs him away with one swing of his right arm. "Get back, you dirty little shit." He smiles sweetly at the girl. "Hi. You're Barbara, aren't you. I'm Sergeant Brock. I'm your friend here."

She licks her dry lips, saying nothing. The guards and the Apache stare.

Brock looks up at them. "Bring me the other," he snarls "The boy, goddamnit. That young fella, Art what's-his-name."

"We might need help with him, Sarge," the pale corporal says. "He's a feisty one. Fierce as a bobcat. Practically had to kill all three of them to get this girl out of there."

"Who told you to put them all into one cell, you dumb bastard? Mangus, give them a hand. Get more help if you need it. And don't kill anybody. I want a heart-to-heart talk with each of them." He claps his hands. "Move."

The men leave. Brock smiles down at Barbara. The music plays "Some Enchanted Evening"—repeating itself every four hours. Sergeant Brock says, "Surprise quiz, Barbara." He strokes her rich dark hair. Moaning, she tries to twist her head away but cannot escape his caressing hand. "Now tell me, quick, no guessing—you have two seconds in which to answer." He clamps her head between his gloved hands, compelling her to look at him, and whispers, "Where is Dixie Dalton?"

Barbara wails in terror, "I never heard of her, I never *heard* of her. . . ."

"Now, now, don't get upset. I'm not going to hurt you. Not if you answer my questions." Brock backs off for a moment and paces about the room; he stops, listening to a clamor of yells, blows, clanging steel grids from inside the cellblock. He comes back to the girl's side, bends over her, and whispers again, "Where is Dixie?"

"I don't know."

"Ah-hah. So you *have* heard of her."

"No, no, I never heard of her."

Brock smiles at Barbara's frightened, sweating face. She no longer looks so pretty. He holds the hand mirror above her face; she turns her head away. He forces her to look. "See? See what you're doing to yourself?" He turns her head toward the brazier, the flaming coals, the red-hot irons. "See that? Mangus used to be a cowboy. Those are what a cowboy calls running irons. He draws brands with them. On cows. On horses. On people. You notice the big scar across his face? A woman did that to him, long ago. But he never forgets, that little Apache. He has a simple mind. Never forgets anything." He lets his words sink deep into her consciousness. "Now tell me, Barbara: Where is my Dixie?"

The girl tries to speak. From the depths of her despair, through a nightmare of overwhelming horror from which she cannot escape, she tries to say something that might save her. The music plays, a voiceless, sexless, mucilaginous, Royal Canadians version of "Bali Hai." She says, "She was with us in the library. In the basement. When the soldiers came. I think— I think she got away."

Brock frowns. His handsome eyebrows twitch with pain, forming a shallow vee. "She got away? Where to? Who with?"

The guards come stumbling into the room, dragging the struggling boy between them. Art sees Barbara strapped to the table. With a howl of rage he frees himself, lunges at Brock, reaching for the throat. Brock belts him to the floor with a blow of his gloved fist, kicks him in the kidneys. The guards hurl themselves on the boy's writhing body, lash him firmly into one of the steel chairs, hands bound, ankles pinioned to the legs of the chair.

All pause, breathing heavily. Sergeant Brock tidies his uniform. Mangus Colorado, eyes on the girl, lights another cigarette with his glowing iron. Delicate white flecks of heat sparkle and fade and sparkle again on the radiant tip of the iron. As the girl stares back at him the Apache grins, shyly, and averts his face. He scratches his armpit. He belches. He yawns.

The boy recovers slowly. Brock opens the vial of ammonia and passes it back and forth under Art's face. The boy jerks his head up and away, tears streaming over his bruised, blood-streaked face. He glares around the room, searching for something. As his vision clears and steadies, his dark eyes come to rest, with murderous hatred, on the face of Sergeant Brock.

"Well," says Brock, "is everybody comfortable? Shall we get started again?" He looks at the boy. "Hello, Art. Nice to see you again. I'm sorry you lied to me last night." He smiles, shaking his head sadly. "Now you'll never get a chance to ride my motorcycle."

Art says, "You're going to die."

Brock shrugs. "All men are mortal." But the shadow of dread comes over him again. He pauses, staring at the instruments on his workbench, seeing nothing. The paralysis of nothingness grips him for a moment. Only for a moment. He overcomes it—*hence, accursed melancholy!*—and turns toward his patients. He pulls up Barbara's shirt, exposing her waist and belly. Her ribs stand out as she takes a deep breath.

"Relax, Barbara, relax. We're not quite ready yet." He opens the jar of K-Y jelly, smears a blob on her stomach, another on her side. He takes a fold of her skin and attaches the first electrode clamp, then a second. She moans. The Apache, the guards, young Art Dekker watch. Brock steps back, turns on the power. The needle on the meter rises a hairsbreadth free of the peg. They hear the gentle humming of the circuit, the murmur of electrons in their current. Barbara stiffens, setting her jaw, shutting her eyes so tightly that a tear is squeezed from each eyelid. "Relax," says Brock kindly, like a thoughtful physician. "You're not feeling anything yet."

"Don't do it!" Art cries. "Don't do it!"

Brock ignores the boy, saying, "Now this will hurt a little. At first." Brock puts his hand on the transformer switch. "Then it will hurt a little more."

"I'll talk," screams Art. "I'll talk, I'll talk, I'll talk!" The words pour out in a garbled rush.

"Mangus, hold the mirror over the young lady's face." The Apache obeys. "Open your eyes, Barbara. I want you to see what this does to your teeth."

"No!" Art howls. "I'll talk. Anything! Everything!"

Sergeant Brock, his hand on the switch, hesitates. He looks at the boy with a smile of surprise. "Why Art. Art Dekker." He pauses in reproach. "I'm ashamed of you. This little girl is braver than you are."

"Goddamn you, what do you want to know?"

The sergeant's smile subsides into a pout of sadness. He looks aggrieved, thinking about his loss. "Where's my Dixie?" he says. "Where is my Dixie Dalton?"

"Dixie? Where is Dixie? Well she—"

"I told you," says Barbara, opening her eyes, speaking rapidly; her face shines with sweat. "She got away. With the others. They—"

Brock claps a hand over the girl's mouth. "Quiet, Barbara. I was talking to Art. Where'd they go, Art?"

Art looks desperately at Barbara but there is no help there, she cannot aid him. "I think," he says, "they were gonna go ... they were gonna meet at, back at, at—Dixie's bar." He glares at the floor, ashamed of his confusion.

The telephone rings on the wall. One of the guards picks it up.

"I think you're both liars," says Sergeant Brock. "Liars!" he shouts. "I don't believe you."

The guard offers the telephone to Brock. "Myers."

Brock takes it. "Yeah!" he growls. "Brock. Yes sir. . . . Jesus Christ . . . yes sir. Thanks a lot sir." He slams the phone back on its hook. He pounds his right fist into his palm, then yells at the guards. "Okay, get them out of here. Back in the cells. The colonel's on his way down to pick up the professor. Move. Move fast!" The guards rush to obey. To the Apache Brock says, "Get that stuff out of sight," indicating the brazier, the irons, the electrical equipment. "Quick, quick."

The guards pull Art and Barbara from the room, leaving their hands bound. But before they go Brock plants one last thought in their heads: "You two were lucky this time. But I'm checking out your lying story. And if she's not there, if my Dixie ain't where you say, then I'm coming straight back here and you two'll wish you'd never been born. I'll show you things you'd never believe." He grins in Barbara's face, leering at her from six inches away, enveloping her in the plume of his whiskey-sweet breath. Terrified, silent, she stares back into his yellow-green eyes—the eyes of a wolf.

Brock vanishes, followed by his Apache. The guards push
Art and Barbara, staggering on their numbed limbs, through the
office and down the hallway to their cell. The gray, steel grid of
bars slides open; the guards shove them inside. The grid slides
back with a clang of iron, clashes, locks.

The boy and girl huddle together, shivering despite the heat.
Cheeks pressed together, they blend their tears and sweat.
"God, I love you," Art says, crying, "I love you, Barbara."

"I know," she says. "I love you too. Now"—she manages a
faint, quavering smile and lifts her bound hands toward his face
—"see if you can get this strap off me."

He unbinds her. She unbinds him. They embrace, and kiss,
huddled in the corner of the cell, hearing the clamor of the
cellblock door and the sound, again, of heavy marching boots
coming down the hall. The sound stops for a moment. Art looks
up to see a tall young officer looking in at him through the
latticework of bars. The man stares, his face without any read-
able expression except, perhaps, a scornful pity. The look, it
seems to Art, that the living cast upon the condemned. The
officer says nothing, and after the brief pause, marches to the
adjoining cell, spurs jingling on his heels, followed by two soldiers.

Again the rattle of metal, a voice of command. Art and
Barbara hear Rodack reply, in a tone of surprise, words inaudible. Then the groan of a tired man rising, the clatter of iron,
marching feet. The officer strides past followed by the soldiers
with Rodack. The professor halts, seeing the boy and girl looking at him from the gloom of the cell. "I'll get you out of here,"
he says.

"We're all right," Barbara says, "but where are they taking
you?"

Professor Rodack smiles. He points upward with one long
forefinger. "Up there," he says, "the Chief—"

The soldiers push him on, out of sight. They hear Rodack's
parting shout. "I'll be back."

Again the clamor of steel on steel resounds through the

cellblock. In the relative stillness following they hear the background rumble, beyond several walls, of the generators.

And another voice from next door, the voice of Jack Burns: "Barb," he says, "Art—that you in there?"

"Yeah," they answer in unison, hugging one another, "it's us."

"Well listen, you two, there's nothin' to worry about. Sam's around somewhere. He'll be along pretty soon. He'll get us out of here. I know that Indian. He don't give up. And what's more" —they hear a shuffling sound—"I got something else. They always forget to search my boots. Now you listen to this, you two. . . ."

Holding one another as close as two can get, Art and Barbara listen, and listen, and after a preliminary snorting and tapping from the adjacent cell, they hear—music. Not Muzak but music: the sweet tones of a harmonica swinging vigorously into the melody of "Oh Susanna!" A simple song of life, and joy, and liberation, and victory. Somewhere, somehow. Someday.

The diesel generators strain their molybdenum entrails, lifting an elevator into the sky.

Rodack is marched out of the elevator on the topmost floor, his hands strapped together before him, through the anteroom and into the heat, the blaze of sunshine, of the penthouse terrace. Waiting for him in the shade of the awning is the Chief, cool and immaculate in his whites, eyes masked by dark glasses and further shaded by the visor of his cap. He is armed only with the sheathed dagger at his waist. The Chief, staring eastward into the shimmering afternoon, toward that vista of mountains, golden desert, ignores the advance of prisoner, guards, Colonel Barnes.

The detail come to a halt in the sunlight, the professor between them, the soldiers at attention. Colonel Barnes advances three steps, clicks his heels, salutes. "The prisoner is here, sir, as ordered."

The Chief continues, for another long moment, to contemplate his destiny. The colonel waits. Without turning to look, the Chief says, "Unbind the prisoner, Colonel. Then take your men and go."

"Yes sir." The colonel nods to the soldiers; they remove the leather strap from Rodack's wrists. "One request, sir."

"Yes, Colonel?" The Chief continues to gaze eastward.

"With your permission, sir, I'd like to have the two young people inducted into a labor company."

"What two young people?"

"Those two I captured this morning. The survivors."

The Chief hesitates. "They should be hanged," he murmurs. "They're all traitors. But do what you think best, Colonel." His voice seems languid with melancholy.

"Thank you, sir." Barnes salutes the Chief's indifferent back, does an about-face, and starts off, followed by the two soldiers.

But he is stopped by an afterthought from the Chief. "Not the would-be assassin, Colonel; that man must hang, along with our other prisoners." The Chief has turned now; disregarding the nearby Professor Rodack, he looks at Barnes.

"Of course, sir," says the colonel. "But as you might have noticed, sir, Myers has been busy today. The cells are cleared of everybody but those two I mentioned. And the assassin. And this man"—indicating Rodack—"here."

"Yes, yes." The Chief sighs, still not looking at Rodack. "Very good. Clear the cells. No more formal executions after today. We have better things to do than entertain these spies, traitors, assassins, terrorists, incendiaries. Of course. No more prisoners, Colonel—get that word out. From now on until we leave, simply have recalcitrants shot on sight. You may regard that as an order, Colonel."

"Yes sir." The colonel waits.

"You may go. Professor Rodack and I have much to discuss. And not much time."

"Yes sir." The colonel salutes once more and strides away, attended by the soldiers.

The Chief and the professor are left alone. Rodack rubs his sore wrists, staring at the Chief, who persists in looking elsewhere, as if Rodack were something too loathsome, or too negligible, to consider directly. The Chief stands in the shade; the professor, bareheaded and bald, in the sun. Despite the intense heat Rodack is not sweating; the aridity of the air, equally intense, absorbs sweat as fast as it appears.

After a long silence, broken only by the sounds of marching men from the streets below, the Chief says, "Come here, Rodack, into the shade. Take a chair." He points to the table and two chairs at his side, under the awning. A fresh pitcher of ice water, and two glasses, wait on the table. "Have a drink of water if you wish."

The professor accepts part of the offer. With shaking hands he pours himself a glass of water and gulps it down. Then pours another. But remains standing, holding the pitcher in his right hand.

"You're shaking, Rodack." The Chief looks half at, half past, the professor. "Sit down." He takes the pitcher from Rodack's uncertain grasp, places it on a flower box nearby, beyond Rodack's reach. "Sit down, sit down." Rodack sits.

The Chief paces about, back and forth in short lengths, generating thought. Philosophy begins as a peripatetic exercise. "You'll forgive me if I seem a little curt, old friend. Many things on my mind; I'm sure you understand. First let me say that we are definitely going to hang you this afternoon. In about three hours, I believe."

The Chief glances at the sun, arching toward the west, and at the pale half moon rising from the east. "I say that simply to ease your mind of any uncertainty. Nothing is more painful, as we know, than doubt."

He walks about. "You will not be tortured. I do not allow torture here. You will be hanged quickly, efficiently, with due ceremony and with as large a crowd of witnesses as we can scare up. Therefore, my friend and former colleague, be of good cheer. The martyrdom that you've been after for all your miserable life will soon be yours. I could hardly think of denying you that much. So—" Smiling, the Chief glances for the first time at Rodack's face, now averted. The professor, eyes pale and weak without his glasses, stares down at his clasped hands.

"You have nothing to say?" the Chief asks.

Rodack is silent.

"Very well. As you wish. I was hoping we might have a little discussion. You were always so garrulous before. But of course we knew, every time, exactly what you would have to say on any topic."

The Chief picks up his riding crop, in passing, from the second chair. "Didn't we, Rodack?" He holds it in both hands behind his back, twitching it from time to time.

No reply.

"Didn't we? That was always the most exasperating thing about you. The predictability of your opinions. The banality of your doctrine. The conformity of your ideology. You called yourself an anarchist. Good God!"

The Chief slashes at a metal stanchion supporting the awning. "Anarchist—while drawing the salary of a tenured professor at a state university. Anarchist indeed. Passionate convictions, or so it appeared—but no courage. No stomach for violence. No more guts than a worm, eh my friend?"

The Chief stops for a moment, staring at the professor. "Care to disagree?"

Rodack says nothing.

"*Fear* to disagree? Perhaps you think I want to kill you, now, with my own hands, and am trying to provoke you, provide a pretext? Wrong, my friend. I prefer not to touch you. It even pains me to look at you, to see you here, on my rooftop, where you have no right to be. Your very breathing is a form of insolence. Your very existence is an insult to everything clean and true and good and proud and manly."

The Chief pauses again. "Ah, but forgive me, dear Professor Rodack, I forget myself, I forget my place here. You are my guest. Please—would you like some more water?"

Rodack does not reply. But his glass is empty. The Chief

refills it from the pitcher, this time leaving the pitcher on the table.

"Drink, my friend. You are pale, very shaky. You look ill. Sick with fear, no doubt. Or maybe with hatred. Is that the meaning of your silence? You wish to express a contempt deeper than words? Beyond speech?"

No answer. The professor drinks the water with trembling hand, empties the glass. Using both hands he lifts the pitcher and fills his glass again. The ice cubes jingle cheerily, cascading from the pitcher's spout.

"But you were always so ready with words before. And worse than words, with organized obstructionism. You and your hordes of fearful allies, those vermin from the universities, reservations, ghettos. Who opposed the nuclear industry, the synthetic-fuels industry, the water-diversion projects that might have saved us? Who cried panic every time some reactor malfunctioned? Who kept whining about air pollution and water pollution and food pollution and made it impossible to get our industrial plant modernized? Who made it so difficult for us to keep our military power at parity with that of our enemies? Our *foreign* enemies, I mean. Who opposed and sabotaged our intervention in Venezuela? in South Africa? in Australia? Even in Mexico, right next door, when there was absolute need for at least a show of support at home?"

Pause. No reply.

"Industry strangled," the Chief goes on, "transit system breaking down, millions of people out of work, communications falling into chaos? And then more sabotage in the nuclear industry, hysterical rumors deliberately reported as fact, mass evacuations in New York, Pennsylvania, Chicago, St. Louis? Martial law—but no power to enforce it? Emergency edicts— and no way to make them public? Mutiny in the armed forces? The loss of deference, the breakdown in respect for authority on every level, in every public institution? Who, my friend, was morally and intellectually responsible for that?"

The Chief pauses for an answer. Rodack makes no answer.

The Chief continues. "It would be ludicrous to blame you person-ally—to give *you* the *credit*, as you might like to think—for that collapse in the moral fabric of our nation. But you did what you could, in your little local way." The Chief waits.

No reply.

"Few dared call it treason in those deluded days. Some of us did but we were ignored, laughed at, ridiculed. But treason it was. I have no doubt that our enemies overseas were involved in the scheme from the beginning. Why they failed to take ad-vantage of our confusion and disunity, and then the collapse, we don't know. Perhaps we'll never know."

The Chief pauses again for reflection, gazing out over his ruined city. "Perhaps they too were betrayed—struck down by traitors in their midst. By a loss of nerve in the governing body, by the failure of power to be exercised when power was avail-able. Leading, step by step, to the loss of power in every form —economic, military, political, spiritual. Decay and disintegra-tion. Exactly what you had wanted and hoped for all along, eh Rodack?"

Silence.

"Speak up, man!"

Silence.

The Chief stares with contempt at the professor, at his bare, bowed, balding head, the pale clasped hands, the slumped and heavy body. The professor seems to be waiting. But waiting for what? Nothing can save him now.

The Chief resumes his pacing, continues the lecture. An interminable lecture in the form of one monstrous and rhetorical question. "Murder, rape, pillage, arson. Millions flee the cities, hunting for food. And then, after a pause, out of the smoking ruins come the rats. The human rats, Rodack, your type, your kind, you and the other vermin. You burn the official records, thinking in your childish way that if the papers are destroyed you can claim ownership of homes, farms, ranches, irrigation systems, the land itself. Pathetic insolence: You've forgotten the military. Islands of decency and tradition in a sea of lunatic disorder. You forgot about us, didn't you, Rodack? Thought we'd been starved out, or fled with the politicians—wherever those swine may have gone."

The Chief halts again, gathering his thoughts, soothing his sense of outrage. He stares at the smoking city, at the deep shadows on the eastern walls and down in the glass canyons, at the barren hills in the desert, at the far-off mountains to the north and east.

"We shall soon find out," he says. "We shall soon find out. But you, Rodack"—he turns to the professor—"you'll never know. As you never really knew anything, outside of your head and your books. And you will die as you've lived, in darkness and in ignorance. Can you deny a word I've said?"

Rodack does not reply.

"Ah well," continues the Chief, "enough of that. It's the future we're concerned with now, Rodack. Not you, you're beyond redemption. But we the living—we have plans. Mighty plans. To create a mighty nation once again. And a new world. The wisest men, Rodack, have known for five thousand years that this world is not sufficient. We are in exile, Rodack, the human race is in exile. This shabby little planet we call Earth is not our home but our prison—our Elba—and its only function is to serve us, eventually, as a launching platform for the journey beyond." The Chief pauses for another glance at his prisoner.

The prisoner says nothing.

"Your time is short, Rodack." The Chief glances at his watch. "Any final thoughts? I'd be interested."

Rodack is silent.

"You have nothing to say? Too bad. And I'd thought we might have one last dialogue. As you can imagine, I'm a lonely man. There's no one I can talk to. The loneliness of power. And the agony of it, too, I might add. Not easy, for example, to condemn you to death, my old friend. Always easier to die than to send others off to death. Something the common folk never have understood."

The Chief hesitates, switching his quirt against the table

leg, against a stanchion, against the flower box as he paces slowly back and forth. "Even so," he goes on, "I feel this ridiculous, last-hour need to justify myself to you. To justify my project, I should say, for what does my trivial self matter? I am merely an instrument, a tool. Inspired by a voice? Not exactly. But by something deeper than intellect, older than wisdom, higher than hope. By something in the spirit of man. And in the soul of the world. Do you remember, Rodack?"

No reply. The prisoner stares at the empty water glass in his hands.

"You were the only man I knew, in that decadent university of ours, whom I had the least respect for. In all that pack of imbeciles—vocational technicians, football coaches, microspecialists in the microsciences, mining engineers, Gödel theorists, literary windbags with their seven types of ambiguity, soft minds, flabby spirits—in that whole swarm of overpaid underworked academics you were the only man I could recognize as an equal."

The professor lifts his gaze to the remote clouds beyond the mountains. The Chief stops for a moment to look in the same direction, his back to the prisoner. Rodack reaches for the heavy water pitcher. The Chief turns.

"Yes? You were going to say something?"

Rodack pours himself another glass of water.

"No?" The Chief resumes. "We were equals, or so I thought at the time. Equals, I mean, in our concern for ultimate things. Rarest of qualities. But no, we were opposites in our interpretation of that concern. For example, your futile faith—typically Jewish, no?—in the bourgeois, eighteenth-century notion of individual liberty. A dead end, as time has shown. An evolutionary cul-de-sac. And your stubborn belief—really irrational—in what you called the 'essential equality' of men. *All* men! Even of women—those soft, squat, lumpy creatures with their venomous secretions of honey and envy. An astonishing idea, refuted by a walk down the street. By anyone with eyes."

The professor makes no statement.

The Chief paces back and forth, back and forth, lashing at things. "Woman *is*. Man *does*. But enough of this trivia. Liberty, equality, fraternity—small ideas for small minds, when viewed under the aspect of destiny. There, my dear Rodack, lay the great divergence between us. For man can never be satisfied with the easy routine you would have us settle for. Your Proudhonian libertarianism, your shopkeeper's anarchism, your Jeffersonian mediocrity. Men require something more difficult, Rodack, more inspiring. Allegiance to a higher purpose. Identification with something greater than themselves."

No word from the professor.

"You agree? Transcendence, Rodack, is what we crave. Transcendence of the self. The corrupt age of individualism is over. Remember the moral decay that preceded the social collapse? We intend to reverse that process, by which I mean we aim at the unification of mankind into a planetary organism transcending individuals, races, even nations. To dare, Rodack, to dare. Ever to dare. *Toujours l'audace!* Even more."

At this point the Chief lowers his voice to a conspiratorial level, as if in dread of some eavesdropping ear, not on the roof of the Tower, but beyond, above, in the sky:

"Revelations, my friend. The ultimate aim of the human project is more than the unification of this planet, more than the conquest of the galaxy. Those are gross, material aims. Beyond the material lies the spiritual. The mastery of the world by the human spirit. We shall conquer death—*Death, thou shalt die!* —and attain divinity, become pure spirit, pure consciousness, bodiless but omnipotent, beyond space, beyond time."

The Chief pauses for comment. Rodack does not speak.

"The ancient sages," continues the Chief, "dreamed of attaining this state through mystical union with God. But we propose to do it through reason, intelligence, science, technique. An insane project, you're thinking, *hubris,* overweening pride. The coward's apology, Rodack. Without risk nothing of value can be gained. If we wish to live like heroes—and what other life is worth living?—then we must be willing to risk a hero's fate."

Smiling, twitching his quirt, the Chief stops for a moment in his promenade to gaze out, proudly, over the wall of the terrace, across the city, toward the drifting, somnambulant clouds, profound in their detachment, heartbreaking in their beauty. "Look . . ."

And as the Chief meditates upon that troubling remoteness, Professor Rodack lifts himself from his chair, seizes the pitcher, and lunges at the slim silent man in the white uniform.

"Death," whispers Rodack, "you shall die." Making a sound like a kind of moan, he swings the pitcher at the enemy's head.

The Chief hears the whisper, the moan. Smiling, he turns in time to take the blow with his left shoulder. The pitcher thuds into flesh and bone, doing little damage, slips from Rodack's grasp, and shatters on the tile floor of the terrace. Groaning with hatred, Rodack reaches for the Chief's throat with his bare hands, finds and grips it.

The Chief staggers back, knocking over the flower box. The force of Rodack's attack carries him against the waist-high parapet. The Chief is bent backward over the wall, his head and shoulders out in space, his cap falling off and twirling down toward the street, fifteen stories below. The cap drifts tangentially on the western breeze, skipping off the tapered wall.

Throttling his opponent with all of the strength left in his hands, heart, mind, glaring into the Chief's bulging eyes, Rodack whispers again in a pleading tone, "Die, you tyrant, die, die, god*damn* you. . . ."

The Chief reacts instinctively, clutching at the grip on his throat. But this is useless. Nor can he reach the dagger pinned between his hip and the wall. Instead he lowers his right hand and drives the heel of it up, like a piston, between Rodack's forearms and into the thyroid cartilage—the Adam's apple.

Rodack shrinks in a convulsion of pain, gasping for air. The Chief draws his dagger, shoves Rodack across the wall, is about to stab and stab again, and push the unresisting body over—but he hesitates.

He hesitates, swallowing his rage, yanks Rodack to safety,

lets him sink to his knees on the rooftop. Holding his dagger, the Chief backs off a few steps, watching the professor's mute agony. Rodack is helpless.

The Chief turns and stumbles toward the telephone on the penthouse wall. The entire struggle has taken less than two minutes. As the Chief unhooks the telephone and starts to dial the guardhouse number, soldiers appear from the anteroom that leads to the elevator, holding their rifles at the ready. Seeing the Chief they stop, looking at him, then at the man on his knees.

"Take that pig," the Chief says hoarsely, "down to the square." His voice failing for a moment, he points to the leather bindings on the floor, then to the professor. The soldiers rush to obey.

The Chief croaks into the telephone. "Myers? Myers? That you, Myers? . . . Listen: I want them hanged at once . . . yes, at once . . . immediately—all four of them. . . . Girl? What girl? . . . Yes, all of them. . . . Him? He's on his way down right now. . . ."

The Chief watches as the soldiers drag the semiconscious Rodack past and through the door. "Yes, disregard the colonel's order. . . . I am countermanding that order. Hang them all. At once."

The four to be hanged are marched into the courtyard and assembled for briefing by Lieutenant Myers. Each with hands bound, they are lined up by a sergeant.

"Dress right!" barks the sergeant. Since some of the prisoners do not understand the command, they are helped to understand by the soldiers of the execution detail, using the customary kicks and gun butts.

"Ten-*shun!*" the sergeant barks, as Lieutenant Myers appears before the condemned. Barbara, leaning on her crutches, has difficulty with this command. One of the soldiers, rifle slung across his back, attempts to assist her by grabbing her neck with one hand and her buttocks with the other. She lashes at him with a crutch, knocks his helmet off. He cuffs her with the flat of his hand, arousing young Art, who breaks ranks to kick the soldier, with the pointed toe of his cowboy boot, hard in the groin. The soldier goes down, curling upon himself. Three soldiers attack Art with gun butts. Order is restored. Some of Brock's motorcycle troopers lounge nearby, watching the scene with lazy grins, fondling their weapons. When all is silent except for the heavy breathing, the lieutenant speaks.

"Well," he says, "I'm not much for making speeches, so this will be short. As you people probably know, you're going to be hung, all four of you, right away. Chief's orders. Now the problem is we have got only a three-place gallows so one of you will have to wait. Any volunteers?"

The soldiers and motorcycle troopers smile. The lieutenant's sense of humor, though familiar, is always appreciated by the rank and file.

"Any volunteers?" the lieutenant repeats. No one speaks. "Okay, who volunteers to go first?"

"I'm ready," says Burns.

"Don't talk to him," the professor croaks in his broken voice. "He's playing games with us. Don't talk to him."

Art steps forward. "Hang me, you son-of-a-bitch."

The squad sergeant steps close to Art; a giant of a man, well over six feet tall, he leans forward to lower his face to within inches of Art's nose, "Say *sir,*" he hisses, "when you answer an officer."

Startled, the boy says, "Yes sir."

"Not to me, you maggot," the sergeant howls, spluttering in Art's face. "I'm a sergeant, not an officer. See these stripes? Sergeant. The lieutenant"—pointing to Myers—"is the officer. You got that straight?"

"Yes sir." Art stares at Lieutenant Myers.

"Lower your eyes!" the sergeant roars.

"What?"

"Lower your eyes! You do not look an officer in the eyes. Never. Absolutely never. You are garbage. A maggot. The lieutenant is an officer and a gentleman. You do not look an officer in the eyes. Got that?"

"No sir."

"Don't 'sir' me, you piece of scum! 'Sir' the lieutenant! The lieutenant is the officer. I am the sergeant. Understand?"

Art falls silent, looking suddenly very tired.

"Understand?" the sergeant bellows. The soldiers grin; the motorcycle troopers nudge one another, chuckling. Young Art says nothing.

"All right, Sergeant," says Lieutenant Myers, "let it go. Enough comedy. These aren't soldiers. Let's get them on the way."

"Yes sir." The sergeant backs away from Art, scowling, draws himself to attention, facing the prisoners, and shouts, "Gallows squad—fall in!" Seven soldiers step smartly into formation, making a hollow square around the four condemned; the eighth member of the squad crawls up from the asphalt and limps into his place. "Ten-*shun!*" The squad snaps to with a clatter of weapons. "Ri-ight . . . *face!*" The eight soldiers turn crisply to the right, facing the open courtyard and the route toward Unity Square. The sergeant waits as the prisoners turn awkwardly in the same direction. Marking cadence, the sergeant bellows, "Foh-waaad . . . *harch!*"

The march begins, at a brisk pace, with Barbara, on her crutches, being immediately overrun by the soldiers behind her. Two of them, at a word from the lieutenant, who is following, snatch her crutches away, pick her up, and carry her along between them, her feet hardly touching the pavement.

Lieutenant Myers skips to the head of the march. The sentries spring to attention, presenting arms, as he leads the procession through the gateway of the compound. The march veers oblique left toward the majestic structure of wood and rope, one block away, in the center of the square. The public-address system, linked to the internal communications of the Tower, fills the open air with the sweet mellifluities of Muzak: "Michelle, Ma Belle," followed by "The Way We Were," followed by "Raindrops (Keep Fallin' on My Head)," as the execution party makes its way past sand dunes, sunflowers, stray horses, foundered automobiles, toward the final destination of revolutionaries. A few civilians—old men, old women, children—watch from the open doors and broken windows of looted banks, ravaged data centers, abandoned office buildings. A battalion of soldiers, some eight hundred men, waits at parade rest in the open square, near the gallows; clusters of officers stand talking together in front of their assembled troops. A red VW, following the burial wagon, creeps beneath the canvas of the stage.

Old Jack Burns, leading the four prisoners within the guard detail, turns his head to speak to Professor Rodack. "They got us an audience this time, Professor. Looks like a full house."

The professor smiles a grim little smile. "Liberty," he whispers in his hoarse, jagged voice, "let others despair of you—I never despair of you."

"You said it, Professor, them's my feelings too."

"Whitman," Rodack says, "not I."

"Don't care who," says Jack.

"Shut up in there!" the sergeant screams. "Prisoners will remain silent."

Tramp, tramp, tramp, tramp, the men march along, across the vast and empty place, through swirls of dust as the wind stirs the air. Fragments of burned paper float on the air, and the smell of smoke, and the buzzing murmur of hundreds of men. The Tower soars above, its glossy walls tapering into the distant blue, the bright strobe light glittering at the tip of the spire. A single cloud hovers in the sky beyond the Tower; seen from the square, it resembles a vaporous dirigible moored to the Tower's mast.

The soldiers wait in the arid heat of late afternoon. The sinking sun pours massive slanting beams of light into the canyons of the city. The moon, pale and translucent as ice, hangs in the meridian. From the mouths of the speakers, plastic goblins, charcoal blue, mounted to light poles, the amplified music blares through the semistillness: the theme from *Exodus;* "Impossible Dream"; "I'll Say a Little Prayer for You." . . .

"The final insult," mutters Rodack.

"Always did love a parade," says Jack Burns.

Tramp, tramp, tramp. Halfway, two thirds of the way across the immense square. The gallows frame, as they approach, looms higher and higher against the sky, grows bigger, heavier, darker, open gate to another world. The ravens sit roosting on the crossbeam, blue-black as demons. Looking up as they come near, the condemned can see the hangman himself waiting for them at the summit of the thirteen steps to the platform, a pot-bellied, stocky man wearing a rumpled soldier suit, the chevrons and diamond of a master sergeant on his sleeves, all but his eyes concealed behind the hangman's black mask.

"Look at that bastard," says Burns; "ashamed to show his sneaky face."

"It's the face of shame," the professor says. He resumes his harsh, broken-voiced, half-whispered prayer as he shuffles forward. "Not a grave of the murdered for freedom but grows seed for freedom, in its turn to bear seed, which the winds carry afar and resow, and the rains and the snows nourish. Not a disembodied spirit can the weapons of tyrants let loose, but it stalks invisibly over the earth, whispering, counseling, cautioning. Liberty, let others despair of you—I never despair of you. . . ."

"Silence in the ranks!"

"Walt—!"

"Silence!"

"—Whitman!"

"Silence!"

The squad marches between two companies of soldiers in formation and into an open area in the shadow of the gallows platform. Marking time, the sergeant stops, facing his men, and shouts, "Guard detail: *Halt!*"

The soldiers halt, the prisoners shamble to a stop. In the sudden stillness—for now someone has shut off the Muzak—all present hear the flapping of the canvas that hangs from the platform's edge; the evening winds are flowing in from the western desert. The ravens squatting on the crossbeam open their yellow bills wide, yawning, and peck at lice under their uplifted wings; they have witnessed the scene before. Many times. Two men watch from far above on the rooftop terrace of the Tower. The solitary cloud, untethered, diffusing, has floated away from the mast and farther to the east.

A squad of drummers breaks the stillness with a flourish on their snare drums. They stop. Major Roland, ranking officer present, steps forward and faces the prisoners. A plump man, anxiety-ridden, pink-faced, he takes a document handed to him by an aide and begins to read in a high, rapid monotone. The words are unclear but apparently deal with charges against the condemned. Names are mentioned—Jack Burns, Noah Rodack, Barbara Weiss, Arthur Dekker. And sundry crimes: attempted assassination of Chief of State; treason against State; conspiracy against State; destruction of public records; assault and attempted murder; conduct detrimental public order ... And the sentence: to be hanged by neck until dead. Et cetera.

Another roll of the drums. The major makes a signal to Lieutenant Myers, Myers to the squad sergeant. The prisoners are herded up the steps, except Barbara, left below, alone between two young soldiers. The hangman watches through his mask, eyes dark and somber, inscrutable. The three prisoners are marched across the platform; the old planking, warped and loosened by the desert sun, rattles beneath the soldiers' boots. Each prisoner is made to take his place on one of the three trapdoors. A big knotted hempen noose hangs above each head. The soldiers withdraw to the stairs, rejoining their comrades below.

The condemned face westward, into the sun, now sinking behind a shoal of crimson clouds. Eight hundred soldiers stare at them from below, each with a rifle slung on his shoulder. The wind, rising again, whirls dust and rags and flakes of soot and ancient yellow newspapers across the general emptiness of Unity Square. The sunlight glances off a mile of glass walls and from helmets and gun barrels ranged in rows and files of geometric precision. Waves of heat rise in layers from the baking asphalt, bending light; seen through the overheated air, walls of buildings on the far side of Unity Square seem to shift and float, like figures painted on a rippling tapestry.

Art on his left, the professor on his right, Jack Burns stands with bound hands and gazes at the battalion of faces facing him. He feels as if called upon to make a speech. His first, last, and greatest speech. There is surely time, at least, for a brave war cry or two. He tries to think of something stunning. From the corner of his good eye he sees the hangman draping a black hood, then the heavy noose, over the head of young Art. The hangman wears moccasins. He is whispering rapidly into Art's ear. Think of something good, Burns tells himself. He feels no fear; he has gone beyond fear.

The professor tries to shout. "Soldiers," he croaks, "remember that we died for—we died—" His voice box fails, trailing off into a gargling stammer.

Burns takes up the cause. "Listen, boys," he yells, "there's bear in the mountains. Forget the war. Let's go huntin'!" He is rewarded by a few scattered cheers from the audience, instantly hushed, before his world goes dark. The hangman has padded behind him and draped the warm, woolly, stinking hood over his face. "Take that off!" Burns exclaims.

"Shut up, boss, and listen close," says the quiet voice of Sam Banyaca. "This is a fake noose. You'll slip right through it when I spring the traps. The hood'll come off. You'll fall eight feet onto a sand dune. Dixie's down there with a little car. Pile in and take off for the mountains. I'll be coming along behind you on a motorcycle. You hear me?"

"Goddamnit Sam," the old man whispers, "why the hell you always wait till the last minute?"

"Don't argue. I got here as soon as I could. Be quiet. The soldiers are watching us."

"But goddamnit, Sam . . ."

But Sam is gone, on to the professor. Burns can only wait, peering at a glow of light through the darkness, hearing the rise and fall of the wind, the fluttering of flags, the sudden harsh barrage of the snare drums.

Sam the shaman steps to the side of the platform and puts his hand on the lever that will release three trapdoors at once. The sergeant of the guard detail is watching the Indian sharply, but makes no move. Yet. Sam waits and watches for the signal from Lieutenant Myers, standing below near the drummers.

The lieutenant raises his right hand. The drummers stop. In the silence the lieutenant's voice rings across the square loud and clear. His finest moment. "Now die," he bellows, "all enemies of the Chief, of the State, and of the people!" Glaring at Sam, he slashes downward with his hand. A whistle blows, the drums thunder once again.

Sam pulls the lever with a hearty heave. The traps drop open. The bodies fall, out of sight. The three nooses hang in place, each ensnaring an empty black hood.

Sam the showman yanks off his mask, flashing a grin at the crowd, and leaps down through the nearest trapdoor. From below comes the clatter of a Volkswagen engine cranking itself into action. The sergeant of the guard detail runs forward, drawing his pistol, and aims at something below the stage. Before he can fire he is cut down by a burst from the automatic rifle of a soldier—Garcia by name—stepping forward from the front rank of Company C.—Charlie Company. Lieutenant Myers, running toward the canvas skirts of the platform, his pistol drawn also, stops for a moment to shoot at Private Garcia. Misses; Garcia disappears into the crowd. The engine of a Harley-Davidson roars into life. A red VW Beetle pops through the canvas and races across the empty side of the square, around the milling troops, and down the avenue toward the east.

As Myers, Roland, and other officers run beneath the stage they are blown out again, uninjured but confused, by a gorgeous purple explosion of smoke and flame. From the midst of this sepia cloud emerges a helmeted fellow on a motorcycle, clinging desperately to the handlebars, crouching low in the saddle, who speeds off with thrashing pistons into the smoky haze of the south. Taking the third corner on the left, he flees the random ricochet of gunfire. Other soldiers, some kneeling, some standing, blaze away at the vanishing Volkswagen, missing their target but wounding a few innocent bystanders who have begun to run, too late, for the shelter of the buildings.

Lieutenant Myers, crouching in combat posture deep in a cloud of lavender smoke, reholsters his automatic and draws the Motorola Handi-Talkie instead. He radios a message to Sergeant Brock and the motorcycle patrol:

"Cougar three-one, Cougar three-one, ten thirty-three, ten thirty-three . . ."

Above the square, over the fading smoke and noise, the ravens flap in circles, squawking in dismay, disgruntled, disappointed, disgusted.

Higher still the Chief—princely in his dignity—puts down field glasses and picks up his riding whip. Smiling a thin smile, without pleasure, he flings it into the air, toward the empty gallows. Colonel Barnes, standing near the wall telephone, observes this demonstration of pique without expression. "Well, Colonel," says the Chief, turning toward him, "are you satisfied? Your children have escaped."

"Brock will find them, I suppose."

"Yes he will. Does that disturb you?"

Barnes is silent for a moment, then says, "I don't think it's necessary, sir, to *exterminate* our enemies. I think we should allow some of them to live."

"You're still annoyed."

"Yes sir."

"Well . . ." The Chief hesitates. "Perhaps I was wrong. Perhaps I made a mistake." He touches his throat, blue-black and bruised, and smiles. "The provocation, you must admit, was extreme. No?" He slaps Barnes on the upper arm. "Come on, my friend, let's go down to dinner. Our so-called officer corps is waiting for us. Some of them have got some difficult explanations to make. Nothing like a failed hanging to whet a man's appetite. Right, Colonel?"

The whip drops in the dust a few feet from Barbara. She crawls deeper into the shadows under the gallows, behind the canvas, and waits for night.

Dixie Dalton clutches the wheel, swerving the VW at top speed in a slalom course through obstacles of junk and debris, wrecked cars, broken glass, billboards toppled across the street. The left wing window, open, is starred with a fresh bullethole. "How're we doing, how're we doing?" she yells.

Far ahead, miles beyond, the desert mountains stand—jagged crags, crumbling talus slopes, the peaks of rosy andesite and iron, all aglow in the sundown light.

"You done great, Dixie, great," the old man says, still struggling with his bonds. "Can one of you boys back there get this thing off me?"

Rodack, in the back seat, his hands freed by Art beside him, gropes between the front seats and fumbles with the straps around Jack Burns' wrists. "Yes, you're doing fine." He glances through the rear window. "No pursuit yet," he croaks.

"Let me out," says Art.

"Keep going," Burns says. "Got to get to them mountains before the troopers come."

"Stop the car," demands Art.

Dixie hangs tightly to the wheel, eyes intent on the streets ahead. She swerves suddenly, barely missing a 1984 Buick (last of the line) parked on four flat tires in the middle of the roadway. "Anybody see Sam yet?" she yells, correcting, as her three passengers are flung back in their seats.

Art grips Dixie's slender shoulders. "Stop," he says, "I want out. We forgot her."

"No sign of him yet," the professor says, peering back. "No motorcycles yet. Thank God."

"Any firearm in here?" Burns asks, rummaging through the glove box. "Under the seat?"

"Any what?"

"Firearm. Pistol. Gun."

"No. Afraid not."

"Barbara!" cries Art.

They are flashing past *Ace Tire Company, Valley National Bank, Sambo's, Hobo Joe's, Big Boy's, Circle K, Whattaburger, Pizza Hut, Holiday Inn* (never a holiday, never an inn), *U-Tote-Em, Qwik Mart, Bashaw's, Safeway, Texaco, Gulf, Shamrock—*

"Barbara!" howls Art. "Barbara! We forgot Barbara!"

"Who's that?" Dixie says.

"He's right," Rodack says. "We forgot poor Barbara."

Dixie lets the car slow down, glances anxiously at Jack Burns. He shakes his head. "We shouldn't do it," he says. "We shouldn't do it. There's a thousand them soldiers back there, mad as hornets. But—turn around."

"No," Rodack says, "stop. Let us out. Me and Art. We're going back anyway. Let us out, Dixie. We'll find her. Then you and Jack go on."

Dixie slows the car, does a broad U turn, and stops, uncertain what to do. Art opens the front door beside Dixie and thrusts his way out. "I'll find her," he says, "you all go on."

"Wait," croaks Rodack.

They argue desperately, frantically, screaming at one another, Art with his head in the little window, the other three jammed inside. From back in the city, off in the golden haze but rising, comes the sound of a motorcycle. Or of many motorcycles.

"We've got to split up," Rodack says. "Better that way. Join us later. We'll be in the old—" He leans close to Dixie and whispers in her ear. She nods. "Now let me out." And he wriggles out on the passenger's side, struggling through the tight passage.

Before he can get clear a lone motorcyclist appears, racing toward them. The red lights blink: once, twice, a third time.

"That's Sam," Dixie says. "That's the signal."

The Indian comes roaring up on his stolen Harley, nearly collides with the VW, skids, falls, stalls the engine. "Damn," he grumbles, getting to his feet. "Damn. Never could manage these things." He becomes aware of the others gaping at him. "Hey, you're going the wrong way." He jerks a thumb over his shoulder. "They're coming. Whole damn motorcycle squad. Let's get out of here."

"Give me that thing." Art lifts the massive bike, straddles the seat, kick-starts the motor. The engine thunders, the machine trembles. "Come on, Professor, climb on. Hurry up! Hurry up!"

Rodack gets onto the rear of the buddy seat, finds the foot rests, wraps his arms around the boy's waist. Without taking further time for hail and farewell, Art guns the engine, engages the clutch, and hurtles off, bearing north up a side street. Red sparks flower from the tailpipe. Art and Rodack fade away under a row of dead and dying eucalyptus trees, through lifeless intersections under bankrupt traffic lights into the gridiron of the tracts.

As the sound of Art's steel horse dwindles to an abstract point, the roar of official motorcycles expands from another direction like the bloom of doom. Sam Banyaca peers down the avenue, shielding his eyes against the setting sun, into the murk of dust, smoke, radiant gold. The sun is setting exactly behind the Tower, a black monolith against the light; the shadow of the Tower falls across the city and into the desert, lengthening eastward.

"Hide the car," shouts Sam; "we'll never outrun them."

Dixie drives the VW onto the sidewalk, through a plate-glass window, and into the showroom of *Abbott Rents: Party & Sickroom Supplies.* Crouching behind wheelchairs, hospital beds, stainless-steel bedpans, and movable screens, they watch half of Sergeant Brock's patrol rumble past at moderate speed, searching, not pursuing. Four men in black uniforms and black goggles, silver helmets adorned with painted flames; red guidons flutter from the handlebars. At the next street intersection the patrol divides again, two going south and two going north. The throbbing motors diminish in the distance.

"Brock's not with them," Dixie says.

"You sure?"

"I'm sure," she says.

"Let's go," says the old man. "Back to my country. Get outa this here devils' country."

"Let's wait for sundown," Sam advises.

They wait. The shadows grow, the sun goes down at last, the cooling begins at once. Around them they hear the ticking, popping, crackling of contracting metal and wood and plastic. The birds, snakes, ground squirrels, coyotes, and foxes begin to creep from hiding places.

No sign or sound of motorcycle. "Let's head for the mountains," Burns says. "Up where a man can breathe."

They get back in the VW and putter toward the east, this time avoiding the broad avenue that becomes, a few miles farther on, the highway to Kansas City and points beyond.

"We could go back to my place," Dixie suggests. "Hide

there tonight." She pokes Sam in the ribs with her elbow. "Hide in comfort, under the covers."

"Exactly where Brock will be waiting for us," Sam suggests. "With his little Apache and his big guns."

"Which happens to be exactly what we need," says Burns from the back seat. "Some weapons. Equalizers. Feel naked as a skinned rabbit without my old cannon."

They drive through the twilight, no lights on. The last radiations of the sun flare on rimrock, on the craggy mountain that rises like a wall, like an altar, like a monumental flatiron, beyond the fringes of the suburbs. They roll through trailerhouse slums and mobile-home barrios where once upon a time, only a decade before, the old folks had come from Wisconsin and Minnesota and Saskatchewan to eke out their golden years in sunshine and peace, eating Purina Dog Chow for breakfast, Fritos for lunch, Holsum Bread and Skippy peanut butter for supper.

"My place is only a mile from here," says Dixie. "We could take a quick look. Maybe Glenn's still there."

"Better not chance it," Sam says. "How much gas in this thing?"

"There's no gauge. It's one of those old ones. The kind that runs forever. Which way then?"

"Not without gas. Which way? Well, yes—which way. Anyway but the highway, I guess."

"Horses," says Burns. "We need guns and horses. Where's your pinto, Sam?"

"Where's your Rosie?"

The old man squints out through the windows, to the left, to the right, fidgeting in the cramped back seat. "Where's Rosie?" he mutters. Nearly forgot her. Growing sentimental and semisenile, he thinks, worrying about a horse. "Where's my Rosie? I wish I knew. But I'd reckon she's well on the way home by now. Yonder somewheres." He jabs his hairy trigger finger over Dixie's shoulder and toward the cactus-covered slopes northeast of the mountain. "Who's that?" he says.

"Where?"

"Right over there."

Two men on motorcycles, waiting in the gloom beneath a shaggy mesquite tree, watch them drive by. A big man with a handlebar mustache and a little man with a scar across his nose. The big man grins as they go by, waves, and leans down to clear the carburetor valve on his black, bright Harley '95.

"My God, that was Brock!" says Dixie as she presses hard on the puny throttle pedal of her VW '59. Patiently, slowly, the car accelerates; gradually it achieves maximum cruising speed. "Which way?" Dixie cries. "Did he see us?"

"Dirt road," says Sam. "Take the first dirt road you see." He leans out his window, looking back. "Yes," he adds. "They saw us."

The motorcycles are coming up fast, easily, gaining without effort. The white grin of Sergeant Brock grows bigger by the second, and the Apache is at his side. Sam fumbles in his baggy sergeant's shirt and pulls out another smoke bomb, yanks the pin, and drops the canister on the road. Brock and Mangus Colorado are immediately engulfed in a violet cloud. Sparks glitter deep in the smoke as one motorcycle goes down. But the other comes through, delayed but upright; on the seat is Sergeant Brock.

Dixie veers to the left, up a rutted rocky dirt track. The car jolts, bounces, rattles with pain, loose and hurt in every seam and weld. Brock follows, reckless, eager, his big bike leaping over ruts and stones. "Goddamn but we need a gun," the old man groans, "we need a gun."

Sam throws out another smoke bomb. Brock disappears in a rich purple fog. "That's it," Sam says. "No more magic." Brock loses ground for a time but soon re-emerges from obscurity, still grinning, gunning his motor as he gears down into low.

"Think of something, Sam."

"I'm trying. I'm trying to think."

The VW chugs up a very steep pitch in the trail, almost stalling. Ahead and far above stand the volcanic cliffs of the mountain. On both sides is the dense forest of saguaro, prickly pear, barrel cactus, and the lush luxuriant spine-covered cholla, shining and poisonous.

"All right," Sam says, "I've got a plan." He glances to the rear again; the enemy follows, keeping up but not gaining. Brock's huge road machine was never meant for Jeep trails. The VW bangs its bottom but keeps going, up the rocky grade. "We're going to get out of this thing," says Sam, "and let it roll back on Sergeant Brock. Then we run for that boulder gulch up in there," pointing upward to a dark gash in the mountain wall. "Ready? Me and Jack first, Dixie, then you. Okay? Keep your foot on the brake, leave it in neutral."

"Yes, yes, I know." Dixie stops the car, letting the engine idle. Sam gets out, followed by Burns from the back. Dixie slides out quickly, releasing the brake.

Both doors open wide like wings, the old car starts rolling backward. A hundred yards below Brock stops his motorcycle to watch. The VW coasts ten feet before the front wheels turn, swinging the car to one side and into the cactus lining the road. The doors slam shut. The car rolls one quarter over and stops, propped on a shrub. Engine running.

"I knew it wouldn't work," Dixie says.

Brock gets off his motorcycle, smiling up at the three fugitives, and unslings his M-16. He levels it at them.

"Melt his gun, Sam."

"He's too far away. It won't work."

"All right, folks," Brock shouts. "Come on down. Hands behind your heads."

"Let's run," Dixie says. "Into the brush."

"Wait," says Sam.

The shrub—a small jojoba bush—suddenly yields beneath the weight of the VW. The car rolls on its back, rolls over again, and once again. It gains momentum, motor still alive, and keeps rolling, directly down the trail toward Brock. Gasoline dribbles from a ruptured fuel line; the rear of the car bursts into a gorgeous yellow bloom of flame.

"Now," says Sam.

They plunge into the shadowy depths of the cactus forest, Sam leading the way in diagonal traverse up the slope at the base of the cliffs. A burst of gunfire stutters below: erratic bullets, hollow-point dumdums, whine past their heads. Sparks fly as metal strikes stone, releasing the odor of flint, saltpeter, gypsum.

"Anybody hurt?"

"Not me."

"Keep going," the old man says, bringing up the rear. "He's coming."

Moonlight and twilight. Stumbling, panting, sweating, they scramble up the steep slope, reach the mouth of the gulch that Sam is headed for, and climb into a jumble of gigantic boulders, the debris of centuries fallen from the mountain wall. Loose stones clatter like broken glass beneath their feet.

Just inside the gulch, under an overhanging ledge, Sam startles a herd of bristling, piglike beasts. The animals panic, explode in all directions, rush among the rocks and down through the cactus on the slope. Snorting and grunting as they run. Which attracts another outburst from the man below, a barrage of automatic fire. A pig screams—one hit. They hear Brock's hearty laugh.

"What in God's name was that?"

"Brock?"

"No, those animals."

"Pigs," says Sam, "wild pigs. Peccaries."

"Keep going," Burns says. "Don't talk."

They work their way as fast as they are able up the gulch, climbing over, under, between the house-size boulders, over taluses of broken rock, through a jungle of vines, thorny acacia, cactus, and mesquite. The air is cooler in this ravine but not cool enough; the heat is dense and oppressive. Silent now, they keep moving upward, encouraged by the noise, not far below, of another animal, armed and patient, bulky and booted and vengeful, crashing through the brush.

Twilight is brief in the desert. Rapidly the evening becomes night, promising secure and sheltering darkness. But the new moon, half full, a waxing shield of silver, glows through a scatter of clouds, balefully bright.

Sam keeps to the shadows. The other two follow as close as they can, though the old man is losing ground. Sam and Dixie pause at the summit of a boulder to let him catch up. The three lean together, panting for breath, wiping sweat from their eyes.

"You two . . . go on," Burns whispers in gasps. "I'll wait here . . . ambush the bastard. . . ."

"With what?" says Dixie.

Burns peers around for a weapon. "I'll . . . brain him . . . with a rock. . . ."

"Naw," says Sam, "not a chance. We best stick together."

"We got . . . no gun. . . ."

Sam pats the big knife on his hip.

"No good . . . not good enough. . . ."

Loose rock clatters below, followed by the sound of a curse. They peer through the gloom but cannot see their pursuer—only a vague moon-spangled complexity of slab-sided rocks, cliff face, the tangled brush, a few great saguaros standing forty feet above the ground. Sergeant Brock, judging by the noise, is somewhere in the darkness of the gulch. Taking his time. He has lots of time. Figuring he's got all night, thinks Dixie, to pick us off, one by one. Or better yet, capture a couple of us alive. She shudders.

"We better get higher," Sam says. "The higher the better."

That seems to make sense, although no one asks why. They go on, climbing, scrambling, pushing their way through the hostile brush. Everything that grows in here seems armed with spines, thorns, needles, stickers, burrs, hooks. They struggle on despite resistance, upward, upward.

"God," says Dixie, "they got me." She stops.

"Who's got you?"

She shows her left arm to Sam. The arm is stuck with a

cluster of silvery cholla stems, detached in joints from the cactus. Sam breaks a stick in two, making tongs; one by one he tugs the evil things away; not easy; they cling with barbs to shirtsleeve and the skin beneath. With each removal Dixie makes a gasp.

Jack Burns comes up slowly, joins them. Blowing too hard to talk, he watches the operation, then turns to stare down into the blackness of the ravine. Half bending, big hands on his knees, he sucks in air with heavy gulps.

A shout from below. "Mangus! Mangus! This way . . ." Brock's voice.

"He's bluffing," Burns says. "Mangus ain't nowheres down in there. We dumped that one for good."

"You certain?"

"Pretty certain. Well, we never did see another motorcycle coming up the road now, did we."

"Maybe he's worried," Dixie says. "I know that ape. He's finally realized there's three of us and only one of him." She plucks tiny needles from her arm.

"But he's got the guns," says Burns. "And he knows we ain't. That's the difference."

Brock calls again for his partner. But his listeners above hear no answer. Sam gazes upward into the shadows of the gulch and at the sedimentary walls towering high on either side —one in moonlight, one in darkness. Unscalable. "We have to go higher," he whispers.

"Sam old buddy," Burns says, "you two're gonna have to go on without me. I am beat."

"No you're not."

"I am beat. I'll wait here for Brock. Tear the son-of-a-bitch's head off with my bare hands."

"You wouldn't have a chance."

"I know it. But I'll try."

"Then we'll all wait here," Dixie says.

"That's right," Sam says. "We'll stick together this time. Maybe we can get him. Somehow. But look,"— the Indian gestures to the cliffs—"if we could get another hundred feet higher, there's a ledge going along the cliff; we might be able to get across up there, go down the other side, get around Brock, go back down the hill, get the VW—"

"That car's finished," Dixie says. "Look—you can still see the fire." She points to a dim glow of flame far down the foot of the mountain.

"Get a motorcycle, I mean," Sam concludes, "and take off."

"We'll need two motorcycles."

"A horse," says Burns. "That's what we need." He looks up at the cliffs. "All right, let's go."

They resume the climb. Dixie takes more care to avoid the cholla. Her arm aches from the venomous spines. Sam pauses for a moment to pass her some small round nuts he has gathered on the way. "Eat," he says. "Good. Jojobas—like hazelnuts."

Panting for breath, Dixie eats one. And then another. "Bitter hazelnuts," she says. "What I really need is water."

Sam shrugs, climbing on. Water: They all crave water. But even more, they crave safety. Escape. And rest. Exhaustion weighs upon them as heavily as fear. Looking up, they can see that the gulch goes on and on, for hundreds of feet, for a thousand feet, toward the impossibly remote rimrock of the mountain. Too much, too far. But they struggle on, up and on.

Sam stops beneath a boulder, digging with his fingers in a sandy basin. The sand is wet. He puts a handful of sand in his mouth and sucks the moisture from it. Dixie joins him, doing the same. They listen for Burns, somewhere behind. Finally he arrives, wrinkled face gleaming in sweat, glass eye glinting, and his good eye dull with fatigue. Stopping to blow, like a winded mule, he looks back and down.

"Can't hear him," he says. "Can't see the . . . goddamn . . . evil bastard. . . ."

"Maybe he quit," says Sam.

Dixie says, "Not Brock. He never quits. He's insane."

"Anyhow," says Sam, "we can't stay here. This is a trap. "We've got to go out on that ledge, get around the cliff."

The old man kneels down with them, digs the hole deeper, waits for a minute to let the moisture drip forth, then scoops a handful of wet sand into his mouth. They sit there, waiting, resting. Burns spits out the sand, takes more. "Somewhere up above," he says, "there might be a seep." The taste of the wet sand in his mouth stirs ancient memories. I've been here before, he thinks, or a place just like it. He remembers old pursuits, old escapes, old times, and smiles an idiotic, half-toothed, useless smile. Last time, he thinks, I swear. Gettin' too old and stove-up for this kind of game. Ain't no fun no more. Old age takes all the fun out of trouble. Like they took all the fun out of war with their goddamn *atom* bombs. "Where's that ledge?" he says. "Let's get out of here."

Sam points to the stone cliff nearby. "Over there," he says. "There's a fault in the rock here."

"Well we can't go out there in the open moonlight. Brock'll spot us for sure."

"We go the other way. Into the shade."

They rise and grope through more brush to the dark wall. Sam with his cat eyes keeps the lead. Dixie in the middle, Burns guarding the rear. Sam steps out on the ledge, a bench of rock two feet wide, leading horizontally across the face of the mountain wall. He holds out his hand for Dixie; she takes it and steps in close, pressing against him. "I hate heights," she says.

"Not all heights."

"What?"

"Heights of passion?"

"Come on, Sam, no jokes. Where does this thing go?"

"Around the cliff, I hope, and an easy way down. But I don't promise anything."

The old man catches up. "What're we waitin' for?" he whispers. "The animal's still coming."

They listen intently and hear, down in the darkness of the black ravine, the sound of a man laughing, singing, forcing his way through the crackling brush. The sound is tricky, hard to locate; Brock might be fifty yards or five hundred yards below. But he sounds confident. Singing,

What a friend we have in Jesus
All our sins and griefs
to bear. . . .

"Gimme your knife, Sam," Burns says. "Three of us running from that lone son-of-a-whore. It's humiliating. Gimme your knife, I'm gonna lay for him."

"No," says Sam, "come on." His dark form moves forward, straight toward the stars now appearing over the northwest horizon. The new moon waits somewhere around a corner, sinking toward the Pacific sea. Dixie follows, afraid to look down, fingers of her right hand hooked in Sam's hip pocket.

Old Jack Burns waits for another moment, squinting with his monocular vision into the gloom below. "Can't be sure," he mutters, "but I think there's two of them." He looks up, sees the faint shapes of his friends fading into darkness before him. He follows—very carefully, keeping one hand against the cliff face for support, watching for loose material underfoot. His sense of balance has never been good since losing that left eye.

The ledge narrows, tapers to a six-inch point. Beyond a two-foot gap the rock crops out again, providing a pathway. The drop off from the gap seems vertical; looking down into it, Sam cannot see the bottom. "Step carefully," he says, stepping across.

"Sam, I don't like this. . . ."

"Grab my wrist." He takes her wrist and helps her across. The old man follows. They go on. The ledge continues, here a bit wider, grading gently upward. They round a corner of the cliff and gain a broader view of the world below. The moon, low in the west, shines on their path. Sam looks for a way down but can see none. They are stepping along an eyebrow of the mountain wall, with near-perpendicular pitches above and below. He sees no footholds or handholds in the sheer, smooth, volcanic stone. Down there in the moonlight, hard to estimate how far, is the foot of the cliff, with a talus slope of loose rock and gravel resting against it. The slope is overgrown with stands of *Opuntia bigelovii*—teddy-bear cholla. They go on, creeping forward on a thin tilted scarp of andesite that may, or may not, lead to safety.

It does not. Beyond the next corner the ledge comes to an end, pinching out to nothing on the face of the wall. Here there is no gap to step across; beyond lies only the vacancy of space.

"Well," Sam murmurs.

Dixie shivers, trembling against him. "I can't bear this. Sam, I can't bear this place."

He puts his arms around her, holding her tightly. "It's all right, we're all right. Don't worry." He runs his fingers through her curly hair, kisses her cheeks, her lips. "We'll get down yet. . . ."

Burns appears, softly swearing, crouching, clutching at the wall with both hands and looking over the edge on his right. He bumps into Dixie and Sam. "Christ . . ."

"Don't push. No jostling here," says Sam.

The old man looks over Sam's shoulder. "Yeah . . . we're there, ain't we?"

Sam nods. "I guessed wrong."

Whispering, more from habit than caution, they discuss their situation, and decide to return a short distance to a wider part of the ledge, where there is at least room enough for all three to sit and attempt to rest. To regain some nerve. Even Sam the insouciant is feeling shaky at this point. They creep back to the wide place on the ledge and reach it as the moon goes down. In what seems at first like complete darkness they sit on the cool stone and dust, the three of them huddled tightly together for comfort, warmth, and lack of any alternative.

A meteor streaks across the western sky, trailing blue flame. A coyote barks to the north and is answered, after a while, by another to the south. Otherwise, all is still. No sound of Sergeant Brock.

"Now what?" says Sam.

"You're the leader."

"You're the boss."

"Well," Burns says, long legs dangling over the verge of the precipice, "looks like we got three easy choices: We can jump off here and get killed. We can go back the way we came and get killed. Or we can sit right here and enjoy ourselves."

"All night long?"

"All night long."

"And get killed in the morning."

"That's right."

"You two are not very funny," Dixie says. "Not funny at all and anyway I want to try to sleep for a minute. So please shut up. Okay?"

They shut up, staring westward at the dim and scattered lights of the far-off city, a few burning buildings, nothing more. Dixie falls asleep in Sam's enfolding arm. She shakes and twitches from time to time, having bad dreams. Sam's head lowers, his eyes close. Only Jack Burns remains awake, aided by an old man's insomnia and the guilt and pleasure of his memories. Dixie sighs. Sam snores, gently, peacefully. The old man listens and keeps listening.

The night is full of little noises.

The sky begins to pale above the skyline. One by one the stars drop out, the brief vernal night blends with the hour into dawn. Some birds, perched like sentries on the tall saguaro, raise timid questions on the air. Things stir in the gloom: Nocturnal creatures returning to their holes.

Or leaving them. Sam is awakened by the noise, more felt than heard, of something heavy crawling over stone. The Gila monster? A dying javelina? The obscure nightmare of an unretrievable dream come horribly to daylight life? Impossible. Sam is a witch doctor, a wizard—he knows better than to trust in the ghosts that haunt the human mind. He glances aside at Dixie and Jack. Both asleep.

Sam hears the noise again, but cannot determine its source.

Gently disengaging himself from the girl, he looks over the brink of the ledge. Down below, things begin to assume their daylight identities, transient but less ambiguous than those of night. He sees the talus slope—not so far down as he had thought last night—and its forest of frosty-needled cholla; slabs and blocks of andesite protruding from the gravel; the humanoid saguaros, the mesquite trees, the waving whips of the ocotillo.

He looks left and right, to where the cliff curves out of sight in either direction. Miles of desert lie below, stretching north toward higher mountains, south toward the barren hills and hogbacks of Arizona. To the west the city still waits, for deliverance, under its haze of smoke and dust.

A trickle of dirt falls on his shoulder. Sam looks where he should have looked in the first place, above, at the crest of the wall above his head. He sees the dawning sky, streaked with salmon-colored vapors. The black *V*-canted wings of vultures circling at a dizzy altitude. And a dark face, scarred, unsmiling, closing on a yawn.

Mangus Colorado in his black uniform squats on the next ledge up, only twenty feet away, looking down at Sam Banyaca and his dozing friends. Mangus holds a rifle in his hands, finger on the trigger, the rifle aimed at Sam. The sun rises behind his head, giving the Apache a corona of blinding gold.

Burns stirs, opening his eyes. "What's wrong, Sam?" But following the direction of Sam's eyes he sees at once what is wrong. Cautiously, Burns draws his legs back from the dropoff and starts to try to stand up.

"No, no, stay right there." Another voice: Sergeant Brock has appeared, coming around the turn of the ledge. "Relax, relax." One hand on the rock wall, the M-16 slung across his back, and a .45 automatic holstered on his hip, the sergeant is genial with self-assurance. He stops ten feet from the half-kneeling Jack Burns. "Good morning, good morning, good morning. Everybody awake?" He draws the pistol, jacks a round into the firing chamber. Avoiding the eyes of Sam Banyaca, he says, "Well—it's been a long night." He sighs, revealing weariness, and glances up, into the sun, toward the squatting Apache. "That you, asshole? Sure took you long enough to get there. Keep your eyes on this Hopi; if he makes one funny move blast him away."

Dixie Dalton is wide awake, curled on the ledge between her two men, both of them on their knees. She stares with fear, with hatred, with contempt, at the smiling Sergeant Brock.

Back pressed against the wall, not much room for maneuver, Brock stares at her over his shoulder, across the sights of the pistol. "My Dixie darling," he says. "My little whore. Have a nice night here? Lots of good screwing, eh? This old man too?"

None of the three makes a move. Dixie says, "Why don't you shoot, you coward?"

Brock smiles. "Now, now, what's the hurry? Relax."

From above, the Apache echoes the lady's sentiment. "Let's kill them, Sarge, and go home. It's gettin' hot."

"You keep your ugly face shut," Brock replies. "You stinking, louse-bitten, ignorant aborigine. If you'd not been so goddamned slow we could've caught them last night."

The Apache scowls but says nothing.

Brock continues: "I been on this project a long time and now I'm going to enjoy myself. We got all day. There's no hurry, Mangus. You'll get some fun out of it too. You'll get your turn. Just keep a bead on that fat-bellied Hopi." He returns his attention to the three crouching before him on the ledge. He wipes a drop of sweat from his eyebrow and reassumes, under the big mustache, his broad and handsome smile. "The question is how to get you three down off of here. Find some place where we can be comfortable."

"Shoot the men, Sarge," the Apache says. "They're no good for anything. Then we take the girl down."

"No, I want them to watch," Brock says, keeping his eyes on Burns' face, on Sam's hands. "Can you get down from where you are, Mangus?"

"No way, Sarge, no way."

"No?" Brock considers the problem. "All right. Let's see."

He focuses for the moment on Dixie Dalton. "Sweetheart, take their belts off and strap their hands."

Dixie stares back at him. "Go to hell."

"I'll blast you."

"Go ahead and blast me."

Brock's flashy grin weakens a bit. "So that's the way it is? Suicide? No, that's too easy." Brock aims his gun at Burns' head. "Look at it this way, Dixie. Do what I say or I blow your friend's head off."

The girl hesitates. "Let him shoot," Burns says. "Then claw his eyes out."

"I'm squeezing the trigger," Brock says.

"Wait," says Dixie. "Wait. I'll do it." She rises, unbuckles the old man's belt, starts to bind his wrists with it.

"Behind his back."

"All right. Behind the back. All right." She does as commanded, but not very well. Burns can feel plenty of give in his bonds.

"Now your little pimp of an aborigine boyfriend," Brock orders.

Dixie removes Sam's belt; the knife in its sheath dangles from the belt. She pulls the sheath from the belt. Brock watches closely. "Throw that knife over here," he says. She starts to remove the knife. "Leave it in the case!" Brock snaps. "Throw the whole thing. Throw it easy. Underhanded." Dixie obeys, tossing it gently in front of Burns toward Brock's feet. The sheath bounces on the stone; the knife slides out, free of the leather. The naked blade glitters in the light, reflecting the rays of the sun into Brock's face. He bends to reach for it.

"Brock!" cries Sam the shaman in a fierce and thrilling tone —like the cry of a hawk. The sergeant hesitates, glancing at the Indian. For a moment their eyes meet and lock. Brock laughs, shakes his head, blinks, and reaches—he can't help it—for the knife. For the knife. But there is no knife.

Instead, there is the snake. A diamondback rattlesnake, thick as a man's wrist, coiled like a rope, the coontail buzzing and the head—shaped like the ace of spades—whipping back and striking forward faster than the eye can follow.

Brock gasps, staggers, the snake hanging from his forearm, fangs sunk in his flesh. He strikes at the wriggling thing with his pistol but the snake, coiling around his arm, clings like a leech. Brock drops the pistol and tries to tear the snake from his arm with his free hand. As he does so, a slab of rock gives way beneath his feet—a grumble of stone, yielding to gravity after a thousand years of hesitation. Brock slides, slides, begins to fall.

The others catch a glimpse of his amazed eyes, his flying hair, as he goes down. Flailing out with both hands, grabbing at the mountain wall with fingers like iron claws, he succeeds, at the last possible moment, in finding a notch in the stone with his right hand, a crevice with his left. He clings, safe for the moment.

He hangs there, fingers locked on the brink of the ledge, head and body below, and feels about with his feet for a foothold, a toehold, that will enable him to support himself, climb back to safety. He finds nothing. He hangs by his fingers.

The rattlesnake has disappeared. Sam's knife lays where it stopped, on the surface of the ledge, shining. But the fang marks on Brock's hairy forearm, twin stigmata oozing drops of dark blood, are real.

From above comes the sound of choked laughter. Trying hard not to, Mangus Colorado cannot help himself; pointing his rifle at Sergeant Brock in his ridiculous desperation, the Apache snuffles and giggles, tears welling in his eyes.

Brock stops grunting and struggling for a moment. Looking up into the sun, he snarls at his corporal. "Mangus, get down here. Help me, damn you, help me."

The Apache cannot stop laughing. Standing for a better look at Brock, leaning forward, hands on knees, tears pouring down his scarred cheeks, he laughs so hard he seems about to strangle. Brock makes a heroic effort, pulls himself up by his fingertips, gets one elbow on the ledge, his head into view. Burns steps forward, puts his foot on Brock's head, and pushes him down again. The Apache shrieks with laughter.

"Mangus," says Sam, staring at him, "look at me!"

Abruptly, the Apache stops laughing, looks down at Sam. Nervously he brings his rifle into play, the black hole directed at Sam. Licking his lips, fascinated, he watches Sam's eyes. Sam speaks to the Apache in Athabascan, a Chiricahua dialect, gently and smoothly and at considerable length. The Apache listens with total concentration, eyes fixed on Sam's face. Sam extends his arms and makes flapping winglike motions. The Apache asks a shy question. Sam nods in agreement. Beginning to smile with pride and happiness, the Apache asks another question. Sam answers with encouraging words.

The Apache straightens himself, standing as tall as he can. He slings his rifle across his back. He extends his arms full length, out from his body on either side. He lifts them tentatively up and down, testing the air currents. Once again he asks Sam a question. Sam nods and offers firm reassurance. Smiling, waving his arms with ease, the Apache makes little birdlike steps to the edge of the rock. He raises his eyes to the horizon. He seems to be gazing not so much outward as inward, sensing the power and the courage grow within his heart. He crouches.

Gently, Sam utters a command.

With a cry of joy Mangus Colorado springs into space, waving his wings. Sailing upward, outward, and down in graceful parabola, he waves them harder and begins to run, as falling humans always do, in the air. As he disappears from view the others hear the swift modulation of his exultance into a waning, Döpplerian howl of despair. Despair cut short, after a moment of silence, by a definitive crash from below, succeeded by the noise of a body bouncing through cactus. Then another, farther, terminal impact.

Sam the shaman shrugs, averting his eyes from the spectacle of failure. "Apaches," he murmurs, by way of explanation. No one present has the stomach to look down except Sergeant Brock, hanging by his fingertips, who finds in the record-breaking descent of his partner the last moments of satisfaction he will ever know.

Afterward . . .

Afterward, they rest for a few minutes before beginning the return traverse along the ledge. Jack Burns, unbound, holds Brock's rifle in his hand, its sling cut through and useless. Brock's automatic rests in Burns' belt. Neither Sam nor Dixie will accept either weapon. The three stare over the edge of the dropoff at the body of Sergeant Brock, two hundred feet below, fetched up against the trunk of a saguaro. Leading down the slope toward Brock is a trail of smashed cholla, marking the path of his descent. Brock's body is furred over, like a porcupine's, with silvery spines; his black uniform, torn and bloodied, can hardly be seen.

Dixie weeps quietly.

Sam wipes the blood and tiny chips of bone from his knife onto the sleeve of his shirt and puts the knife away, back in its case. Burns stares down at the body of Brock and at that, much farther away, of the Apache. Watching closely, he sees a twitch of movement in Brock's body, one arm with its blood-smeared useless hand groping over the dust and gravel, feeling for something. Searching. The hand bristles with cactus needles. The old man, horrified, sucks in his breath.

Sam and Dixie see that movement too. "Oh good God," moans Dixie, "he's not still alive?"

Sam looks up, briefly, at the eyeless face of the sun. At a pair of vultures soaring on the sky. "He won't be for long."

Burns swears. He goes down on one knee, sets the M-16 on semi-automatic fire, and aims with care, left elbow propped on knee, at the inert, semihuman form of Sergeant Brock. He fires once, pauses to resteady his aim, and fires a second time. All can see the body jerk as the bullets strike.

Slowly, creaking at the joints, Burns rises. "Let's go," he says. Cradling the rifle in his left arm, like a hunter, holding with his right hand to the stony wall, he starts back the way they had come. Dixie Dalton watches the body of Brock for another minute; she wipes the tears and sweat from her face and follows. Last to leave is the Indian. Unobserved by his friends, watching their backs, he picks something up from a crevice under the ledge, eight small fleshy objects sticky with blood, and drops them into the beaded medicine pouch that hangs, hidden by the shirt, from his neck.

Later, as they work down through the brush of the ravine, stumbling with fatigue, the old man will draw Sam aside for a few minutes, away from Dixie, and ask, "Sam, how could you do a thing like that?"

Sam shrugs again. "Boss . . . I don't know."

"Dixie was shocked."

"I know." Sam avoids Burns' penetrating eye, looks away. "Maybe," he says, ". . . maybe I really am an Indian."

Burns stares at the Hopi's ageless, brown, wholesome, contented face. "How did it make you feel?"

Sam looks back at the old man, straight into the dark and questioning eye. Sam is not smiling. "Good," he says. "I feel good."

Nor does Burns smile. "That's what I wanted to hear." He claps a big hand on Sam's shoulder. "I feel the same way, partner. I'm glad you did it. And I'll even bet—" He stops.

"Yes?"

"That Brock liked it too. Wanted it that way."

Sam considers. "He died like a warrior."

"Yes . . ." Burns turns to look at the cliffs, the rim of the mountain. "The only good thing he could ever do, he finally did it." Another pause. "Well, we got the little ones, Sam. Or you did. Two of them, anyhow. But the big ones are still alive."

"That's the way it always goes, boss."

"Maybe it ain't too late to change that."

"You can. I'm going home."

"Going home, Sam?" Jack Burns smiles at his friend, hugs him around the shoulders. "Yeah, you should do that. It's about time for you."

"Come with us, boss."

"Us?" Burns looks surprised. "Who's this us?"

"Dixie is coming with me."

"Well I'll be damned. Well, I'll be goddamned." Burns and
the Indian look down through the boulders, trees, and cactus of
the gulch, at Dixie on her knees by a seep of water. "Good for
you, Sam. I'm mighty glad to hear that. That Dixie is one fine
woman."

They walk toward her, over the loose stones, under the
thorny branches of the mesquite. Far to the west in the forenoon
light, a plume of dust rises from the city.

"Come with us, Jack."

"Naw, Sam, you know I can't do that. I got my own place
to take care of. And besides—I ain't finished here. You know
what I mean."

"Do I? Listen, boss, I learned one thing at Harvard. There's
one thing wrong with always fighting for freedom, and justice,
and decency. And so forth."

Burns looks up at the blazing sky. "Only one thing? What's
that?"

"You almost always lose."

The old man laughs, reaches out, and squeezes Sam's near
arm. "Well, hellfire, Sam, what does that have to do with it?"

L‾‾

ate afternoon. Once again the sun descends toward the west. One more time the new moon sails high across the sublime, imperial, grandly indifferent blue of the desert sky. Once more, and once again, out of the past and into the unknown, an army departs from a ruined city to seek new adventures, more glorious conquests, greater disasters. Once more and once again, over and over and over again. Seen from the foothills of the mountains, a plume of dust signals the Army's movement, bearing east and northeast toward the high country. The glitter of arms reveals its character. The echo of drums, the bray of horns, announce its purpose. Once more, once again, always and always again.

Far in front of the main body rides a party of scouts,

mounted on good horses. A proud young lieutenant, flanked by two soldiers, rides the point. His other men are spread out, here in the plain, for half a mile on either side. Where the road enters the hills the scouts will converge on one another.

One mile behind the scouts appears the bulk of the Army, ten companies of cavalry, two thousand soldiers on horseback. There is no infantry, no men on foot. After the cavalry comes a herd of horses—fresh mounts—and a herd of cattle—fresh meat —kept together and driven forward by cowboys in uniform. The rear guard to this enormous procession is formed by a final troop of well-armed and mounted men.

Still in the city but preparing to leave is a motorized column —a few light tanks, a few armored cars, tanker trucks filled with gasoline and diesel fuel, and a fleet of 2½-ton supply trucks loaded with the dunnage, water, dried food, canned food, ammunition, tents, and other equipment required by an army on the march. The motorized column, starting now to move out, will swing past the cavalry and leapfrog ahead to the first night's camp.

This is the picture of the Chief's Army as seen by an eagle high on the air. From the point of view of spectators on the ground, a few furtive men and women lurking in the shadows of abandoned buildings in the suburbs, the array of power presents more detail.

Leading the grand parade is the color guard, six horsemen in battle dress bearing ensigns, guidons, and flags. The Chief's gold eagle on a field of scarlet; the red, blue, gold, and copper of the State of Arizona; and on the right and in the fore the red, white, and blue of the United States of America. Red for courage. White for loyalty. Blue for honor.

Next is the Chief himself, sitting easily and well on a great, lively, nervous Arabian gray. At his side but one deferential step behind is the colonel, riding a tall sorrel with golden mane. They both are dressed in field uniforms of desert khaki, the broadbrimmed campaign hats of cavalry troopers. The Chief, as usual, wears no insignia of rank. Each man carries a pistol strapped to his waist, a saber slung on the left.

After the Chief and the colonel rides the Chief's personal guard, one hundred of his finest soldiers mounted on their best horses. These men are armed with revolvers, sabers, carbines in saddle scabbards; in addition they carry lances—*lances!*—each with pennant fluttering below the bright, sharpened, steel point, held upright and catching the sunlight. An archaic touch, these lances, but impressive. The Chief's idea. A spear, he would say, is hurled at your enemy but a lance—ah, the lance!—is thrust into him. More intimidating. Most intimidating.

Behind the guard come the regulars, the working soldiers. Each company with its captain; each platoon with its lieutenant and staff sergeants; each squad with its sergeant and corporals. Some of the officers wear sabers; the men are armed with pistols, revolvers, carbines, automatic rifles. Mounted infantry rather than true cavalrymen. There is a heavy-weapons platoon attached to each company; these men and their pack mules carry machine guns, mortars, flamethrowers, and rocket launchers.

Near the middle of the long column, which extends for three miles as it emerges, at intervals, from the fringe of the city, is a military band. The musicians are the only men on foot. At the limits of the city they withdraw to the side of the highway, assembled in formation, and bray through their brasses and beat their drums as the remainder of the mounted troops pass by. One of the drummers is a small, wizened fellow with close-set eyes, a drooping nose, a ragged little gray beard on his chin. Like the others in the band he will be left behind to share the fate of the city.

The band plays "The American Emblem"—a bold, stirring anthem that rings out across the plain, audible and manifest from the rear of the column to its head. Even the Chief and the colonel, well beyond the city, can hear the faint music, remote but haunting, that ushers them toward the unknown East.

And as this army moves across the plain, toward the mountains, under the moon and through the long light of evening, one man comes to meet them. A single horseman, eluding the scouts, emerging from the shadows at the base of the cliffs, he rides at walking pace across the golden desert in a line that will intersect exactly with the vanguard of the column.

"Well Charles," says the Chief, "I'd say we got out of there in good order. Not a shot fired. Not one bomb thrown. Not even a jeer."

The colonel urges his horse closer to his Chief. "Too easy, sir. They were glad to see us go. Roland's the one who will catch it."

"He's expendable." Pause. "Of course we're all expendable —as individuals." His face shaded by the hat brim, eyes hidden behind opaque sunglasses, the Chief's smile is ambiguous. "Some more than others, of course. You don't mind if I call you Charles?"

"No sir."

"It's going to be a long march. We can be a little less formal now. With each other." The Chief sits straight in the saddle, as tall as a god can be. "Christ but it's good to be on our way at last." He swells his chest with a deep draft of the dusty air, gazing proudly ahead into the rose-and-purple sky of the East. "The greatest adventure, Charles, our greatest yet. And a clean departure." But an irritating recollection intervenes; the smile becomes a frown. "Although, I must say, I was annoyed by those damned flowers." Absorbed in his own thoughts, the colonel makes no reply. "The flowers, Charles," the Chief repeats.

"Flowers, sir?"

"Those brats with the flowers. Strewing flowers in our path. Someone put them up to that. A cowardly insult. Using children."

"Just kids, sir. They thought it was a parade."

"I suspect somebody with a Platonic sense of humor." The Chief falls silent, thinking of his enemies.

"You mean Rodack?"

"Don't mention that name, Colonel. Let's forget that name. Put it clear out of our minds. Brock will find those scum."

"Brock seems to have disappeared, sir."

The Chief looks sharply at Barnes. "Disappeared? Brock? No, I don't believe it."

The Colonel shrugs. "He never came back to headquarters. No word from him or of him for"—Barnes looks at his watch—"for about thirty hours."

"I can't believe it," the Chief murmurs, looking vexed again. "He's one of our best men."

In a soft but stubborn tone, as if speaking to himself, the colonel says, "We're better off without him."

"How so, Colonel?"

"Brock is a criminal."

The Chief smiles. "Now Charles, you're getting moralistic again. Of course Brock is a criminal. That's what makes him useful to us."

"He's a torturer."

Eyes fixed straight ahead, his back straight as a post, the Chief speaks coldly to his companion: "Sergeant Brock is not a gentleman, that's true. But try to understand something, Charles." The Chief hesitates, selecting his words with care, before turning on Barnes the full magnetic luster of his smile. "It's like this, my boy: An historical note: Without criminals and torturers like Sergeant Brock—there could be no gentlemen like us."

For a moment the Colonel stares at the blank, hidden eyes of his Chief, at the satisfied little smile. Then he looks away, murmuring, "That can't be true."

"But it is," the Chief says gaily. "You think I'm being cynical. Maybe so. But cynicism, my boy"—the Chief sounds happy again, delighted with his wit—"cynicism is the cutting edge of truth."

Two armored cars speed by on their left, racing forward over the paved highway. The cars are followed by four light tanks and a file of trucks. As the last truck diminishes ahead and the roar of engines dies away, the Chief says, "Where's the rest of our armor, Colonel?"

"Sir?"

"Where's the rest of our armor?"

"We had to leave the heavy stuff with Major Roland, sir. Don't have enough fuel to move them all. And if we don't find more fuel on the way we'll not get all of these beyond Kansas City."

"We'll find fuel."

"Roland will need the heavy tanks anyway, if he wants to hold the Tower." The Colonel is peering far ahead, at something distant, vague, improbable. He lifts his binoculars to his eyes.

"Ah yes, poor Roland. What do you see out there, Charles?"

"Well sir . . ." The Colonel's horse shies sideways, drops a pace behind; Barnes touches him with a spur, brings him prancing abreast of the Chief. "It's a rider, sir. One man." He looks through the glasses again. "He's in uniform. Must be one of the scouts. But he's coming this way. At a walk."

"The scouts should have radios."

"They do sir. Most of them. I don't know what this fellow is up to." The colonel lowers his binoculars, turns to the Chief. "With your permission sir—"

"Go ahead. Check him out."

Pleased, smiling with pleasure, Barnes spurs his horse, dashes past the flag bearers, and rides at a canter across the open desert to meet the approaching horseman. The Chief keeps his place in the column but turns to signal one of the lancers behind him. A captain answers the summons, saluting.

"Follow Colonel Barnes," the Chief orders. "Stay close behind him."

"Yes sir!" The captain salutes again and races off at a gallop, the red pennant streaming from his uplifted weapon.

Colonel Barnes intercepts the lone horseman a mile ahead and to the right of the vanguard of the Army. The rider makes an attempt to get around Barnes but his horse is no match for the quick and agile mount of the colonel. Cut off, stymied, the rider glares at the colonel, then advances closer, recognizing him. Both men halt their horses, a few paces apart, staring for a moment in silence. The captain comes riding up; at a signal from Barnes he stops some distance in the colonel's rear.

"Well," says the colonel, "it's you again."

The old man grins his yellow-toothed grin. "It's me, Charlie." His mismatched eyes shine in the western light; bareheaded, his tangled shock of white hair tosses in the breeze. Tobacco juice dribbles down his beard. Senile, thinks the colonel, and a madman, riding that scarecrow horse. How can this man be my father? Why should my father become like this?

"Where'd you get that uniform?" he demands.

Burns is wearing the khaki uniform borrowed from Sam, which Sam had obtained by dubious means. On the sleeves are the chevrons of a master sergeant—a hangman's grade. "This?" says the old man. "This soldier suit? Well—Sam found it."

"Who is Sam?"

The grin on Burns' face grows wider. "Your hangman-for-a-day, Charlie. Remember him?"

The colonel is silent for a few seconds. Then he says, "Why are you so eager to die, old man?"

Burns looks beyond his son's face, far past him, at the distant procession, the flags, the guard of honor, the slim small solitary man on the gray Arabian. "Charlie," he says, "I want to do the one decent thing that's left for me to do."

"You never did a decent thing in your life."

"That's your mother talking, Charlie. Not you. You got to know better than that."

"I can see what you are."

"I'm your father, Charlie. You're my son. There's nothing we can do about it." Nudging his gaunt mare a few steps closer, peering into the colonel's face, Burns says, "Come with me, Charlie. Let that evil bastard over there—let him go on without you. Let him disappear into the goddamn miserable dying cities where he wants to be. Where he came from. Where he belongs. Let him go, Charlie."

"Impossible."

"Let him go. We'll forget him. Let him go, son."

"No," the colonel says. Studying the one-eyed man before him, Barnes says, "I keep my promises."

The old man flushes with anger. "Don't say that, Charlie. You don't know what you're talking about. Don't say a thing like that."

"I know what I'm saying."

"Oh God, Charlie. Goddamn it all anyway, Charlie." Old Burns' voice breaks with anguish. The easy tears of age appear in his good eye. "Charlie," he goes on, "one last time: Come home. Come home with me."

"No, Jack."

"I'm your father."

"Not anymore."

"Call me—father. Dad." The old man grins again, through the tears trickling into the stubble of his beard. "Call me Paw. Pop, even. Something family-like. Just once. Just for the hell of it, Charlie, what the goddamn hell. Only this once."

The colonel hesitates. He says, "I can't. I can't."

Burns laughs, a laugh as harsh as a wolf's bark. "That's all right, Charlie. I can understand. You're a pitiless son-of-a-bitch but that's all right. I used to be that way myself. We know where you got it. Okay then, Charlie, I got to ask one more favor of you. Stand aside here, let me ride in and kill that other son-of-a-bitch." He pats the butt of the automatic in his belt. "Loaded and locked."

"You're insane."

"That man is poison, Charlie. He's a plague on the land."

"You are wrong. You are terribly wrong."

"Got to do the decent thing, Charlie. Got to kill that fella before he starts the old merry-go-round all over again."

"You're insane, old man."

"Never saner in my life. Him and me, we'll go down to hell together." Burns tries to jockey his horse around the colonel; the colonel again blocks his path. The captain watches closely, from ten paces away. "Let me by," says Burns.

"Never."

Burns draws the automatic, points it at his son, snapping off the safety. "Stand aside, Charlie."

The colonel draws his own pistol and aims it at the old man. "Go home, Jack."

They glare at each other across their gunsights.

The captain comes closer, his gleaming lancehead leveled straight ahead. With questioning eyes he watches his colonel. Take him? Shall I take him?

Burns saws his horse to the left, to the right. The other two block his way. The three horses, overexcited, rear, snort, trample the dust with agitated feet. The dust rises and floats away on the wind, through the long and golden evening light.

"Let—me—through!" bellows Jack Burns, spurring his horse savagely in the flanks, driving it forward and between his son and the captain. For a moment he seems on the verge of breaking free, into the open. Still aiming his pistol, the colonel does not shoot, is not able to shoot, not quite willing to pull the trigger. But the captain does not hesitate: As Burns forces his way past him the captain draws back his right arm, lunges forward, and thrusts the shining blade of the lance into the old man's side, between the ribs, into the lungs.

Burns gasps in agony, his head twisting toward the sky. He groans from the pain, drops his weapon, tugs with both hands at the haft of the lance, trying to pull it out. His horse, reins trailing, veers in a circle; Burns topples from the saddle, taking the lance with him, and crashes to the ground.

Sprawled on the stones and sand, he pulls again, feebly, at the unendurable thing imbedded in his body, then surrenders to the pain, to the blackness sweeping over him. On his back, he clutches at the sand, at a clump of dried-out weeds. His fingers flex, digging into the earth, as if he were clinging to the revolving world, spinning at a giddy speed, whirling into oblivion.

He makes no further sound. The rich, warm, foaming blood,

milky and pink from his lungs, pours out his mouth and nostrils in a flood. The dark, venous blood streams from the wound in his side, soaking the shirt, seeping through the rent in the cloth, and trickling down the polished shaft of the lance. His fingers grow still, still. Jack Burns stares up at the immense sky, lavender blue in twilight, and at the towering ranges of the clouds that hold in their vaporous masses the final great radiance of the sun. Whatever it is that he sees up there now, with his one true and dimming eye, he tells of it to no one.

The captain dismounts, pulls the lance free, presses an ear to the fallen man's chest, listening for a time. He holds the old man's left wrist, forefinger on the pulse, then checks the carotid arteries of the neck.

The colonel sits still on his horse, watching. Burns' mare stands ten yards off with empty saddle, looking back over one gaunt hip at the men, the other horses. She lowers her head to sniff at the tawny desert bunch grass.

The captain looks up at the colonel. "He's a goner."

The colonel nods. "Have him buried right here. If the ground is too hard, have him covered with stones."

The captain stabs his lance into the earth at Burns' side, making the spot easier to mark from a distance.

"Search him," the colonel says.

Still on one knee, the captain goes through the pockets, finding the old, thin billfold, which he gives to Colonel Barnes. "Did you know this man, sir?"

Barnes looks through the billfold. "No," he answers, "never knew him at all. But I do now." He finds the wad of greenbacks, long obsolete, and the bleached-out photographs of a woman and a boy. There is nothing else. Nothing, nothing, less than nothing. Nothing but a slip of yellow paper, years old, which seems to bear a message, a kind of poem written by hand, the ink turned pale green from time. Silently he reads,

There was so much I wanted to do,
And never did.

There was so much I wanted to understand,
And never could understand.
There was so much I wanted to be,
And never was.

The colonel replaces the fragments in the billfold and slips it into his shirt. The captain climbs on his horse and sits there, waiting. "Go on," Barnes says, "rejoin the column. I'll be there in a few minutes."

The captain salutes and rides off. Failing to return the salute, not even seeing it, the colonel sits slumped in his saddle and stares for a long time at the man on the ground. The sun glares from low in the west, under an armada of motionless clouds. The wind dies out as evening quiets the world. One bird sings—solitaire—over and over again, the same lovely but unchanging song, from the thickets of mesquite and acacia along the dry bed of a desert ravine. There is the murmur of insects—nothing seems to change. The colonel watches the body of his father, and what he thinks he feels is not sorrow, nor regret, nor pride, nor anger, but instead a sense of ever-growing wonder.

After a time he turns his horse, leaves.

The young man is gone. Burns' horse, left alone in a wide and empty horizon of space, sand, mellow light, shuffles in slow stages, in contracting circles, back to her fallen rider. The mare nuzzles the old man's face, her velvety nostrils expanding, her slow and solemn consciousness puzzled by the wonder of this curious, unprecedented repose. After a while the horse lifts her head to watch the far-off and departing Army. She stands in place, waiting.

The colonel rides again on the right hand of his Chief. "You look abstracted, Colonel. Distracted."

The colonel murmurs something unintelligible.

"Heard about your little engagement, Charles. Nasty business, that lance work. Actually, though—a rather noble way to die."

Barnes says nothing.

"Who was he? Another spy?"

"It was that old man, sir. Your would-be assassin."

"Ah-haaah. Come back for another try."

Barnes remains silent.

"Who was he anyway?"

"There was nothing on him. No ID at all. We learned nothing."

"I see. Just another wanderer out of nowhere. Well." The Chief is getting bored with the subject. He changes it. "We're getting messages from Major Roland, Charles. Claims he's in trouble. We're not even out of sight of the city and already he says he's under pressure. That rabble can't give us a decent interval of peace before resuming their sneak attacks."

Barnes eases himself half around in his saddle, looking back. The city is miles behind them now but the great blocks of steel and towers of glass remain visible, stark in silhouette against the yellow sky of sunset. Tall thin black rags of smoke lean toward the clouds, toward the brightening moon.

"Don't bother looking back, Colonel. It's not worth it. Might even be dangerous." The Chief chuckles. "You're the best man I've got left; can't have you turning into a pillar of sodium chloride, you know."

Barnes is about to face forward when he sees a flash of light in the center of the city, among the tallest towers, and the rise and fall of rose-colored fire. He waits, listening, and after a time hears a low, rolling rumble, like summer thunder. Some of the men behind him stop to look.

He turns to the Chief. "Big explosion back there, sir. About where Roland's ammo dump should be."

"I heard it, Colonel."

"Maybe we should send a troop back, give him a hand."

"No." The Chief remains imperturbed and imperturbable. "Let Major Roland handle it himself. He can hold the town."

"Against whom, sir?"

"He'll do his job." The Chief refuses to slow the pace of the march; he does not condescend to give a glance to the rear. Eyes steadfast on the high country ahead, on the east and the future, smiling, never hesitating, voice cheerful and resolute, the Chief says, "In any case it doesn't matter much." Still not looking to either side, riding straight ahead, the Chief concludes, "You know, Colonel, poor Phoenix—it never was a real city."

The colonel makes no reply. He turns to the captains behind, as they hesitate, and gives them the clenched-fist, rising and lowering arm signal that means, Come on. Move them out. Follow me.

Forward! Advance! Onward!

Onward.

Sam and Dixie rest most of the day in the shade of an iron-wood tree, down by a pool in a breezy arroyo at the foot of the mountain. They are awakened, near sundown, by the muted thunder of a distant explosion. Dreaming of rain, Sam opens his eyes and looks up, but there is no rain. Not yet. He sighs with longing, feeling Dixie stir in his arms.

In the soft sweet coolness of twilight Dixie and her man walk through the empty ruins, past the abandoned slums, toward the Dalton Bar. They watch and listen but neither see nor hear any sign, any trace, of the Chief's long-gone Army. Nearing her place, they do hear, though, coming as if from everywhere, the bright swift exact configuration of cascading notes from a worn but wearable *pianoforte*. Dixie presses the shaman's arm.

"Glenn's there. He's still alive." She hurries forward, down the alleyway and into the back entrance of the saloon. Sam stops to roll up the pantlegs of the oversize dress suit he has found and liberated from a housetrailer closet, then follows Dixie.

They find Swingin' Glenn in the gloom of the bar, hunched before his piano, long fingers dancing up and down the keyboard in the actualization of an abstract theorem of tone and tempering worked out some two hundred and seventy years before, by a bewigged German organist trying to hold down a good job. Glenn, as he plays, intones the theme through his nose, a ghostly moan that seems to hover above, within, behind the music.

On top of the piano is a bottle of bourbon, half empty, and next to it an open family-size can of Van Camp's pork and beans with the handle of a spoon sticking out. Without a break in his play Glenn reaches for the bottle, takes a quick slug, sets it back, and rolls on in a crescendo of interbraided melodic line: the *stretto* coming up, *stretto allegretto molto fortissimo*. One slice of eternity, captured from space-time and deity, writ down plain, once and for all, for all to hear. Conclusion.

Sudden silence. After the perfect music, a perfect silence, rich in intellectual reverberation. Hands at rest on the keyboard, Glenn stares into space, entranced by the afterglow of the music, unaware of the man and woman standing nearby, watching him.

"Glenn? . . ."

He seems not to hear. Dixie speaks his name again. The old pianist turns, stares, begins to smile. He stands slowly and holds out his arms; Dixie steps into them; he hugs her to the drapery of white beard on his chest, kissing her in the curls, on the ears, cheeks, lips. Looking up, he sees the Indian, and offers his hand. They shake. Glenn puts his bottle and beans on a nearby table, pulls up chairs. The three sit, pass the bottle, and tell their news.

"Where's Singin' Bob?" says Dixie.

"He joined the Army. They needed another drummer boy." Glenn smiles his broad and wicked smile. "Old Bob always did like to go with the crowd." Glenn takes a deep swig from the bottle. "The human weathervane: As the wind blows so turns Bob." He looks out over the swinging doors of the entranceway. "You saw the Army going by?"

"We saw it."

"Thank God that plague has passed."

"Not all of it," says Dixie. "They left a rear guard in the city."

"Ah yes. Of course, they would." Glenn turns his bloodshot, gentle gaze on Sam Banyaca. "And where's your friend? The old cowboy with the long-range eye?"

Sam shrugs, smiling. Dixie says, "He went back to the city for one more look. Found his old horse along the trail, got restless, took off. We couldn't stop him."

"One more look?"

"For his boy."

"Yes, the boy. The jealous lover." He winks at Dixie. "So he's in there too?" Cocking a thumb to the west, cityward.

"They're all in there," says Dixie. "All but us. And you, Glenn."

Glenn smiles. "My home is here." He indicates a cot against the wall, the screwed-down piano stool, the piano. "My music's coming back, Dixie. I'm very happy. It's all coming back."

"We heard."

"I'm staying right here until the world becomes sane again." He fondles his bottle. "Or until I drink myself to death. Whichever comes first. If there's any difference." He looks at Sam once more.

"And you? Back to your Enchanted Mesa, I suppose?"

Again Sam shrugs, smiling, and says no word. Dixie speaks for him. "We made a decision. It took us all afternoon to decide but we decided. We decided to go after old Jack and help him find the boy. We're going to find Art and the professor and their gang of outlaws and then—we're going to join."

"Join? Join what?"

"Join them."

"Oh Dixie . . ." Glenn's face saddens; tears start in his eyes. "You're no revolutionary, Dixie darling."

"I am now." She smiles happily, looking younger, rosier, prettier than ever.

"No, Dixie, no. It's all insanity." Glenn reaches across the table and places his large, pale, graceful hands, gently but firmly, on her breasts. "Dixie, Dixie, Dixie Dalton—you're meant to be a mother, Dixie. Look at these marvelous things. A mother. Your part is not to destroy, your part is to bring new life into this corrupt world."

"I can do both," says Dixie. "And I will." She looks aside, with warm and loving eyes, at Sam. "*We* can do both. Besides" —she giggles—"we've got two motorcycles now."

Glenn groans, half in despair, half in amusement. He turns to Sam. "You're a sensible young man. Take her out of here. Take her back to your village on the mesa. Save her."

Sam speaks at last. "I'm in love," he explains, smiling. As if that explains anything.

Glenn stares at him. "You're crazier than she is. Is that why you're wearing that awful suit? For a wedding?" He grins. "Actually, it's not such a bad suit. In fact it's beautiful. Too bad they didn't have your size." Nobody laughs, they've heard it before. "Sorry." Hopefully he says, "Well, at least you'll spend the night here. I'll open a new can of beans." He takes a drink from the bottle. "And another bottle. We'll have a party, by God. We've got something to celebrate at last. Two things: Dixie Dalton's engagement and the Chief's disengagement. We'll have music, my friends. I'll play 'Hail to the Chief.' Hail and farewell. We hope."

"We'll have supper with you, Glenn. But then we've got to leave. It's safer in the night—where we're going."

Glenn looks to Sam. Sam nods.

"We'll be back," says Dixie, laughing. "Don't look so glum. And when we come back we'll have our friends with us and we'll have the biggest party you ever heard of." She laughs again, with only a hint of malice. "You stay here and guard the piano."

Glenn says, "I'll guard the music. Yes." He stands. "Very well. Okay. My blessings on you both. I can see you're not to be swayed." He looks about. "Candles, candles, we must have candles. Champagne and caviar, pork and beans and Norwegian sardines. I'll fix you two a dinner you'll never forget. And oh yes"—he reaches inside his shirt collar and pulls a necklace up over his head—"look what I found." He hands the thing with its medallion of gold-veined turquoise and shining silver to Sam. "I want you to give this to Dixie. For good luck. She'll need it more than I will."

Sam takes the necklace in his hands, kisses the amulet, and drapes it once again around Dixie's neck. He kisses her, and whispers in her ear, "This time—three of us. Forever."

Beginning to cry, she smiles, nods, cannot speak.

The burial detail report to their sergeant. The sergeant reports to his lieutenant. The lieutenant reports to his captain. The captain reports to his colonel.

"Colonel, the men couldn't find the body."

The colonel looks cross. "That's absurd."

"Yes sir."

"Did they really look? Couldn't they find our tracks?"

"Yes sir, they followed the tracks and they found where the old man was. Found the lance. Dried blood all over the place. But no body."

"Absurd. What about the horse?"

"The horse was gone too."

"Ridiculous."

"Yes sir. Maybe coyotes dragged the body away."

"That's really absurd."

"I know, sir. But no body."

"Absurd."

"Yes sir."

"Absurd."

"You're right, Colonel."

A pause. "Captain . . ." The colonel pauses again.

"Yes sir?"

"We'll say nothing about this to the Chief. You understand. You know how he"—the colonel hesitates—"how he detests any sort of disorder."

"I know that."

"What's the latest from Major Roland?"

"He says he's busy. Surrounded by barbarians and infidels and what not. Having a lively time."

"He make any requests?"

"Says he'll fight to the last man, Colonel."

"Tell him Charles will never get there."

"He knows that, sir."